OTTO PENZLER PRESENTS
AMERICAN MYSTERY CLASSICS

VULTURES IN THE SKY

TODD DOWNING (1902-1974) was an author, reviewer, and teacher of mystery fiction, as well as an expert on the Choctaw language. Born in Atoka, Indian Territory, he is remembered today as one of the first mystery authors of Native American descent. He wrote six titles in the Hugh Rennert series, then turned to nonfiction, at which point he produced books on Mexican history and Choctaw grammar.

JAMES SALLIS is the award-winning author of eighteen novels, including the Lew Griffin series, the Driver series (inspiration for the 2011 film, *Drive*), and the John Turner series. He has also published numerous short story collections, poetry collections, literary biographies, and criticism.

VULTURES IN THE SKY

TODD DOWNING

Introduction by
JAMES SALLIS

AMERICAN MYSTERY CLASSICS

Penzler Publishers
New York

This is a work of fiction. Names, characters, places, and incidents either are the product of the author's imagination or are used fictitiously. Any resemblance to actual persons, living or dead, businesses, companies, events, or locales is entirely coincidental.

Published in 2020 by Penzler Publishers
58 Warren Street, New York, NY 10007
penzlerpublishers.com

Distributed by W. W. Norton

Cover image: Andy Ross
Cover design: Mauricio Diaz

Paperback ISBN 978-1-61316-180-7
Hardcover ISBN 978-1-61316-179-1

Library of Congress Control Number: 2020916519

Printed in the United States of America

9 8 7 6 5 4 3 2 1

VULTURES IN THE SKY

INTRODUCTION

> There was always a faint tremor underneath one's feet, in the air one breathed. As if the volcanoes far to the south were stirring ominously in their sleep.
>
> —*Murder on the Tropic*

Salvage is an occupation rife with foolhardiness and hope. There's a staggering amount of junk down there out of sight—rusted hulks, baubles, skeletons, old shoes—and bringing it to the surface takes herculean effort. But great finds wait as well. Ask any treasure hunter.

Published in 1935, *Vultures in the Sky* was Todd Downing's third novel, following upon *Murder on Tour* (1933) and *The Cat Screams* (1934), the latter having won wide acclaim for its fair-play plotting and atmospheric writing, and for its warm embrace of the Mexican landscape and Mexican folklore, all of which became fundaments of Downing's work.

His active career as mystery writer would run only eight years and span nine novels, seven of them with the same character as those of the first three, US Customs Agent Hugh Rennert. *Night Over Mexico* in 1941 was the last. A "towering, important novel of Mexico in the early 1820s" announced by *Publishers Weekly* for 1942 never appeared.

Todd Downing was born in 1902 at Atoka, in Indian Territory that's now Oklahoma, of direct Choctaw ancestry. He received bachelor's and master's degrees from the University of Oklahoma, studying Spanish, French and anthropology both there and at the National University of Mexico. Following graduation he became an instructor at the University while contributing reviews of mystery novels and nonfiction to the Daily Oklahoman and Books Abroad and leading summer tours in Mexico. The cancellation of one of those tours found him writing his own first novel. That novel's modest success led him to dig in as fulltime writer, the acclaim afforded *The Cat Screams* furthering his resolve. In the Forties, once the wellspring for whatever reasons went dry, Downing worked as an advertising copywriter, then in 1954, following the death of his father, returned to Atoka to live with his mother, teaching Spanish and French at Atoka high school. Later he taught the Choctaw language at Southeastern Oklahoma State University.

The time in which Downing wrote was a transition period, as the classic mystery scrunched over to make room at the table for evolving new forms—some of them comic, some less stylized or more patently realistic, others simply oddball—and the list of lost and misplaced writers is a long one. Curtis Evans made a fine foray towards remembering Todd Downing with *Clues and Corpses* (Coachwhip Publications, 2013), balancing a couple of hundred pages of information about Downing and his books with another couple of hundred gathering his book reviews, these latter offering valuable documentation of how the genre was changing even as he brought his own novels into it.

Downing's work is masterfully carved to the golden age template: stylized plotting; violence offstage and abstract; essential clues carefully placed, carefully biased; feints and end runs; a final escalade. It's the tension between so formalized style and the darker, deeper substance of Mexican folklore and attitudes that more than anything else can serve to shift Downing's mysteries into overdrive, especially when lent force by such atmospheric writing as exemplified by the endless rain of *Night Over Mexico*, or the animal cries prefiguring each murder in *The Cat Screams*.

"Death's a gayer partner for him than life itself," Downing wrote in *Night Over Mexico*. "He plays jokes on it it just as it plays jokes on him. . . . the Mexican hugs it, sleeps with it, dances with it."

In *Murder on Tour*, Rennert plays with a Day of the Dead toy, making "the little skeleton" jump into life in its macabre dance.

And then, of course, there are the vultures, ever circling. When Rennert notes them, ugly blotches moving in downward spirals, round and round, a crew member responds.

> "It is the *zopilotes*." There was something incongruous about the hollow voice that emerged from the folds of fat about the Mexican's throat. "I do not like them. . . . All morning the sky has not been clear of them. It is," the voice echoed in a shell, "as if they were following this train."

Vultures in the Sky takes place aboard a train making its way along the tracks from Nuevo Laredo to Mexico City carrying nine passengers, three of whom will survive, along with assorted crew. The novel follows the classic pattern of Christie's *And Then There Were None*, serial murders among a small group closely confined, which Downing had employed in *The Cat Screams* (a house under quarantine) and to which he'd return in *Night Over Mexico* (a house in the mountains, isolated by violent weather).

Here, the situation is compounded by engine trouble, an impending railway strike, possible sabotage, and a kidnapping. The cars bearing the passengers get uncoupled from the rest, leaving them stranded in the desert, in darkness.

Giving reader and writer, one might add, perfect clearance for ever mounting tension and wonderful portraiture. The reader comes away feeling that Todd Downing was right up there with the best of his time.

Pure folly and conjecture, to ask why Downing's career as novelist ended after eight years and nine novels. The life of a freelance writer is never an easy one, of course, aswarm as it is with insecurities, misadventure, changes in fashion, happenstance, self doubt, and simple inertia. For many it becomes increasingly difficult to rally belief in the value of what we do, and to abide the expense of same.

In his reviews, again and again Downing champions practitioners of classic mysteries, "brilliant variations on the same theme." The once popular and now forgotten Rufus King, for instance, author of 26 novels and collections, Downing's "greatest early direct influence" and "the best living writer of mystery stories." Yet, with all his love for the classic mystery and personal investment in writing them, Downing freely acknowledges the innovations of such as Hammett, Cain, and Jonathan Latimer in their motion towards a more expansive literary aspiration. Maybe this stretching, this *reach*—changes within the genre itself—hints at Downing's silence?

Or maybe not.

Downing ends his 1943 essay "Murder Is a Rather Serious Business," following upon a fairly comprehensive survey of the field, with this sentence: "For, the author should bear always in mind, this is nothing else than the literature of escape."

Of the classic mystery, of that literature of escape, Todd Downing was unquestionably a master. He constructed his landscapes, his vast deserts and tiny towns that are little more asterisks on a map, his characters' lives and thoughts, convincingly and with great care, great skill.

In *The Last Trumpet*, Rennert's friend Sheriff Bounty refers to a novel that Downing much admired, Susan Smith's *The Glories of Venus*.

> "Remember this definition of *vacilada*? 'Life is the greatest insult that can be offered to a human being,' he read, 'and yet if you will only accept that fact, you can manage to enjoy yourself thoroughly a great deal of the time.' Mexico, huh?"
>
> "Um-huh," Rennert agreed. "Mexico."

That awareness, that central node of his fascination with the Mexican spirit, was in everything Todd Downing wrote. He knew also that much of what is the best in humankind comes from the collision and intermingling of cultures. This, too, is everywhere in his work, and another of many reasons it's so good to have that work back among us.

—James Sallis

VULTURES IN THE SKY

PART ONE

TIME-TABLE OF NATIONAL RAILWAYS OF MEXICO

Monterrey	*Lv.*	*8:30*	*A.M.*
Santa Catarina	“	*9:09*	“
García	“	*9:38*	“
Rinconada	“	*10:20*	“
Hiqueras	“	*10:50*	“
Ramos Arispe.	“	*11:25*	“
Saltillo	*Ar.*	*11:50*	“
Saltillo	*Lv.*	*12:10*	*P.M.*
Encantada.	“	*12:44*	“
Agua Nueva.	“	*1:01*	“
Carneros	“	*1:14*	“
Gómez Farías	“	*2:06*	“
La Ventura.	“	*2:56*	“
San Salvador.	“	*3:08*	“
El Salado.	“	*3:31*	“
Vanegas	*Ar.*	*4:18*	“
Vanegas	*Lv.*	*4:28*	“
Catorce.	“	*4:54*	“
Wadley.	“	*5:03*	“
*Tropic of Cancer	“	. . . .	“

*Non-agency, flag station.

Chapter I
THE PASS OF THE DEAD
(9:25 A.M.)

"BLAST THE train?"

"Yes, that's what he threatened to do. I thought I ought to warn somebody."

Worry edged the querulous voice of Jackson Saul King as he stood upon the observation platform and wiped Mexican dust from his forehead. He passed the handkerchief over his thin iron-gray hair and struck a few ineffectual blows upon the sleeves and trousers of his gray suit. He returned the cloth to his pocket and stared backward over the rails.

His companion, a somewhat elderly man with homely but not undistinguished features, was regarding him thoughtfully.

"You say your wife overheard this conversation last night?"

"Yes," King cleared his throat. "She was worried over these rumors of a railroad strike on the Mexican line and sat up until we got to the border. I went to bed. It was when she was getting off at Laredo that she told me about what she had heard. She didn't want me to come on."

"She remained in Laredo?"

"Yes. She has a sister living there and decided to stay with her rather than come on into Mexico." King blinked weak myopic eyes in the sunlight as he removed his gold pince-nez and began to polish them with a piece of chamois skin. "Mrs. King," he said carefully, "is rather nervous about traveling. She has never been outside of the United States." He paused. "So you can understand, Mr. Rennert, how she would be alarmed over all these reports about a strike," he left the sentence halfway between a statement and an interrogation.

"Yes," the other's clear brown eyes were on the dust that whipped the rails. "Suppose you repeat exactly what your wife told you."

King nervously adjusted the pince-nez upon his nose. He carefully folded the chamois skin and put it into the breastpocket of his coat.

"It was sometime after midnight," he said in a low voice that had a slight nasal resonance. "She was sitting in one of the berths that hadn't been made up. She heard two people talking somewhere behind her. One of them mentioned the station at San Antonio. Then he said: 'I'll get off with you at Monterrey and you can get the money. If you don't, I'll blast the train on this trip.' She says the man who was talking got up then and started to walk away, so that she didn't hear his last words very plainly. She thought, though, that he said something about earrings and cuffs and 'don't forget the extra edition.' "

He met Rennert's stare and smiled weakly.

"I know it sounds rather senseless but my wife insisted that that's what it sounded like. Earrings and cuffs and 'don't forget the extra edition.' I didn't pay much attention to it at the time because I was sleepy and I knew she was rather wrought-up, but I got to thinking about it this morning and decided I'd tell you and see what you thought I ought to do. Of course," the smile lingered a moment and vanished, "there's probably nothing to it."

Behind them Monterrey was lost behind the folds of the gray-brown mountains whose serrated peaks were shattered battlements jutting against the sky. A haze of heat was beginning to cloak the barren desert that stretched away on each side of the track, fusing cactus and mesquite and slate-gray dust into a wavering mirage.

"Did your wife hear the voice of the second person?" Rennert asked.

King hesitated. "No," he said after a moment, "I don't think she did. At least, she didn't say anything about his words. She did mention something about the voice of the person who was talking, though."

"Yes?"

"She said it was rather soft and she thought the English had a slight foreign accent."

Rennert considered this a moment. He knew the readiness of sedentary people to attribute a foreign accent to any strange voice.

"About this reference to the station at San Antonio," he asked. "Did that mean anything to you?"

"What?" King held a hand cupped behind one ear.

Rennert repeated his question, raising his voice.

"No," the other shook his head, "I can't say that it did."

King clutched desperately at the railing as the train swerved around the spur of a mountain that had been sliced as with a gigantic knife. Jagged brown rocks shot up on both sides of them and dust was choking in the confined space.

"Suppose we go back into the car," Rennert suggested, holding open the door.

King passed through and paused in the narrow passage. He coughed and asked: "What do you think I ought to do?"

"Forget it, at least for the present," Rennert tried to make his smile reassuring. "As you say, there's probably nothing to it."

King's fingers toyed with a lodge emblem upon his watch-chain. "You don't think that we're in any danger, then? I had thought of getting off at Saltillo and waiting for the next train."

"I'll talk to the train officials and find out what the situation is. Then you can decide what you want to do."

"I'll appreciate it if you will. I don't speak Spanish, you see."

Rennert watched King's narrow stooped shoulders disappear around the bend in the passage, then followed him into the Pullman. He sat down in the rear seat and stared thoughtfully out the window.

Despite his assurances to King, a doubt kept nagging at him. They had been delayed the night before at San Antonio by rumors of a strike of Pullman employees on the Mexican National Railways and when they had crossed the border early that morning there had been but one Pullman available—the last, they had been told, that would be allowed to run until the strike was settled. Conferences between the workers and officials of the Railway were being held in Mexico City. It had all been of little concern to Rennert—no club car, of course, and limited dining facilities—but he had looked forward to no real discomforts on the trip southward. And now this worried little man, presuming upon a brief acquaintance in the smoker, had come to him with the incoherent words which his wife had overheard, or thought she had overheard, during the night.

Rennert knew from long experience how readily the eternally tautened atmosphere of Mexico responds to the most nebulous touch of rumor and he was mildly surprised at himself for letting these vibrations disturb him. He had the curious feeling (and told himself that he was a fool to admit it) that the masses of contorted stone were closing in imperceptibly upon the train. Perhaps, he reflected, it was due to the fact that the morning was unusually warm and that there was a peculiar breathlessness about the air impounded by the stark Gothic cliffs of El Paso de los Muertos.

Electric fans droned discreetly and the car was very still.

Rennert stared at earrings and told himself sharply: *Don't be a damn fool!*

She sat in the seat in front of him—a thin angular woman of slightly more than medium height. She was dressed in black taffeta whose severeness was emphasized, rather than relieved, by a white, stiffly starched collar. Faint streaks of gray showed in her light brown hair. The earrings were small old-fashioned pendants of twisted gold wire to which were attached oval black cameos.

She sat stiffly erect, holding in her left hand a thin paper-bound volume, the pages of which she cut at regularly spaced intervals with a long bronze knife. About the wrists of the hand which held the book and of that which manipulated the knife were wide cuffs of the same starched whiteness as the collar.

She had been sitting, Rennert remembered now, in exactly the same position when he had gotten on the train in San Antonio the night before. He had retired soon to the smoker and had seen no more of her until breakfast, an hour or so before they reached Monterrey. She had been at a table by herself then, orange juice and dry toast lying untouched before her (strange, Rennert reflected, how these details came back to him now) as she stared at the mountains with eyes that forgot the other breakfasters.

Two seats beyond, on the other side of the car, sat a tall man whose narrow head was plastered with glossy dark-brown hair. As Rennert watched, he turned large dark-colored glasses toward the window and half rose in his seat to pull down the blind. His body seemed to uncoil, slender and ungainly in gray shirt and corduroy trousers but giving the impression of a vast amount of concealed wiry strength. He sank back onto the seat and threw one long leg over the other.

Rennert got up and walked slowly down the aisle in the direction of the smoker. There had been, he believed, seven passengers besides himself in the Pullman when the train had left San Antonio . . .

To his right, in the center of the car, sat an elderly man with gray hair cut *en brosse.* He wore an ill-fitting suit of black serge and his hands, bleached-looking and delicate, rested upon his knees as he stared fixedly at a point above the doorway.

In front of him was a middle-aged, narrow-shouldered individual whose jet-black hair, sallow olive complexion and prominent cheek bones denoted a strong mixture of Mexican blood. With the thumb and forefinger of one hand he was caressing the end of a thin drooping mustache. As Rennert passed, he glanced up quickly, searched his face for an instant with obsidian-black eyes and as quickly lowered his gaze. His face remained impassive but there had been, Rennert was positive, a certain furtiveness deep in his eyes.

King sat across from him. He was bending forward, rummaging among the contents of a black gladstone.

Rennert walked on, past the door of a compartment, to the smoker.

Two men sat upon the leather seat. One of them looked up and greeted him with a friendly nod. He was a tall fellow, probably in his middle thirties, with a well-proportioned athletic figure. He had a long clean-shaven face, slate-blue eyes beneath sparse lashes and corn-colored hair combed back from a wide forehead.

"How're you this morning?" he asked, taking a cigarette from the corner of his mouth and flipping the ashes to the floor.

"Very well," Rennert drew a package of cigarettes from his pocket and selected one.

"I don't believe I remember your name," the other said, "but I met you in here last night, as we were leaving San Antonio. Mine's Spahr." His voice had a soft pleasant drawl.

"Rennert is my name," as he held cupped hands over a match

"Oh, yes. This is Mr. Radcott, Mr. Rennert."

Radcott looked up at Rennert over the top of a newspaper. He was a heavy-set man with a round pleasant face upon which stood beads of perspiration. His blond, carefully brushed hair did not conceal incipient baldness. He wore no coat and his shirt clung damply to his torso.

"Hot, isn't it?" he remarked in a perfunctory tone as Rennert sat down beside him.

Rennert agreed and glanced at the front page of the newspapery which Radcott held in his short pudgy fingers. He felt a faint twinge of surprise.

Exclamatory red letters proclaimed it an extra edition of the San Antonio *Express.*

They smoked for several moments in silence. The whir of the diminutive electric fan set in the wall mingled with the steady rhythm of the rails to give the room a soporific effect.

Rennert found his thoughts refusing stubbornly to respond

to the stimuli that had awakened them before. It all seemed so silly now. A frightened woman leaving a train in the small hours of the morning and translating a sleepy conversation into incoherent phrases. Earrings and cuffs . . . and don't forget the extra edition . . .

Looking back upon it—this brief interval of comfortable after-breakfast relaxation in inviolable masculine surroundings—Rennert was to think of it as a definite period punctuating the uneventfulness of that strangely prolonged journey, during which those words would assume unexpected proportions.

"Going to Mexico City, Rennert?" Spahr broke the silence.

"Yes. I suppose you are, too?"

"Yeah. I'm with the San Antonio *Express.* Going down to do some stories on the new President." He took a last draw upon his cigarette and flipped it into the cuspidor. "What do you think this strike is liable to amount to? They say there's a streetcar and bus strike in Mexico City and that the Pullmans are tied up all over the country."

Rennert smiled. "Strikes are about the same in Mexico as in the United States, I've observed. Maybe a little more fanfare and oratory, but nothing to worry about."

With a barely suppressed yawn Radcott got to his feet and dabbed at his pink face with a wadded handkerchief. "Thanks," he folded the newspaper and tossed it to the seat beside Spahr. "I think I'll walk back and get some air. I'm about to suffocate in here."

They watched his broad moist back disappear through the green curtains.

"It is hot, isn't it?" Spahr said. "What about a cold bottle of beer?"

"Thanks," Rennert said, "a little too soon after breakfast for me."

The diminutive Mexican porter entered and walked quickly across to the windows.

"What's the matter?" Spahr asked as he watched him lowering them. "It's hot enough in here as it is."

"Tunnel, sir," the Mexican replied in careful inflectionless English as he recrossed the room.

Spahr glanced out the window at the wall of brown rocks that seemed to be thrusting their knife-edge sides in on the train.

"I think I'll get that beer," he said, rising. "You won't change your mind?"

"No, thank you. This your paper?"

"Huh? Oh, yes, but go ahead and read it if you want to. I'm through with it." Spahr stuck a hand into the pocket of his loose-fitting seersucker trousers and lounged from the room. He was whistling a low tune as the curtains fell to behind him.

"The eyes of Texas are upon you . . ."

Rennert sat, gazing upward at the smoke of his cigarette as it rose in slow spirals that were suddenly caught, twisted and whirled into invisibility by the current from the fan.

These were the seven passengers. King, Spahr, Radcott, the furtive-eyed Mexican, the gray-haired man, the tall fellow who looked like a ranchman, and the lady in black taffeta who wore earrings and cuffs.

Rennert picked up the newspaper.

PILOT AND PASSENGER DIE IN AIR CRASH was the headline that was spread across the front page. Rennert glanced down the column. An airplane had crashed to the ground outside San Antonio about sundown the day before, carrying with it two men. . . .

A low, heavy rumble from ahead came to his ears and he became aware that the room was growing dark. He glanced out the window and saw the wall of rock close in upon the train.

They were in the tunnel.

There was something about the abrupt departure from hot blinding sunlight into rock-incased blackness that always gave Rennert a queer other-dimensional feeling. Sitting there with his cigarette a pinpoint of light in the darkness, he remembered with a smile how, as a small boy taking his first long train trip, he had held his breath and clutched the seat in an agony of heart-stopping apprehension as he had passed through a tunnel in the Alleghenies. The sensation, he imagined, must be something like that which an inexperienced diver feels when he opens his eyes to another element . . .

He opened his eyes now, as it were, to the increasing light ahead and blinked as the train emerged from the rocks, like a plated serpent drawing its ungainly length from a crevice.

He resumed his perusal of the newspaper. Baseball results, a speech by a political candidate, the weather report . . .

"Do you know," King asked from between the curtains, "where the conductor is?"

Rennert looked up. "No, I don't." He saw King's gray-white face. "What's the matter?"

"It's a man back in the Pullman. He's fainted, I think."

Rennert got up and thrust the newspaper into his pocket. "Let's see."

King stood aside and allowed Rennert to precede him back down the passage.

"He's across the aisle from me."

Rennert stepped inside the door and looked down at the Mexican. His body was slumped now against the frame of the window. His hands dangled from the edge of the seat and swayed helplessly to and fro with the increasing motion of the train. His head had fallen slightly forward so that he seemed to be staring at the floor.

Rennert leaned over and caught hold of his shoulder. He must have grasped it with more force than he thought, for the body became dislodged from its position and fell forward. Rennert pushed it back against the rear of the seat. For an instant, as he felt for the pulse and looked at the still wax-like face, he had the feeling that the eyes of glazed obsidian were staring purposefully into his.

"What's the matter with him?" King demanded in a sharp frightened voice.

Rennert straightened up.

"This man," he said soberly, "is dead."

Chapter II
WATCHERS IN THE SKY
(10:20 A.M.)

"Dead?"

The word stuck in King's throat, obstructed by a sick gulp in the taut cords. He stepped back, one hand groping for the seat behind him, and stared at the face of the man across the aisle as if unable to take his eyes from it.

Rennert cast a comprehensive glance down the length of the car.

The gray-haired man in the seat behind sat in the same rigid posture but he was staring now at Rennert's face as he had stared before at the woodwork above the doorway. There was an odd dazed look in his liquid light-blue eyes, as if he had been jerked violently out of a reverie and were trying to order his thoughts. The tall man on the other side was leaning slightly forward and peering with his dark glasses at the black arc of hair that topped the back of the seat. The woman in black taffeta seemed not to have noticed the disturbance, as she continued to hold the book in a steady hand, her gaze intent on its lines.

Across the aisle from her the little porter was straining to open a window.

Rennert called him.

He looked around, nodded his head with a quick bird-like movement and came forward. In his eagerness he stumbled against a battered hat-box of black grained leather which stood in the aisle, against the seat of the gray-haired man. He stopped, picked it up and placed it upon the vacant seat behind. He moved forward again, a curious suggestion of a trot in his short-legged gait, and came to a halt before Rennert, his quick black eyes searching his face.

"Yes, sir?" his English was mechanical.

"Find the conductor," Rennert told him, "ask him to come into this car as quickly as possible."

"Yes, sir."

As he started to move forward he glanced down at the seat beside which Rennert stood. Not a muscle moved in his wooden face and his eyes were small unmoving pebbles. It was a strange anomaly of a face—that of an old old man, with the aspect of leather and corrugated with wrinkles, set on the yet unformed body of a youth. His hair was black and vigorous, with the mere suggestion of a curl rippling through it.

"Get the conductor," Rennert said sharply, "at once."

"Yes, sir," the porter took his eyes from the countenance of the dead man and kept them averted as he ambled toward the door.

Rennert turned to King, who stood at his elbow, a fixed stare on his face. "What happened?"

King looked at him blankly for a moment and said in a smothered voice: "I don't know. After we got out of the tunnel I just happened to glance over there and saw him—like that. I thought he had fainted. I went to get the conductor." He tightened his grip upon the back of the chair. "I didn't know he was dead."

"You say he is dead?" the man with the stiff gray hair rested a hand upon the edge of his seat and leaned forward. His voice was low and well modulated and only a faint trace of cultured precision betrayed a foreign origin. The hand which lay upon the green fabric was a sensitive one, with long tapering fingers.

Rennert nodded as he studied the man's face.

It was a strikingly handsome face, with a curious mingling of asceticism and virility in its finely cut features. It had the bleached pallor that comes from long confinement indoors. The nose was thin with a slight flaring of the nostrils. The hair above the wide forehead was, Rennert saw now, not as gray as it had appeared at first sight. It might have been until fairly recently dark brown, but now was shot through with gray. The full lips gave the impression of being held in temporary immobility and lent a note of sensuality oddly at variance with the rest of the features.

"But he was alive a few minutes ago," the man went on, "just before we entered the tunnel." His eyes had lost some of their mildness and there lurked in them now a sharpness, an unrelaxing vigilance which he could not entirely mask.

"You are sure of that?"

"Certainly, I saw him glance back over his shoulder."

"What's the matter?" the tall man had stepped forward and stood in the center of the aisle, looking down at the side of the Mexican's face. His hands were thrust into the pockets of his worn corduroy trousers, bulging the cloth as if they were doubled into fists.

"It seems," Rennert said, "that this man died while we were passing through the tunnel."

The other emitted a long-drawn-out whistle of surprise. He stood for a moment, a frown contorting his features. His face was long and roughly featured, with a squared-off jaw and flat cheeks. His mouth was small and not unpleasant. What held Rennert's gaze was the sunburn. It was the worst case which he had ever seen in long years of experience along the sun-baked reaches of the Rio Grande. The man's face might have been seared unmercifully with a flame. The skin must have been unusually white before its exposure but now it was a virulent red, with dried brownish particles clinging to it like scales. Seen in combination with the blank dark glasses with concave lenses, it gave the effect of a grotesque mask.

"What was the matter with him?" the question came in a soft even voice.

"That remains to be seen."

As Rennert turned his head at the sound of footsteps and excited voices in the passage, he saw the blue eyes of the man in the seat fixed with curious intentness upon the side of the other's trousers, where the fists bulged the corduroy.

"*¡Pues, hombre, te digo que no puede ser! Es imposible——*"

The conductor stood just inside the door, transfixed by shock. He was short and plump, with a lunar face and eyes that protruded in an unreadable stare behind the thick lenses of huge tortoise-shell spectacles.

"This man," Rennert gestured toward the seat by his side, "is dead. I asked the porter to call you at once."

He fixed Rennert with his stare, then moved forward and bent over the inert figure. He shook it by the shoulder but withdrew his hand as if he had experienced an electric shock. His lips mumbled something unintelligible as he turned to Rennert.

"What——?" he stopped as if at a loss for words.

Rennert guessed that his English had fled along with his composure and said in Spanish: "I found him like this—dead—

when we came out of the tunnel just now. He evidently died while we were passing through it, since he was alive shortly before."

Relief had flooded over the Mexican's face. "Ah, señor," he shrugged his pleasure, "you speak Spanish! It is well. My English is very very little. I——"

"Is there a doctor on this train?" Rennert cut short his flow of words.

"A doctor?" another shrug and a drawing-down of the corners of the lower lip. "No, señor, I am very sorry but there is no doctor." He pulled out a massive gold watch and consulted it hopefully. "In forty-five minutes we arrive in Saltillo. There we will find a doctor."

Rennert frowned. "And in the meantime?"

Yet another shrug, expressive of matter-of-fact acceptance of the inevitable. "In the meantime, señor, there is nothing to do. There will be authorities in Saltillo who will know about the regulations in the case of a death on the train. Myself, I do not know. This is my first run on this line. I was transferred yesterday from the run between Monterrey and Torreón because of the strike."

Rennert was conscious of the scrutiny of the three men about them. "Is there some place where I can speak to you in private?" he asked.

The conductor looked doubtful.

"There is a compartment up there. Why can't we use that?" Rennert suggested.

A decisive shake of the head. "It is occupied, señor—by a lady. We cannot go there."

"The smoker, then. It might be well to have the porter cover this man and stay with him until we get to Saltillo."

"*¡Cómo no!*" the conductor turned to the porter, who was standing in the door, a quiet little gnome whose eyes glinted as they darted from one face to the other. He gave staccato orders. The porter vanished.

The corduroy-clad figure still stood planted in the center of the aisle, his bulk swaying slightly to and fro with the motion of the train. "What's the confab been about?" he demanded of Rennert. "What are they going to do with the body?"

"It will have to stay here until we get to Saltillo, I'm afraid. A doctor can examine it then."

The other grimaced slightly. "Thank God it's not far to Saltillo. In this weather——" he wheeled about abruptly and lurched back toward his seat. A hush had settled again upon the car.

The man in the seat behind sank back against the cushion and passed a hand across his eyes. Rennert thought, but could not be sure, that his lips were moving, although no words came from them.

King still stood, holding tightly to the back of his seat and staring out the window opposite.

The porter trotted in with a sheet. They stood aside as he tossed it over the body and tucked in the edges with as much unconcern as if he had been making a berth.

The head of the gray-haired man was bent and his fingers were going swiftly through the motions of the cross.

There was a choking sound and King sank onto his seat.

The porter stood up. "*¿Estâ bueno?*" he addressed the conductor.

"*Sí. Quédate aquí hasta que lleguemos a Saltillo.*"

"*Bueno.*"

The conductor turned to Rennert. "*¿Pues, señor?*"

Rennert nodded and led the way to the smoker.

The room was close and warm and the odor of cigar and cigarette smoke still hung heavy in the air.

Rennert stood for a moment, his lips pursed in thought. At a sudden resolve he took from the pocket of his coat a long manila envelope, opened it and tendered it to the conductor.

"Here are my credentials," he said, "to prove my identity. Any of your immigration officials will recognize them."

The Mexican took the envelope and glanced through its contents. His eyes might have been those of a fish peering out of the glass walls of an aquarium. "*¡Pues!*" he exclaimed softly. "The Treasury Department of the United States!" He carefully returned the contents of the envelope and handed it back to Rennert. There was a slight note of deference in his voice as he asked: "Very well, señor, what is it that you wish?"

Rennert lit a cigarette. "I should like to ask a few questions with regard to this man who has just died."

"*Cómo no.*" Ready acquiescence, noncommittal attention, and a certain amount of defensive wariness shaded the words.

"Did this man get on the train at San Antonio?"

The conductor drew from his pocket a sheaf of envelopes and shuffled through them. He opened one of them, looked at the ticket which it contained and nodded. "Yes, he had lower berth number three, San Antonio to Saltillo."

"A one-way or round-trip ticket?"

"One-way, señor." He returned the tickets to his pocket, the operation seeming to absorb all his attention.

Rennert regarded him thoughtfully. "Did you have occasion to notice him particularly last night or this morning? Did you see him talking to anyone, either one of the Pullman passengers or anyone else?"

The Mexican gave this a great deal of thought before he replied. "No," he said at last, "I did not see him talk to anyone."

Rennert propped a foot against the seat. "About this tunnel through which we passed," he stared down at his cigarette, "is it not customary to turn on the electric lights of the train when passing through one?"

The conductor's face, as smooth in texture as the woodwork behind him, began to look unpleasantly moist. "Certainly, señor," his cheeks bulged with a pleasant smile, "when it is a long tunnel such as this one."

"But the lights were not turned on this time."

"No," the other very carefully smoothed the cuffs of his coat, "the porter will have forgotten to do this. He, too, is new on this run and is not accustomed to the work on a Pullman. Everything is so difficult now, with this strike." He paused and went on with lowered voice: "I, too, do not work any more on the train when we get to Mexico City."

"You are joining the strikers?"

"No," his eyes darted to the window, "but it is that I have a wife and children."

"You have fear of the strikers?"

A shrug and an increasingly glassy stare behind the spectacles that were directed at the window.

Rennert had the curious feeling that an invisible curtain of reserve had been lowered between this man and himself. He took his foot from the seat and sent his cigarette spinning toward the cuspidor.

At the movement an alertness seemed to come over the Mexican. He took his eyes from the window and regarded Rennert for a moment. Some of the glassiness vanished, replaced by an unexpected amount of shrewdness. "What is your opinion, señor Rennert, about how this man died? You found the body."

"I found the body, yes, but I did not examine it carefully. I saw no traces of a wound."

The other did not relax the vigilance of his gaze. "You expected," came the soft question, "to find a wound?"

Rennert did not reply for a moment. That, he told himself, was exactly the trouble. He had expected to find a wound. This man's death had followed too closely upon his conversation with Mr. King. And yet, he admitted, there was really nothing to connect the two events. It might be that he was too hasty at jumping at a conclusion.

"I thought it possible," he said at last, noncommittally.

"But might it not have been heart failure?" the conductor dangled hopefully. "The air in the tunnel is very bad, they say."

"Yes," Rennert nodded, "it might have been heart failure. We shall find out when we get to Saltillo." He turned to the door. As he parted the curtains he was aware that the Mexican was still standing in the center of the room, gazing steadily at his back.

He almost ran into King, who was standing in the passage, nervously running a finger underneath his wilted linen collar. There was the same worried frown on his face. He moistened his dry lips and said: "I'd like to talk to you a minute, Mr. Rennert."

Rennert, wondering if the man *had* been listening to his conversation with the conductor, replied: "Very well. Shall we go back into the diner?"

King nodded acquiescence and followed Rennert toward the adjoining car.

On the platform between the two cars stood Spahr, smoking

a cigarette and gazing out at the landscape through eyes partially covered by drawn lids. He turned and grinned at Rennert.

"Thought you'd change your mind about that beer," he said. "It helps."

Rennert made some reply and was about to continue his way when the newspaperman stepped forward and caught hold of his elbow.

"Say," he demanded, "who's the tall dame back there in the diner? First time I've seen her on this trip."

"You mean the elderly lady in black?"

"No, no—this is another one. Looks like one of those society women who endorse cigarette ads."

Rennert smiled. "I'm sure I don't know." He paused. "She is probably the occupant of the compartment. I believe the conductor mentioned that a lady had it."

He pushed open the door of the diner.

The shades on the east had been lowered against the glare of the sun and light filtered coolly onto white linen and polished silver and tall glass bottles of Arkansas mineral water.

Smoke was a halo about the head of the woman who sat at a table on the opposite side. She smoked a cigarette in a long jade holder and let the ashes fall at random on the tablecloth or in the plate that held a cup of black coffee. She smoked slowly, inhaling deeply and allowing the blue wisps to trickle from between her red arched lips. She was tall and slender, in a severely plain dress of jade-green chiffon. Her shining honey-colored hair was parted in the middle and drawn back like two lacquered wings to a smooth knot on the nape of her neck. She was gazing out the window with an expression in her eyes that might have been either infinite boredom or intense inner concentration. Rennert wondered, as he passed her table, how much art had contributed to nature in the production of the fragile beauty and clarity of complexion of her long face.

He led the way to a table at the far end of the car and sat down. King sank into the opposite chair and removed his pince-nez. As he polished them with the chamois skin Rennert observed the lines etched deeply under the man's tired eyes.

"What is it?" he asked, when the other had restored the pince-nez to the bridge of his nose.

King cleared his throat and his fingers fumbled with a knife upon the top of the table. "I have just remembered something," he seemed to be experiencing difficulty in choosing his words. "You asked me this morning if the reference which my wife heard to the platform at San Antonio meant anything to me. I told you then that it didn't. Well," he paused, "I remember now that something did happen there. I don't know whether it's important or not but I thought that I ought to tell you—in view of what has happened back in the Pullman."

Rennert was immediately alert. "Yes?" he prompted.

"It was last night, while we were waiting for the Pullman to be opened. A man fainted on the platform and had to be carried away."

Rennert waited and when King did not go on said: "And that's all?"

"Yes, that's all. There was a crowd there waiting on trains and this man was quite a distance away from my wife and myself, so that we didn't see him very plainly. There was some confusion, though, and someone told us that a man had fainted. We got on the train soon after and that's the last I thought of it until a few minutes ago."

Rennert's gaze was on a stunted mesquite tree that perched in utter isolation on a rocky slope far above them. It stood silhouetted sharply against the hot blue sky and in the sky, lazy and black and sinister, floated a *zopilote,* the gaunt vulture that is a sentinel of every Mexican landscape.

Rennert's thoughts were attuned to the stark grimness framed by the window. Last night a man had fallen unconscious upon the platform at San Antonio. Some time after midnight an individual on the Pullman (an individual with a "foreign" voice) had threatened another individual with—what? Exposure, probably, unless the latter got off the train at Monterrey and obtained some money. The train had passed Monterrey; none of the Pullman passengers, as far as he had ascertained, had left the train; and a man (who would, judging by his appearance, have a distinctly "foreign" voice) had died in the darkness of the tunnel. It all fitted, he told himself soberly, too well to be explained by coincidence.

He said to King: "I think that if I were in your place I should keep your information to myself for the present. We shall be in Saltillo in a few minutes and I shall consult the authorities there, have them wire back to San Antonio for particulars of the man who fainted on the platform."

He must have allowed more of his own apprehension to tinge his voice than he had intended, for King's face grew grayer.

"You think there *is* some connection between what happened at San Antonio and what happened on the Pullman then?" his voice was blurred.

"I think," Rennert leaned forward and discreetly lowered his voice, "that it is very probable that there is a connection, although there's no certainty of it yet." His eyes were very clear and penetrating as they studied King's face. "About the death of this man in the tunnel. You were sitting across from him the entire time, were you not?"

"Yes."

"Did you hear him cry out or make any disturbance?"

"No," King shook his head slowly, "I didn't. The train was making so much noise, though——"

"Did you," Rennert put careful emphasis upon the words, "see anyone approach his seat?"

King lowered his eyes and regarded the silverware with drawn brows. "I hate to admit it," he said at last, slowly, "but I'm not sure. When we got into the tunnel the dust and smoke choked me so that I had a severe coughing spell. I think, though, that someone was in the aisle between my seat and his for a moment or two."

"Did you get any idea of this person's actions?"

"No," King ran his tongue over his lips again, "I didn't. He just seemed to be standing there. I supposed it was the porter, he had just been through, lowering the windows. When we got out of the tunnel whoever it was had gone."

"It might have been the porter?"

"Yes."

"He was wearing a white jacket, remember."

"Oh," King stared down at the tablecloth, "that's right. I don't believe, then, that it was the porter. I think that I would have noticed the white jacket."

"Can you recall anything at all as to the size or height or dress of the person whom you saw?"

"Nothing at all, I'm sorry to say. It was dark and I had my handkerchief up to my face most of the time. I may have been entirely mistaken."

Rennert was sure that King had not been mistaken, that someone had stood by the Mexican's seat, had accomplished in some way his death while the car was plunged in darkness. He thought a moment.

"And what have been the comments of the passengers in the Pullman since the conductor and I left?" he asked.

"There was considerable excitement, of course. Everybody seemed to take it for granted that it was—well, a natural death. Mr. Searcey said that it was probably heart failure."

"Mr. Searcey?"

"Yes, he's the tall man in corduroy trousers. Seems to be a competent sort of fellow, not the kind to lose his head."

The train was slowing down at a station and Rennert glanced out the window at slate-gray dust and blank adobe walls and hot white sunlight.

"Suppose," he said, "that we go back into the Pullman now."

"All right."

They rose.

King stood still in the aisle and asked hesitantly: "You're going to question the passengers in the Pullman?"

"Yes."

King stared at the doorway.

"You won't mention my name in connection with any of this, will you?"

"You would prefer that I didn't?" Rennert watched his face.

He drew out his handkerchief and passed it over his forehead, where stood tiny beads of perspiration.

"I'd really rather that you didn't," he said, his lips drawn into a sickly smile. "If there is any—well, any foul play—about this I might be in danger."

"I understand," Rennert turned down the aisle. "I'll do my best not to involve you in any danger."

A haze of smoke hung in the still air about the head of the woman in jade green. She had inserted another cigarette in the holder but otherwise might not have moved since they had passed her when coming into the diner.

At the door Rennert paused.

Upon the platform between the cars stood the conductor. His face was smooth moist clay worked to mask-like immobility. His eyes stared without expression at the sky. As Rennert watched the thick lenses moved almost imperceptibly round and round, in a regular orbit.

As the door opened the man wheeled about suddenly, as if a galvanic shock had gone through his body. He closed his mouth and seemed to be rubbing his thick lips together with a curious rotary motion.

Rennert stood aside and motioned King to precede him into the Pullman.

When the door had closed he asked casually: "Was there a Pullman reservation made out of San Antonio last night which was not taken?" His eyes covertly studied the sky.

The Mexican swallowed and nodded quickly. "Yes, señor. Number seven—lower berth—was reserved but the passenger did not come."

"Do you know when the Pullman ticket was purchased?"

"Last night, I think, while the train was waiting in the station. Earlier, it had not been taken."

Above the flat roofs of the little town the sky was cloudless and blue, bright with a sheen of heat. Two ugly blotches moved in lazy downward spirals, round and round.

Rennert watched them, his eyes narrowed against the glare.

"Something worries you?" he asked quietly.

"It is the *zopilotes,*" there was something incongruous about the hollow voice that emerged from the folds of fat about the Mexican's throat. "I do not like them."

"God knows they're common enough in Mexico!"

"But today there are so many. All the morning the sky has not been clear of them. It is," the voice echoed in a shell, "as if they were following this train."

Rennert's laugh sounded harsh in his own ears. "There has been a drought in this section of the country, hasn't there?"

"Yes, señor. For many many weeks it does not rain."

"That explains the *zopilotes* then. Livestock and wild animals have died out on the desert, of thirst, and the vultures are waiting for more to die."

The conductor's back was framed by the door. "Of course, señor, that explains them." The door closed behind him with a soft swish.

Rennert stood and felt the tremor of the train's starting vibrate beneath his feet, watched the drab desert buildings slide by. They were humming in his ears again—those intangible wires that mesh the atmosphere of Mexico, dried to brittleness by the Mexican sun and charged with the electricity of the thin air that speeds the pulse-beat.

He began to whistle "La Cucaracha," defiantly, as he pushed open the door of the Pullman.

"¡La cucaracha, la cucaracha
Ya no puede caminar!
¡Porque le falta, porque no tiene
Marihuana que fumar!"

He walked down the passage past the smoker and the compartment.

Spahr was propped in the doorway, an unlighted cigarette dangling from his lips and an alert expression on his long clean face. He glanced around as Rennert approached, straightened up and jerked the cigarette from his mouth.

"Say," he exclaimed eagerly, "what's the dope on this man's death? Just think, I was back in the diner drinking beer while something like this was happening right in the next car! What was it, heart failure? I can't get anything out of that gargoyle over there," with a nod of the head toward the porter, who sat, as if shriveled within his white jacket, on the seat opposite the sheet-draped figure.

An expectant hush had fallen upon the car, rustled at the edges by the faint stir of bodily movements. Rennert pitched his voice to carry through its length.

"Nothing can be learned about the cause of his death until the body is examined in Saltillo," he said.

"It will be taken off there?" Spahr was standing with one foot braced against the arm of King's chair and was studying Rennert's face with quick eyes.

"Yes," Rennert's gaze wandered past Spahr to the other occupants of the car.

At the rear the woman in black taffeta sat as before, upright in her seat. She had laid aside her book and her head rested upon the back of the chair. She was gazing at them with an absent expression upon her placid face. Radcott stood in the center of the aisle, swaying back and forth with the motion of the car like an erect bear. His face was pink and warm and his mouth was partially open. Beside him the tall sunburned man whom King had named Searcey sat upon the arm of his seat, one leg extended along its length. One hand was still thrust into a pocket and the other lay like a chunk of dried meat upon the corduroy that covered his thigh. He regarded Rennert steadily from behind the colored glasses. The gray-haired man sat very still and looked at Rennert with eyes whose liquidness seemed suddenly filmed by thin ice. His lips were held very firmly pressed together and his breath came and went irregularly.

"All of you are aware by now," Rennert said, "that a man has died in this car. Did any of you know him?"

No one spoke. Radcott made a slight negative motion of the head but the others did not move.

"He's probably got a passport on him," Spahr suggested. "Why don't we look for that and find out who he is?"

"We shall have to let the authorities at Saltillo do that, Mr. Spahr. Mexican laws regarding the disturbance of corpses are exceedingly strict."

Spahr's broad shoulders shrugged indifference.

"Since there will be a certain amount of investigation by the authorities," Rennert went on, "it has occurred to me that it would avoid delay and possible complications if we were all prepared to give them any information possible without delay."

"But what worry is it of ours," Radcott blurted out, "if he's a Mexican? I don't see how it concerns us at all if a Mexican chooses a Mexican train to die in."

Rennert frowned. "It happens, Mr. Radcott, that we are in Mexico now and the death of a Mexican on a train or elsewhere is of considerable more importance than back in the United States"

Radcott's face flushed and he seemed about to reply, but restrained himself.

The right side of Searcey's mouth moved slightly as if he were beginning to smile. The hand upon the corduroy flattened itself a bit.

"This man died while we were passing through the tunnel," Rennert went on imperturbably. "Did any of you hear any outcry or any sound of a disturbance during the time we were in the tunnel?"

Silence.

"Did any of you see anyone approach his seat?"

The train was going up a steep grade now and had slackened its speed. The silence seemed intensified, heavy with some of the engine's labor.

"I was back on the observation platform," Radcott volunteered suddenly.

"And I was in the diner," from Spahr.

Rennert, glancing sideways at him, caught a glimpse of King's gray tight-lipped face behind the newspaperman. There was a frantic look of appeal in his eyes.

"One person in this car approached him," the voice of the grayhaired man at Rennert's left sifted clearly across the train's noises. He sat forward upon the edge of his seat and held himself braced, as it were, with his hands upon the knees of his black trousers. The blood had drained from his face, leaving the skin with an odd transparent look.

"How do you know?" Rennert asked quietly.

"While we were passing through the tunnel," the man spoke slowly and with the same careful precision, "I was aware that someone was bending forward over the back of this seat in front of me. He was there for only a moment. I think that he went toward the rear of the car then."

"Did you hear any sound?"

"I thought, yes, that I heard a slight choking sound but when we came out of the tunnel I saw that this gentleman," the blue eyes rested on King's face, "was coughing violently, so I supposed that the noise which I heard came from him."

"Did you," Rennert asked evenly, "recognize this person?"

As he put the question he saw the ice harden in the man's eyes until they glittered in the light that struck them from the window. His hands pressed so tightly into the trousers that the knuckles stood out sharp and white like polished skulls across his skin.

"No, I did not recognize him—but," he squared his stooped shoulders, "I believe that I could identify him."

The silence that followed his words was punctuated by a sharp intake of breath from Spahr, at Rennert's elbow.

"How's that?" came the eager question.

The other looked at Spahr for an instant, then turned his head and let his eyes travel slowly about the car.

"I am very, very sorry that it is necessary for me to speak," he seemed to be addressing all of them, "but to conceal the truth is to lie. We humans try to salve our consciences by flimsy fictions that only mask our fear of meeting an issue face to face. One of you is concealing the fact that he leaned over this seat because he fears the consequences. It would have been much better if he had admitted it. I am but the agent——"

"Yeah!" Spahr broke out impatiently, "but tell us how you could identify this person."

The man looked at him and smiled. The smile lent a strange attractiveness to his face.

"I beg your pardon," he said, "for having tried your patience with my words. When this person bent over the seat ahead my hand was resting upon the arm of this chair," he moved his hand and laid it upon the wood in front of Rennert's knee, "I felt very distinctly the material of his trousers. It was rough corduroy."

Chapter III
THE MOUNTAINS OF MEXICO
(11:35 A.M.)

THE TRAIN was nearing the top of the grade and its motion had slowed perceptibly. Ahead, the engine emitted regular puffs of travail and the shrill creaking of metal and wood tortured their ears in the stillness which had fallen upon the car.

Searcey had risen very slowly from his seat upon the chair's arm and had advanced unhurriedly and deliberately down the aisle. His face was as expressionless as a mask but a faint derisory smile played about the corners of his mouth, making the thin lips the only living part of his features. He still held his hands buried in the pockets of the corduroy trousers.

"Would you mind repeating that?" he addressed the gray-haired man in an even voice that held a distinctly metallic undertone.

The other looked back at him over the rear of the seat. "Certainly." His smile was so nebulous that it seemed merely a shifting of the light-and-shadow effect upon his pale face. "I had hoped that you would speak out and save me the pain of doing so. As you did not——"

"Go ahead," the metal cut through the softness of Searcey's voice. "Cut the preliminaries!"

The other made a slight deprecatory gesture with his hands. "I was about to repeat that, as we were passing through the tunnel, someone approached the seat in front of me and bent over it. My left hand was lying upon the arm of my chair and this person's clothing brushed against it. The clothing was of rough corduroy."

Searcey's lips curled, twisting painfully the flesh of his flat cheeks. "And exactly what is it that you accuse me of, may I ask?"

"Of nothing at all, my friend, except of having come to this man's seat and of having failed to admit the fact."

Searcey's mouth looked cruelly feral as he said: "Stay off the pipe, fellow, stay off the pipe! It always gives you dreams like that."

The dead surfaces of his glasses traveled about the circle of faces and came to rest upon Rennert's. His lips relaxed a bit.

"See here," he said with a visible effort at pleasantness, "it strikes me that we're getting all excited about nothing here. You seem to have been getting the lowdown on this business. Suppose you tell us what it's all about."

Rennert shrugged. "Really, there's not much to tell. The man is dead, with no apparent trace of a wound. Exactly what caused his death cannot be known until we reach Saltillo."

"No trace of a wound?"

"No."

"There's no reason, then, to suspect that he died anything except a natural death?"

"No," Rennert's gaze glanced against the opaque glass that shielded the other's eyes. "I merely suggested that we be prepared to give our statements to the authorities at Saltillo in case they require them."

"Well," Searcey took his hands from his pockets and leaned against the back of a seat, "in that case, suppose we all get acquainted and cut out the dramatics. This looks like a pretty respectable bunch of travelers to me. Since this gentleman," he nodded with exaggerated politeness across the car, "has been so thoughtful as to drag me into it, I'll be the first to introduce myself. My name is Searcey, William Searcey, from Forth Worth, Texas. I never saw the man who died before last night, in the smoker. I know nothing at all about him. I didn't leave my seat while we were in the tunnel." His laugh was mirthless. "Is there anyone else here who thinks he felt my corduroys?"

The glasses traveled slowly about the circle, the muscles about them contracting into a squint.

"Very well," he shrugged his loose shoulders, "I guess that finishes me."

A rather uneasy silence followed.

Rennert broke it: "Since Mr. Searcey has started the introductions, I'll continue. My name is Rennert, from New York among other places. I was back in the smoker while we were passing through the tunnel. I returned to this car after Mr. King here had noticed that this man was lying in a peculiar position upon his seat and had called me. I touched him and found that he was dead. I called the conductor immediately."

The train had reached the top of the grade now and was increasing its speed. Wheels clicked against rails in steady crescendo.

Spahr's elbow was propped upon his knee and his chin rested in the palm of his hand as his quick eyes surveyed the group.

"I'll be next," he spoke up. "Name's Ed Spahr. With the San

Antonio *Express*. I was back in the diner drinking beer while we were going through the tunnel. The waiter can testify to that, I think, also a lady who was at a table back there. I didn't know that anything had happened in here until we'd been out of the tunnel for some time." He shifted his position and looked down at King.

The latter caught Rennert's eye for an instant before he spoke.

"I am Jackson S. King, of Dallas, Texas," unconsciously probably a note of self-importance crept into his voice, "the King and Dysart Cotton Mills. I was seated in this exact spot during the entire time we were going through the tunnel. I know nothing whatever of the man who died. I never saw him before this morning, while we were in the station at Monterrey." He adjusted the pincenez and stared past the sheeted figure at the baked barrenness of sand and cactus outside the window.

Radcott was rolling up his sleeves, exposing thick moist arms.

"I'm Preston Radcott," he said, a forced smile upon his lips, "of Kansas City. I'm with the Southwestern Novelty Supply Company. I was back on the observation platform when we started through the tunnel. I stepped back inside and closed the door but stayed there until we were through. I came back here a few minutes later. I——" he stopped and drew out his handkerchief. "I guess that's all," he surveyed the begrimed cloth doubtfully before he began to mop his forehead.

Expectant silence fell between them. The steady rhythm of the rails had become again a regular restful monotone.

"Our friend in the seat there seems to have forgotten that

he is included in this truth session as well as the rest of us," Searcey's voice was edged with unveiled sarcasm.

The man had turned about in his seat to face them. His shoulders were squared and his slightly cleft chin was drawn up. His eyes had lost all of their vagueness and were clear and bleakly cold.

"Not at all, my friend," he spoke kindly. "I had not intended to avoid an introduction, but was merely waiting until you had all concluded. My name is Paul Xavier Jeanes. My home is in San Antonio. Of this poor soul," his eyes went for an instant to the sheet that lapped over the seat in front of him, "I know nothing whatever. All of us are upon a journey. His has ended sooner than ours. Let us hope that he was prepared." He paused. "Of what happened while we were passing through the tunnel I have spoken. I know nothing more."

A queer silence followed his words. A puzzled frown was on Radcott's face as he stared blankly at him.

Spahr stood up and ran his lingers through his hair. "Well," he said, with an effort at joviality that fell flat, "I guess that finishes the inquisition. Who'll have a beer?"

"I think I will," Radcott jammed the handkerchief into a hip pocket and started forward.

"Have you gentlemen forgotten me?"

Radcott turned at the sound of the quiet pleasant voice from behind him.

The woman who had sat at the rear of the car stood now in the center of the aisle, regarding them with a mild and slightly absent expression.

Radcott and Searcey stepped to one side and she advanced into the center of the group.

"Masculine conceit, I suppose, that always leaves the women on the sidelines when anything that they consider unpleasant is going on," she said with an abstracted smile. "Or is it the protective instinct we read so much about?"

Her face had probably always just missed being beautiful. There was a regularity of features which cosmetics might have emphasized over a coarseness of the lips and nose. The white pearl-like beauty of her teeth was marred by a slight protuberance. Her brown hair, streaked with gray, was twisted carelessly about her head into a tight knot at the back. Her smile was pleasant, lending a certain gentleness to her face.

"I am Miss Talcott, Trescinda Talcott," she said. "My home is in Coyoacan, a suburb of Mexico City. I am returning from a visit to the States. I was reading during most of your conversation, but I believe that I heard you say that someone had died." Her eyes, gray and kindly behind white gold spectacles, were on Rennert's face.

"Yes, Miss Talcott," he gestured toward the sheet, "a man died while we were passing through the tunnel back yonder. We were wondering if anyone on this car was acquainted with him."

"I'll look at him and see if I knew him, though I'm sure I didn't. I seldom pay any attention to my fellow-travelers—they are all so much alike."

She stepped forward and calmly threw back the sheet with her right hand. The light from the window struck the large diamond in the ornate old-fashioned setting upon the third finger so that the stone glowed with sudden fire.

"No," she shook her head slowly as she looked down at the dead face, "I don't remember ever having seen him before." Her voice had not lost its pleasant dispassionate tone. She let the sheet fall, folded her hands before her and said, still smiling: "But then all Mexicans are so much alike even when alive that one can't be expected to tell them apart when they're dead."

An awkward silence held them for a moment. King cleared his throat, very loudly it seemed.

"But Miss Talcott——" Jeanes had half risen from his seat, his face a shade paler than before.

"Yes?" she had turned to go but paused now and looked at him. She repeated: "Yes?" patiently.

A subtle change was taking place in the man's face. The skin seemed stretched very tightly across the thinly chiseled bones, so that they were whitely visible through its transparency. In his lips alone was perceptible a slight quivering, unable to be repressed. Some of this quivering was in his voice as he spoke in a strained unnatural tone: "But surely you cannot mean what you say! You cannot be so callous in the presence of death!"

She laughed, with singular lack of mirth. "No? What would you have me do—get as excited as the rest of you because a man has died?" Her eyes went to the window.

The train's speed had slackened and close to the tracks an occasional low, flat-roofed building was to be seen. Beyond these impudent evidences of man's intrusion the barren terrain rose and fell until it merged with the barren, shadow-flecked mountains.

"While you are here wrangling over this man—who he was and how he died—the mountains of Mexico are passing by that window and you are not seeing them."

Jeanes had gotten to his feet and was grasping the back of the seat with both hands. Beneath the ice of his eyes fires were alive and glowing as he stared unblinkingly at the woman.

She raised her right hand, as if in admonition to a child, and said very pleasantly: "Yes, yes, I know what you are about to say, Mr. Jeanes. About the sanctity of human life and all that. It's really not worth your while repeating it to me——"

She lowered her hand to steady herself as the train came to a sudden stop, moved forward with a convulsive jerk and was still again. Sudden uproar of porters' cries poured through the windows.

They were in Saltillo.

Chapter IV
CARNATIONS AGAINST A WALL
(11:55 A.M.)

A SCARRED veteran dreaming of battles, Saltillo, capital of the State of Coahuila, basks in the sun in a cup of the Sierra Madre Oriental more than five thousand feet above the level of the sea. Ancient adobe and stone houses spread away from green plazas and gray-white pavements and the heaven-jabbing tower of the Cathedral to flow like lava up the slopes of the mountains, toward the grim crumbling reminders of a sanguinary past.

The train rested in the Saltillo station for twenty-five minutes, the third of the series of delays that were to mark so fatalistically their southward course.

The twenty-five minutes were for Rennert minutes of confusion, of much pointless talk and of conferences as grave as they were futile. Officials of ascending degrees of importance in the railway hierarchy and an officer of the Mexican army, hastily summoned by the conductor, had boarded the Pullman and looked at the body. There had been a discussion of whether the man had died in the State of Nuevo Leon or of Coahuila and of jurisdiction. Dusty manuals were brought out and passed from hand to hand. His tourist certificate, issued by the Mexican consul in San Antonio, was examined and commented upon in low excited tones. His name was Eduardo Torner, of San Antonio, and he was—unexpectedly—certified as being a citizen of the United States. His age was given as thirty-eight and his profession as that of real-estate agent. This information had required the summoning of someone (Rennert never did find out exactly whom) who proved to be out of the city at the time. The air of tension that prevailed was due in part, Rennert surmised, to the strike which was threatening to tie up all traffic on the lines of the National Railways of Mexico. As yet no violence had occurred, but the railway officials evidently regarded this as being the first of a series of attempts to intimidate the workers. The army officer disagreed—volubly—although he maintained a discreet reserve on the subject of his suspicions.

At this point the doctor arrived, a stiffly dignified white-haired old gentleman who seemed to see no necessity for haste. His examination of the body was perfunctory. He found no traces of a wound upon it and was of the opinion that the man had died from natural causes, probably heart failure. He agreed, however, that a more detailed examination would be necessary before he could give a definite statement. The body was at last removed from the train, together with the single imitation-leather bag that had comprised the man's luggage.

Throughout all this Rennert had remained a silent, alert and grimly amused spectator. He had accompanied the group from the train, stood on the outskirts of another conference upon the platform and now sat in the small cluttered office of the station-master, across the table from the latter and the army officer.

Upon the boards of the table had been strewn the contents of the dead man's bag. There was little of importance there, it would seem. Two silk shirts and collars, a few handkerchiefs and socks, underwear, a few toilet necessities, a paper-backed Spanish novel—*El Cerro de las Campanas*—of the kind hawked in railway trains on both sides of the border. His pockets had contained, besides the tourist certificate, the usual masculine impedimenta—a few loose coins, a ring with two keys, a cheap pocket-knife, a packet of matches, Mexican cigarettes, a billfold containing fifty pesos in Mexican currency.

The room was close and fusty with the smell of human beings, of stagnant smoke, of long undisturbed dust.

Rennert was saying, a bit wearily, as he leaned forward in a creaky chair: "Of course it may turn out that this man died, as you think, of perfectly natural causes. On the other hand, I have given you my reasons for believing that he was murdered, as he had told of the words overheard in the Pullman the night before." He had evidently been affected more than he realized by the strained atmosphere, for the word had a sharp ugly sound in the still room. (The Spanish *"matado"* clicks like a knife-blade against the teeth.)

"But Señor Rennert, how?" the officer dropped his brown hand from his glossy waxed mustache and gestured widely.

"As to that," Rennert had to admit, "I do not know. Probably the doctor's examination will tell us. I have wired back to San Antonio, Texas, to learn the particulars about a man who fell unconscious upon the platform there last night before this train left. It is possible that I shall learn something which will aid us in this case. I should have a reply to my telegram by the time we reach Vanegas this afternoon. If so, I shall notify you."

The officer watched him with opaque black eyes. "Who was this man of whom you speak?"

"I have no idea. One of the passengers in the Pullman told me of the incident."

"You think that the same person killed both these men?" there was careful lack of expression in the question.

"I have no grounds for more than suspicion at present."

The stationmaster shifted his position in his chair. He was a very worried man. He was young (younger than his leathery face and the sparse black hair that lingered about his bald dome would indicate) and the past few hectic days had kept him in a state of continuous nervous tension. Two days before, when relations between the labor organizations in the Capital and the Railway had reached the breaking point, a train had been derailed just outside Saltillo. Little damage had been done and the train had continued on to the border within a few hours, but the incident had begun to assume ominous proportions in his mind in view of the increasing frequency of reports of sabotage at various points along the National Railway lines. He felt that he ought to come to some decision in this matter of the man who had died upon the Pullman; he felt that he would have done so at once had not this army officer intruded his presence, to complicate still further the already complicated question of jurisdiction.

"You are going on to Mexico City on this train?" he asked Rennert. (A sister of his wife's had married a mining engineer from the United States and this relationship had given him a feeling of confidence in the presence of the cool air of self-assurance of this type of American.)

"Yes." Rennert's eyes had rested momentarily upon the section of the platform visible through the open window. The tall woman whom he had seen in the diner was standing at the foot of the steps, idly surveying the scene. Her hair was gold in the sun, contrasting pleasingly with the jade green of her dress. From time to time she raised the cigarette holder to her lips and let blue clouds of smoke drift upward into the hot still air.

"In that case," the stationmaster summoned up courage enough to speak directly to the army officer, "might it not be well for us to keep in touch with Señor Rennert? In the event that this Eduardo Torner was involved in a plot to blow up the train, there may yet be danger. He may have confederates at some place along the line. There may have been a quarrel and one of them, or some enemy of his, may have killed him in the Pullman. From what Señor Rennert tells us, it would seem that the person who killed him is still on the train. Señor Rennert knows these people and can watch them. If you would detail some of your men to aid him——" the suggestion dangled.

The officer was again stroking the sparse hairs of his mustache. His dark amber face was expressionless.

"But there are soldiers on the train," he said at last. "Since the beginning of this strike all the trains have carried them."

"You will give them instructions, then, to be on their guard? To make an arrest in case Señor Rennert discovers that one of the passengers is threatening the safety of the train?"

"It is a question of authority," the other said pompously. "I must get in touch with my superiors."

"You will do it, then—at once?"

The hot heavy silence of a Mexican noon lay stagnant upon the little room as the officer pondered.

"Yes," he said at last, heavily.

Trescinda Talcott lowered the blind against a brown hand that was holding a pottery bowl of unsavory-looking food up to the window and a brown Indian face that was regarding her with pleading black eyes and repeating "*¡Ta-a-acos! ¡Ta-a-acos!*" with almost hysterical intensity. She marked her place in the novel with the bronze paper-knife which had come from Acapulco and moved an inch or two along the seat the large bag of plaited fiber which she had bought in Oaxaca. She relaxed a bit as she regarded with slightly amused eyes the man who sat opposite her.

She thought of him as a young man—a very young man despite his prematurely graying hair—and was amused by his perfervid air of seriousness. She had thought, after those trying yet bittersweet weeks through which she had just passed, that she could never again be amused by serious people. She had even grown a trifle bitter about them lately, she realized now. Yet this young man was different somehow. She tried to remember where she had seen a resemblance to him before—to his pallid face that seemed planed in ice yet reflected glowing fire somewhere beneath. There was a painting of El Greco's somewhere.

She brought herself back sharply to his words (he had just said something about the danger in which she stood) and realized that she had not been following him very closely. He had paused now and seemed to be waiting for her to say something.

She said, hoping that there would be some kind of connection between her reply and the question which he had evidently asked: "But it's because young peoples like the Americans have such a few generations of their dead beneath the soil of their country that each addition seems so important now."

She saw by the tensing of the muscles in the hands that grasped the knees of the shining black cloth that he was about to break out in protest but she went on imperturbably: "But, you see, I've lived in Mexico too long to go back to that way of thinking. For twenty-five years I've lived in a house which is built on the cemetery of a former monastery. Below that—far below—is the burial place of a people who lived there before the

Aztecs came to the Valley. Archæologists come and dig around the foundations of the house and find ugly little urns and statues."

She paused and thought: *I ought to stop now because he won't understand.*

"The flowers in my garden," she went on, "literally grow out of human bones. The back wall of my house was used by the Huertistas as a place of execution during the Revolution. The bullet marks are still there. Below them I planted the *xempoaxochitl,* the Indian's yellow death flower—wallflowers, we call them—but for some reason it wouldn't grow. I planted carnations then. Now they are the largest and the brightest in Coyoacan. I sometimes think——"

She wasn't sure whether her words had followed coherently upon his or not. *(That flower-bed behind La Casa de los Alamos, with the pearl and white snows of Popocatepetl in the distance! With the dampness of morning on them, the carnations lived, took on the pink and crimson tints of the flesh for which they were named—petaled carnivores.)* She passed a hand across her eyes, wondering if she had really fallen asleep.

The young man was leaning forward, one hand resting upon the edge of the seat opposite him. The ice of his eyes was clouded by bewildered frustration as he stared at her.

Behind them a door slammed and Radcott came into the car. He was perspiring profusely but his cheeks bulged with a boyish smile. Across one arm he held draped a large *sarape* with alternating stripes of brilliant reds and purples and yellows framing a huge purple eagle poised upon a cactus and devouring a writhing brown snake.

He came to a pause before them and held the *sarape* out. "Look what I bought out on the platform!" he said proudly.

Jeanes looked up and seemed to be trying to concentrate his thoughts. His right hand moved over the surface of the seat and came into contact with the fiber bag.

Miss Talcott was regarding the *sarape* with an attempted show of interest. She turned her head as Jeanes started to his feet. She looked at him for a moment with a puzzled frown. He was staring fixedly down at the bag and his lips were bloodless. "Pardon me," he murmured and walked uncertainly down the aisle.

She stared at his back for an instant, before turning her attention to Radcott again.

"How much did you pay for it?" she asked, her thoughts elsewhere.

Rennert walked through the sunlight toward the steps of the Pullman. The platform was deserted now save for two or three men who were regarding the windows of the train with flat black eyes.

At the foot of the steps stood the woman in jade green. Ed Spahr had joined her and they were examining some pieces of pottery which a smiling Indian woman held in a basket. Spahr was delving excitedly into the basket and holding up jars for the woman's inspection. She shook her head from time to time with an air of patient boredom and brushed away a fly with a little bunch of yellow wallflowers which she held in her hand. She made some remark to Spahr and turned toward the steps. He thrust the jar which he had been fingering back into the basket. As Rennert came up he turned to him and remarked: "Awfully cheap ugly stuff they have for sale here, isn't it? Miss Van Syle says that one can pick up much more artistic things in Indo-China."

Rennert wondered afterwards exactly what expression had been on his face, for Spahr laughed rather self-consciously and said: "Oh, you haven't met Miss Van Syle yet, have you?"

"No, I haven't had the pleasure."

"Miss Van Syle," Spahr called eagerly, "I'd like to present another of the passengers in the Pullman." As she turned her head slightly, "Miss Van Syle, Mr. Rennert."

"How do you do, Mr. Rennert?" her voice was low and resonant (with, Rennert couldn't resist the thought, a slightly affected cooing quality) but her eyes held the same look of languid boredom as she gazed for an instant into his. She turned then and resumed her way to the steps.

"Miss Van Syle is of the Long Island Van Syles," Spahr whispered to Rennert as he moved forward with alacrity to assist her.

Rennert followed them. They turned to the right, in the direction of the diner, while he started down the passage toward the Pullman. Here he met the porter, who was moving forward with his quick short steps, a folded sheet thrown over his arm. Rennert stopped him, his eyes on the sheet.

"Has the Pullman been cleaned out this morning?" he asked.

The brown little face moved from side to side in negation. "No, sir. The berths have been made up. That is all."

Rennert looked at him thoughtfully. "You closed the window beside the seat in which the dead man sat before the train entered the tunnel, did you not?"

"Yes, sir," the black pebbles held no expression whatever.

"Are you sure that he was alive then?"

"Yes, sir."

"Did he make any motions or say anything to you so that you can be positive of this?"

"Yes, sir." A pause. "He moved his feet so that I could reach the window."

"You saw this man when he got on the Pullman in San Antonio last night?"

"Yes, sir."

"Do you know what time he retired?"

The man's small dry lips seemed to move like those of an automaton. "No, sir."

"Did you see him after most of the other passengers had retired—say along about midnight?"

"Yes, sir."

"Where was he?"

"Last seat on the right, sir, number twelve."

"It is unoccupied, isn't it?"

"Yes, sir."

"Was he alone?"

He thought for an instant that there was about to be a shifting of the pebbles. They remained motionless, however, as the toneless reply came: "Yes, sir."

"I want you to think carefully now, over the time before the train arrived in Laredo. Did you see anyone near this man or talking to him?"

The wrinkles on the brown forehead deepened and the claw-like little hands moved about among the folds of the sheet, as if the effort of thinking moved responsive muscles in his body. "I did not see anyone."

"You came into the Pullman when the lady got off at Laredo, I suppose?"

The clanging of a bell and the sibilant hissing of steam echoed into the narrow passage. Wheels turned protestingly.

Rennert glanced sideways at the slowing moving platform of Saltillo.

He turned his head to meet the steady unblinking gaze of the pebbles. An odd light glinted against them now, however, almost but not quite penetrating their opacity.

Rennert repeated his question.

The little man shifted his weight from one short leg to the other, tightened his grip upon the sheet and said: "But no lady got off at Laredo, sir."

Chapter V
QUANTITY X
(12:20 P.M.)

RENNERT STARED at him. "You are sure of that?"

"Yes, sir."

"You were awake, of course, when the train stopped at Laredo?"

The porter's head moved quickly up and down. "Yes, sir."

Rennert started down the passage past him, stopped and asked: "Was there a lady with the man in berth number four, behind mine, when the train left San Antonio?"

"No, sir. There were eight passengers at San Antonio, seven lower berths and one upper. All of them are still here, except—" an almost imperceptible pause "one."

Rennert nodded abstractedly, reached in his pocket for a coin and handed it to the porter.

"Thank you, sir," the man inclined his head, revealed small firm white teeth in a smile, and walked on.

Rennert continued his way. He was confused and angry. The confusion was that of a person who surveys the surface upon which a sudden unexpected gust of wind has disarranged the pieces of a puzzle which he has so painstakingly fitted together.

The anger was at himself. Of a vocation which demands unceasing vigilance and the assumption that every individual, however innocent his exterior may seem, is a potential lawbreaker (sometimes, bitterly, thinking of past experiences with customs evasions, he wondered whether the assumption were not well founded) he found it a necessary relief, nevertheless, to indulge in thoughts about the up-rightness of human nature and to view the pillars of society with an unquizzical eye at such times as he could permit himself normal human relationships. That, he told himself severely, was exactly what he had been doing, without being aware of it, in this case. He had allowed the lodge emblem which hung from King's solid gold watchchain to carry over into his mind a connotation of solid businessmen's-luncheon-club dependableness. But what, he demanded of himself, could have been the purpose of the man's fabrication of this tale of a wife who had listened to a half-understood conversation in the middle of the night?

He stood in the door of the Pullman and glanced down its length.

In the second seat upon his right King was bending over, trying to unfasten shriveled limes from two thin sticks tied in the shape of a cross. He was frowning in concentration over the task. Jeanes sat rigid in his seat and stared straight in front of him. At the rear Miss Talcott held in both hands the edge of the *sarape* which was draped over Radcott's arm. She was smiling pleasantly and loosening thread after thread with her dexterous fingers. Radcott stood in the aisle and stared down at the *sarape*. His round face looked redder and graver than usual.

Rennert started down the aisle.

"But look at the weaving in it!" Radcott was protesting in a hurt voice. "It must have taken weeks of work to do that." Miss

Talcott was saying with a patient smile: "One glance should have told you that it is factory and not hand made. They always sell tourists worthless things like this. You shouldn't have bought it, at least not in a railway station. What earthly good is it to you? And you paid too much for it. Thirty pesos!" She let the edge of the blanket fall from her fingers. "You could have gotten it for ten, if you had waited until you found some Indian who was hungry or who wanted to get drunk. That's the way to get things cheap in Mexico."

Rennert stepped past Radcott's obstructing bulk and sat down in the seat beyond, number twelve on the right side. He had been bound here when he had met the porter in the aisle.

He leaned forward and began a deliberate and minute examination of the seat opposite.

He had no particular hope of finding anything there but at least the deceased had sat there the night before, with or without a vis-à-vis. Also, it gave him a routine procedure to go through with while he was deciding where to begin fitting the scattered pieces of the puzzle together again. Shaving, he reflected as he surveyed the blank unresponsive surface of the green cloth, would have done as well or better. There was something about the face-to-face communion with one's self in the mirror. . . .

Of course, the most obvious explanation was that King had fabricated this story of a mysterious individual who had been in conversation with the Mexican the night before in order to furnish a convenient quantity *x* in the equation which would result in case the latter's death, *which had not yet occurred*, should be attributed to other than natural causes. In that case was he, Rennert, to read some meaning into the words "earrings and cuffs" and "don't forget the extra edition?"

He bent over the floor next. There was always the chance

that one of those ubiquitous clues which one read about would present itself obligingly for labeling as Exhibit A. Too bad that footprints and fingerprints were out. The butt of a cigarette might do, if it were of an exotic brand smoked by one—and only one—individual in that car. No, that wouldn't do. In the smoker the unknown might have lit a cigarette while conversing with his intended victim, but not in the Pullman,

The floor was kinder than the seat. Or, Rennert wondered as he stared down at the objects which lay upon it, was it?

Below the seat in which he sat were two kernels of molasses-coated popcorn, a crumpled carton and, next to the wall, a cheap brass stickpin. With exaggerated gravity Rennert moved the kernels of popcorn about with the toe of his shoe, studying them. He contemplated picking them up and consigning them carefully to an envelope for future examination by a chemist. There was always poison to be considered, of course, in anything edible which remained on the scene of a crime. But if Señor Eduardo Torner had eaten popcorn here it must have been the night before and not just previous to his death. And that death had coincided so neatly with the passage of the train through the tunnel that Rennert firmly refused to allow the popcorn a place among lettered exhibits. The stickpin he wasn't at all sure about. He leaned over and picked it up. It was an exceedingly cheap sort of affair. The head of it was a small white horse of what had evidently been intended to look like pearl. Rennert could not picture anyone wearing such an atrocity. He turned it about in his fingers, wondering whether it deserved the primary place among the letters of the alphabet. Considering the lack of any other claimant for the place. . . .

"Clues?"

There was pleasant raillery in the voice. He looked up at

Miss Talcott, who was standing in the aisle, regarding him with a smile. Radcott had disappeared.

Rennert had to laugh. "Frankly," he said, "I don't know. I'm afraid I am in the awkward position of not being able to recognize a clue when I see one." He extended his hand, upon the palm of which rested the stickpin. "What would be your verdict on this?"

She took the pin and glanced at it. She frowned slightly and her eyes became a bit vague. "If it were found on the scene of the crime now," she said, "it might mean something. But found back here where no one was sitting." She looked at him oddly. "Why were you searching the floor back here?"

"I understand that the man who died this morning was sitting here late last night, before we reached Laredo."

"Well?"

"I thought, Miss Talcott, that perhaps he were talking to someone here."

The fixity of her gaze became disconcerting. "A peculiar time to be indulging in conversation," she said.

"Exactly, Miss Talcott, a very peculiar time." He glanced across the aisle. "Your berth is the first one forward, isn't it?"

"Yes."

"I don't suppose you heard the sound of voices back here?"

She smiled slightly. "No, but that means nothing. I usually sleep very soundly at night." She gazed down at the pin, as if fascinated by it. Her absent expression did not change as she said quietly: "There's one explanation, of course, for this."

"Yes?"

"It's the white horse. Do you know what one means in Mexico when he says that someone rides a white horse?"

Memory stirred in Rennert.

"It means," she went on without waiting for his reply, "that the person referred to is going to his death."

Rennert nodded slowly, thoughtfully. "I had forgotten."

She handed the pin back to him. "That sounds like something out of a thriller, doesn't it?" Her eyes were searching his face. "I'm surprised that you don't laugh at me for suggesting it."

Rennert pushed the pin into the cloth of the underside of his lapel. "In Mexico," he said candidly, "one gets accustomed to the fantastic."

She had turned to pick up the fiber bag from her seat. At his words she looked at him quickly. "You've had experience with Mexico?"

"A great deal, Miss Talcott."

She slipped the handle of the bag over the white starched cuff of her left sleeve. "No wonder you don't laugh at me then," she said quietly as she started down the aisle.

Rennert sat with his head half turned and watched her disappear in the direction of the diner. He moved then to the seat opposite and sat by the lowered blind, staring thoughtfully down the car, deserted now save for Jeanes, whose motionless gray head projected above the rear of his seat.

Earrings and cuffs. Don't forget the extra edition. It was nonsensical, he told himself. The whole business verged on nonsense so blatant that it was insane. By no stretch of the imagination could the earrings and cuffs belong to anyone except this quiet Miss Talcott. And if King had intended to implicate her in the affair why hadn't he said simply that it was a woman's voice which had been heard? But no, he had been insistent upon the fact that it was a man's voice and that it had had a "foreign" accent. There was nothing masculine about Miss Talcott's soft tones and nothing that could be termed foreign-sounding.

The extra edition. Rennert drew the San Antonio newspaper from his pocket again and carefully went from paragraph to paragraph of it, rereading every item that might by any chance have a bearing upon the business in hand. It seemed to him that the pages were remarkably sterile in reader interest, as if, with the heat, doldrums had settled upon Texas, the Southwest, and the nation. There was a great deal about the drought and governmental plans for aiding the stricken regions. Cattle were dying of thirst and hunger on the West Texas plains. In a syndicated article a well-known scientist advanced a complicated theory to account for the unprecedented heat wave, something about sunspots which appeared over long periods of time. The Governor of Oklahoma had proclaimed a day of prayer for relief from brazen skies. The Hopi Indians of New Mexico were holding a snake dance for the same purpose. Even politics, which in Texas usually rise in fervor with the thermometer, seemed to be in a state of temporary lethargy. The sensational Montes kidnapping case, which for so long had been a godsend to news-avid reporters appeared to have been drained dry of material for copy. The nurse of the abducted boy had been released from custody at last, for lack of evidence of her implication.

On the next to the last page, below the comic strips, a signature over a feature article caught Rennert's eye. The name was that of Ed Spahr.

Rennert ran his eyes down the lines.

As Aztec drums beat again in remote mountain villages of Mexico, what strange rites will be performed unseen by the eyes of white men? the writer queried.

Does the strange stone altar recently discovered on a mountain peak in Michoacan await some bloody oblation to unforgotten gods?

Will the approaching eclipse of the sun bring forth from its centuries-old hiding place the obsidian sacrificial knife or its modern equivalent—the *machete* and the bayonet?

These are the questions that are being whispered in the cities of Mexico as astronomers adjust their instruments to study the eclipse of the sun, which on May 27 will be total in the arid section of north-central Mexico lying about the Tropic of Cancer and embracing portions of the states of Tamaulipas, Nuevo León, San Luis Potosí, Zacatecas, Durango, and Sinaloa.

The white man's culture is at best but a thin veneer in Mexico and the districts which the eclipse will plunge into total darkness at midday comprise some of the least known parts of the country.

It was in this region that there appeared a few years ago the Child Fidencio, whose fame as a healer grew so rapidly that the government was forced to send troops to keep in order the frantic throngs that sought to reach the worker of magic cures. And the Child's string laid upon the sands proved more potent than the guns of the State!

And it is not so many years ago that the little mountain village of Tomochic, in Chihuahua, became a Mecca for religious fanatics, under the apostalship of the Maid of Cabora, and led to one of the bloodiest wars of the Diaz Regime.

Small wonder then that with these and countless other examples of curious interminglings of pagan and Christian worship in their minds, city-dwellers are not at rest in Mexico today.

Recently a German explorer returned to the Capital after a three months' stay in the mountainous regions of the Southwest. He reports the discovery, on an isolated mountain peak south of Lake Patzcuaro in the state of Michoacan, of a rude altar, made of stones laid one upon another in the shape of a small pyramid. This, he affirms, shows indications of having been recently erected, although there were no human-habitations near by and the dwellers in the nearest villages professed ignorance of the altar and of its purpose.

This discovery, which is causing considerable consternation in that section of Mexico, calls to mind the hideous human sacrifices with which the ancient Aztecs worshipped their gods and sought to propitiate them in times of danger.

Such occasions were particularly those when the heavenly bodies left their ordered routine in the skies. Greatly dreaded were the demons Tzitzimime, whose advent to destroy the world was greatly feared during eclipses.

When the eclipse came dogs were pinched to make them howl and a noise was made by striking the doors or furniture of the huts, thus frightening off the Tzitzimime. The Emperor Montezuma, who was in constant consultation with the astrologers, kept in his zoological gardens a collection of albinos, reserved for sacrifice at such times.

Many educated Mexicans, who are inclined to make light of rumors of survivals of pagan practices such as human sacrifices by the knife, admit nevertheless that propitiation of the elements of nature may take other forms.

In this connection reported renewal of the Cristero outbreaks, which in 1927 plunged Mexico into turmoil, takes on added significance.

Under the guise of defenders of the Church against governmental persecution, native fanatics who have confused the forms of Christianity with those of pre-Conquest paganism may, it is admitted by many, substitute for the ancient knife of sacrifice the more modern but no less effective rifle and bayonet.

Blood may yet induce the sun of Mexico to uncover its face!

Spahr had evidently ransacked several encyclopedias for information, striving to refurbish timeworn properties of horror. The result was a rather dismal failure, Rennert reflected as he read on to the end.

He glanced at his watch, decided that food would help, and got up, thrusting the paper back into his pocket.

As he advanced down the aisle he saw Jeanes glance about quickly. His gaze rested for an instant on Rennert's face then traveled about the car.

When Rennert came abreast of him he said with lips that scarcely moved: "I should like to speak with you, Mr. Rennert."

Rennert sat down opposite him.

For several moments Jeanes said nothing but sat staring at a point just above Rennert's head as if he had become all at once unaware of the other's presence.

Rennert regarded him curiously. The man puzzled him. He thought of him (as had Miss Talcott) as a man consumed by some inner white-hot fire which sent occasional curious strainings to the surface of his ice-fragile face. Somewhere, at the back of Rennert's mind, recognition tapped elusively. (Of the passengers in that coach during those tense twenty-four hours, this man was to remain longest in his memory. Probably because the man himself, as well as the mission which had brought him to Mexico, remained to the last partially unexplained. Whether Paul Xavier Jeanes were his real name or an assumed one he was never certain. The silence of Mexico was to envelop him as effectively as the gray adobe wall behind which he disappeared the next morning, at the little railway station outside Mexico City where the sun glinted against naked bayonets.)

At last Jeanes lowered his eyes to Rennert's face. The ice in them was deep and hard and misty blue.

"I have done a terrible thing," he said in a low vibrant voice. "I have presumed to bear witness against a fellow man too hastily, without asking myself if my weak human senses might not err. Yet I was so sure——"

"What is it that is troubling you?" Rennert asked quietly.

The words slipped slowly through Jeanes' lips: "I was sure that I felt the corduroy trousers of Mr. Searcey when someone leaned over the seat in front of me. Now, I am not sure."

"What has caused you to believe that you might be mistaken about the corduroy?"

"A few minutes ago," Jeanes held his hands spread out in front of him and stared at them, "I felt an object exactly like that which touched my hand in the tunnel. It was," he paused and said almost inaudibly, "a fiber bag."

Chapter VI
HELIOPHOBIA
(1:15 P.M.)

SUNLIGHT POURED in below the lowered blinds and bathed the diner in glare. A pencil of it, striking the water-bottle on the table across the aisle, was shattered to glittering bits of crystal.

The dark concave lenses of William Searcey's glasses stared at the vacant tables by the windows to his left. He stood in the aisle for a moment, hesitantly, then approached the table where Rennert sat alone.

"Mind if I sit here?" he asked as he laid a hand upon the back of the chair opposite Rennert's.

"Sure not. Sit down." Rennert took his gaze from the contorted masses of rock through which the train was passing and his thoughts from the words which he had just heard from Jeanes' lips. He watched Searcey lower his weight into the chair and glance out the window. The muscles about the oval panes of his glasses twitched spasmodically.

"Going right up, aren't we?" Searcey remarked conversationally. "You can feel the difference in altitude already."

"Yes, the engine seems to be having difficulty in making the grade."

"Do you have a watch?"

"Yes," Rennert drew it out. "One-twenty."

Searcey frowned. "We're running late, aren't we?"

"Yes."

The small lips tightened a bit. "That will put us into Mexico City late tomorrow morning, I suppose."

"Trains are usually able to make up their lost time when they get up onto the plateau."

There was an interval of silence. Searcey had reached forward for a menu and was studying it. He had put on a loose Norfolk jacket, of the same material as his trousers, and looked warm and ill-at-ease. Rennert had an opportunity to observe the man's sunburnt face. None of its surface had escaped the cruel searing of the sun's rays, although the throat below his squared-off jaw showed a splotch of whiter skin. Shaving had evidently been a painful operation, for a stubble of dead-white hairs protruded from the blistered flesh of his cheeks, his upper lip, and his chin. The effect of these colorless hairs was rather startling, seen in contrast with the glossy dark-brown hair that covered his head.

He pushed the menu aside and looked up at Rennert. A halfsmile was on his lips.

"I suppose," he said, "that I ought to apologize for forcing myself on you like this."

"Not at all. Glad of your company."

"As a matter of fact," Searcey said a bit awkwardly, "I didn't want to sit on the other side because of the sun. Its glare hurts my eyes." A large hand went up to his glasses and adjusted them more securely upon the bridge of his nose. "I've been exposed to the sun quite a bit lately, as you've probably noticed."

"As a matter of fact, I had noticed it," Rennert said with a sympathetic smile.

"I've been down in the lower Rio Grande Valley, having some land cleared for growing citrus-fruit. That sun's no place for a white man to be."

The middle-aged *mestizo* waiter set Rennert's dessert before him and thrust an order-blank and pencil in front of Searcey. He picked up the pencil, held it poised over the paper as if in indecision, then hastily scribbled upon the surface. He pushed the blank toward the waiter.

When the latter had left, Rennert thought that Searcey's gaze rested for a moment upon the ice-cream which lay before him.

"Go right ahead," the man said, "don't wait on me."

Rennert began upon the ice-cream.

At the next table Spahr and Miss Van Syle sat across from each other. Several diminutive bottles of Hennessy cognac stood before the newspaperman, empty. He was leaning forward, elbows on the table, and talking rapidly and a bit too loudly. "Of course you'll probably find Mexico City rather dull after Paris," he was saying, "at least judging from what friends of mine have told me about it. But I've got the addresses of some people down there—in the American Colony—who ought to be able to give us some pointers. One of them has promised to give me a card to the American Club." The woman rested against the back of her chair and looked at him through the coiling smoke of a cigarette. From time to time she delicately sipped Sauterne from the glass in front of her.

Beyond them the silver-gray knot of hair at the back of Miss Talcott's head was visible above the starched white collar.

Searcey sat staring out the window until Rennert finished his ice-cream.

He leaned slightly forward then and asked in a lowered voice: "What happened back in Saltillo when they took that Mexican's body off the train? Did they find out the cause of his death?"

"No," Rennert set down his glass, "the doctor was unable to say from a brief examination."

"There's still no reason to think it wasn't heart failure or something like that, then?"

"No."

Searcey's fingers slowly and methodically marshaled the silverware into position. "All that excitement for nothing, then," he said without looking up.

"Perhaps."

"Perhaps?" the blank dark surfaces of the glass rose to meet Rennert's gaze.

"It is possible, of course, that a more careful examination in Saltillo may reveal particulars about his death that will necessitate further investigation."

"Of the passengers in the Pullman?"

"Yes."

Searcey compressed his lips and silently watched the waiter place a sandwich and a cup of coffee before him. When the waiter had gone he said, without making any motion to begin his meal: "But they let us go ahead on this train?"

"Yes, there was not sufficient reason to stop anyone."

Searcey picked up his sandwich. Rennert glanced for a moment from the window. The train had come to a panting stop at a little dusty station of gray stone.

"I noticed that several extra soldiers got on the train at Saltillo."

Rennert turned his head and saw that Searcey was holding the sandwich in his hand, regarding it thoughtfully.

"Yes," he said, "doubtless as extra precaution in case of trouble caused by the strike."

"Oh!" Searcey said with, Rennert felt, a careful lack of expression, "I had been wondering why they got on." He bit into the sandwich, hungrily.

Miss Van Syle rose and walked slowly down the aisle toward the door. Spahr followed her.

As she passed their table Rennert saw Searcey look up. The muscles of his eyes looked as if they were contracting into a nearsighted squint as he stared at her face. As if conscious of the directness of his gaze she turned her head and looked down at him. He made a slight uncertain inclination of the head and moved his lips as if to speak. There was no recognition in her cycs, however, as she moved forward with a graceful studied gait.

"Funny," Searcey remarked when the door had closed behind her and Spahr, "I thought for a minute I knew that woman. I thought I recognized her when she was standing on the platform at San Antonio last night, but I guess I was mistaken. Know who she is?"

"Miss Van Syle," Rennert replied—and added with a touch of malice, "of the Long Island Van Syles, I believe."

Searcey shook his head and took another bite of the sandwich. "Don't know her," he said.

Rennert glanced out the window again. The little station still stood motionless, bathed in the glare of the sun.

"I've been intending to ask you something," he said carefully, "about last night."

Searcey's jaws were still. "Yes?" he said indistinctly.

"Some time before we got to Laredo the Mexican who died in the Pullman this morning was sitting on the last seat in the rear of the car, two seats beyond your berth. You have number eight, don't you?"

"No, I was sitting there this morning but I have upper six, above Radcott."

"Well, it makes no difference really. I was merely wondering if by any chance you had heard the sound of voices back there."

"Voices?" the glasses were staring directly at Rennert. "He was talking to someone?"

"Not that I know of but it struck me as a rather late hour for him to be sitting up, unless he had company."

Searcey was silent for a moment. He laid the remnants of the sandwich carefully upon his plate and asked: "I suppose it was the porter who saw the Mexican back there?"

"Yes."

Searcey thought a moment. "I was trying to remember," he said slowly. "I was wakened by the noise when we crossed the border but I don't believe that I heard anyone talking in the car then. I had been asleep for some time before that."

"Did you observe this Mexican very closely when you saw him last night?"

There was no expression at all on Searcey's face as he stared at Rennert and said: "When I saw him?"

"Yes, in the smoker."

"Oh." (Rennert's eyes narrowed ever so slightly. As flat as the monosyllable had been, he thought that he detected a faint note of unguarded relief in it.) "I'd almost forgotten that. No, I didn't pay any particular attention to him. Why?"

Rennert took the stickpin from the lapel of his coat and held it out. "Do you remember," he asked casually, "if he was wearing this in his tie or elsewhere?"

Searcey's brows contracted into a thoughtful frown as he looked at the pin. "Yes," he nodded slowly, "I believe he was wearing that in his tie—or at least one like it."

Rennert returned the pin to his lapel. "I supposed that it was his."

"Where'd you find it?"

"On the floor by the seat where he was sitting last night."

Rennert glanced out the window again. The train's delay at this little station was beginning to worry him. Nervousness was so rare with him that he recognized its symptoms with something approaching alarm.

"If you'll pardon me," he said, "I think I'll get out and stretch my legs. We seem to be delayed here for some reason."

"That's bad," Searcey's frown deepened. "The fourth time it's happened. San Antonio, the border, Saltillo, and now here. Looks as if the cards were stacked against us on this trip." He paused. "By the way, do you ever play poker?"

"Sometimes."

"What about a game this afternoon? It'll help kill the time and may take our minds off—other things."

"Sorry," Rennert said frankly, "but I don't think I could keep my thoughts on cards. I'm a poor player anyway."

He thought that Searcey looked at him oddly. "Worried?" he asked quietly.

"Frankly, yes."

"About what's happened or what's going to happen?"

Rennert laughed and got to his feet. "Both, I suppose."

"What time is it now?"

Rennert consulted his watch again. "One thirty-five."

Searcey kept his gaze on Rennert's face. "Let me know what you find out about the delay here, will you?" he asked. "I don't want to get out in the sun." He paused. "I expect I have more reason to worry than you."

"How's that?"

"It's important that I get into Mexico City on time in the morning. I've got an offer of a job down there—and it closes at noon."

"Even with a few delays we should be in Mexico City long before noon," Rennert said as he turned down the aisle.

He stepped out upon the platform and half closed his eyes against the glare.

The station was Carneros.

It lay lethargic and baking beneath the afternoon sun. Far away, across the cacti-sprinkled desert, the austere brown and blue mountains, flecked with cloud shadows, were wavering mirages.

The conductor stood beside the car, gazing with a worried expression in the direction of the engine. "What's the matter?" Rennert inquired.

The man shrugged wearily. "It is the engine, señor. They are having trouble with it. Up to this point the grade has been very steep. We are almost to the level of Mexico City now." He pulled out his watch. "We are very late but we will make up the time when the new engine meets us." He returned the watch to his pocket and glanced around nervously.

Rennert noticed the direction of his gaze. He looked up into the sky. It was clear and blue, with an occasional fleecy white cloud close upon the horizon. High overhead another vulture floated in almost imperceptible spirals.

"You are getting a new engine?" he asked, as he took his gaze from the sky and felt in his pocket for cigarettes. There was, he had to admit, something rather disquieting about the unfailing presence of those damned *zopilotes*.

"Yes," the conductor was starting toward the steps, "they have wired to San Luis Potosí for another engine to meet us at Vanegas."

"The grade is downward from here to Vanegas, isn't it?"

"Yes, there will be no difficulty, I am sure. And with the new engine all will go well. *Con permiso, señor.*"

Rennert drew soothing smoke into his lungs as he looked about him.

By the corner of the station Preston Radcott stood, bareheaded in the sun. His arms were crossed and he was staring absently across the desert at the mountains.

The platform was deserted save for a beggar who crouched in the dust and looked with motionless eyes across the glare.

Below the observation platform King stood in the shade of the Pullman and drew contemplatively upon a thin cigar. There was a look of concentration upon his face as he gazed beyond the train and from time to time turned his head nervously in the direction of the engine.

"God, it's hot!" Spahr stood upon the lower step and passed a handkerchief over his face. "Texas doesn't know what heat is."

Rennert turned, agreed, and came a step or two nearer. He took the stickpin from his lapel and showed it to Spahr. "Ever see that before?" he asked.

Spahr looked at it and grinned. "No. Looks like the bargain counter at a five and ten cent store."

Rennert turned the pin about in his fingers. "I was wondering if it belonged to Torner, the Mexican who died this morning. Did you see him last night in the Pullman?"

"Yes, I saw him," Spahr said readily. "He was in the smoker when I was getting ready to go to bed. He didn't have that pin on though."

"You're sure?"

"Well, fairly sure. I remember noticing his necktie, a loud one with pink and green checks. If he'd had that pin on I think I'd have noticed it."

"Thanks," Rennert returned the pin to his lapel. "I may have been mistaken."

Spahr looked at him with some interest. "Where'd you get it?"

"I found it in the Pullman. No one seems to want to claim it."

"I don't blame 'em. I wouldn't wear it on a bet."

Rennert changed the subject. "By the way, I was just reading one of your stories in the San Antonio *Express*. The extra edition that came out last night."

"Yeah?" Spahr was looking over Rennert's head. "Which one?"

"The one about the eclipse and human sacrifices in Mexico."

"Oh," the young man grinned. "Pretty lousy, wasn't it?"

"I did miss the sacred virgins thrown into the sacrificial well."

Spahr's blue eyes were partially closed as he stared upward into the sky. "I'll have to put them in the next one," he said absently. "I wrote that story when I had a hangover, maybe that accounts for the worst parts. I'd just gotten back from a trip down into the country around El Paso, following up a lead in the Montes kidnapping case, when I ran across an old college prof of mine. He gave me the dope on Mexico, seemed to take it all seriously. I thought I might as well make a story out of it."

"You covered the Montes case?"

"Yes, while it was news. Everybody's tired reading about it now so I got 'em to put another man on it while I came to Mexico."

"What's your idea as to the identity of the kidnapper?"

Spahr laughed. "You're about the thousandth person who's asked me that. I haven't got any idea, to tell the truth. I always thought the kid's nurse was mixed up in it but they've released her now. I don't suppose they ever will know who did it. What're those—buzzards?"

Rennert's eyes followed the direction of his gaze. "Yes, *zopilotes* they are called down here."

"A lot of 'em, aren't there? There are three—no, four—in one bunch. Something must have died." His jaw fell suddenly. "Think I'll try another beer," he said as he turned.

"Mr. Rennert!" King's voice was thin and brittle in the heavy heat-laden stillness.

Rennert turned and walked toward him.

From the doorway of an adobe hut an Indian face stared blankly past pink and scarlet geraniums at the train. There was an inveiled look about the unwinking obsidian eyes that reminded one of a lizard, lying upon a sunlit wall and staring at nothingness.

King coughed nervously. "What's the matter up there?" there was no attempt to conceal the anxiety in his voice. "According to the time-table we're only supposed to stop here a minute or two. We've been here fifteen."

Rennert explained.

King stood for a moment, drawing furiously upon the cigar.

Dust filmed the lenses of his pince-nez so that his eyes looked remote. He spoke hurriedly. "Something queer happened back there in Saltillo. I thought I ought to tell you about it. This is the first chance I've had to get you alone."

Rennert noticed that he kept his eyes averted. "Yes?" he prompted.

With a forefinger King carefully flicked the ash from the cigar. "I was standing on the platform, watching the crowd. An old Indian woman came up with some limes on a stick. My throat was dry so I thought I'd buy them from her. I was trying to find out how much they were when I noticed a man standing close by, watching me closely. He was well dressed, looked—well, white, if you know what I mean. He came up, said something to me in Spanish that I didn't understand and shoved a piece of paper into my pocket. He disappeared into the crowd before I could stop him."

He paused and thrust the cigar back into his mouth. He put a hand into the pocket of his coat and brought out a folded piece of paper. He handed it to Rennert.

Rennert unfolded it.

It was an ordinary sheet of cheap ruled writing-paper. Upon it had been typed, with frequent erasures: *"Nuestros amigos en San Antonio advierten que el peligro vuela sobre su tren. Se le espia. ¡Cuidado!"*

Rennert stared at it, read it again.

"It's Spanish, isn't it?" King queried. "What does it mean?"

Rennert shrugged and folded the paper. "Do you mind if I keep this for a while?" he asked. "I'd like to study it over. I'm not sure, you see, exactly what it does mean."

A queer startled look flitted across King's face. "It's nothing serious, is it? Nothing to do with the train?"

Rennert did his best to smile reassuringly. "It probably means nothing at all, it was evidently given to you by mistake."

"You think it was meant for someone else on the Pullman, then?"

"Yes."

"But how could that man have made a mistake? I don't resemble anyone else on the train."

Rennert had been staring thoughtfully at the mountains. He brought his eyes back to King's iron-gray hair, silver in the sunlight.

"You were buying limes, you say?" his voice sounded abstracted.

"Yes."

Rennert was thinking of the fruit which King had brought back into the Pullman. Limes upon two sticks arranged in the shape of a cross. A message which, translated into English, read: *"Our friends in San Antonio warn that danger hovers over your train. You are being watched. Take care!"*

Up ahead the engine was disturbing the brooding peace of the desert with its puffings and janglings.

"¡A bordo!" came the conductor's warning cry.

Radcott strolled toward the train, his hands thrust into his pockets and his shoulders thrown forward. He stopped to toss a coin to the beggar, who sprang at it with the agility of a monkey.

Rennert asked as he walked by King's side toward the steps: "I believe you said that you didn't see this man Torner last night?"

King looked at him quickly. "No, not until this morning, while the train was at Monterrey. He was walking up and down the aisle then."

Rennert held out the stickpin. “I don’t suppose, then, that you could identify this as having belonged to him?”

King glanced at the pin. “No,” he said, “I couldn’t.”

They walked on, their feet making crunching noises in the gravel that sounded unnaturally loud in the hot heavy silence.

Rennert said: “I wish that you would do something for me when we get to Vanegas, Mr. King.”

“All right,” King had turned his head to look at the beggar. “What is it?”

“I want you to send a telegram to your wife in Laredo.”

King kept his head turned away from Rennert and did not answer at once. “Sure,” he said after a moment, “I’ll be glad to. What about?”

“I want you to ask her about the location of the voice which she heard last night. You said, I believe, that it was behind her. That might have meant either the front or the rear of the car, depending upon which way she was facing. She can send you the answer to San Luis Potosí.”

King was frowning. “There’s no need to wire her about that,” he said shortly. “I can tell you. She was facing the front of the train. She always does. It gives her a headache to ride the other way.”

“Just the same, I want you to wire her—to make sure.”

“All right,” King’s voice was smothered, “I’ll wire her.”

He paused at the foot of the steps and allowed Radcott to precede him. He turned once more and glanced across the sunlit ground at the beggar, who was sitting in the same posture, motionless, staring at the train.

A slight tremor passed over his thin gray-clad shoulders. He asked: “Does Mexico make you afraid too, Mr. Rennert?”

Chapter VII
THE SWEETNESS OF THE MANGO
(4:20 P.M.)

Coralie Van Syle closed her eyes in delicious relaxation and, after a long time, opened them again, hoping to catch once more that breathtaking stab of excitement which had gone through her that morning when she had awakened in her berth and looked out over the desert into the unreality of the mountains of Mexico. It was gone now—never, she knew, to be recaptured—but there remained something distinctly more pleasant, something which took away awareness of the cool shaded compartment in which she sat and the fabricated comfort of her surroundings, something which drew a merciful screen between her and the scalding heat of the sun on alkali-crusted sand and rock, the ugly distorted little trees and the diminutive whirlwinds that writhed between her window and the mountains. The mountains were blue and haze-dimmed, hovering in the air like mirages—and she was moving between them, as unreal as they.

She leaned back in her chair, carefully inserted a cigarette in the jade holder and pressed the catch on a gold lighter. She gazed over the tiny flame into the mirror on the door and studied her reflection. She flexed her thumb, adjusted the holder between fore and index finger and was satisfied. She drew upon the cigarette and laid the lighter upon the top of the table. She looked for a moment at the bright upraised surface of the lighter, paneled by smaller receding surfaces, and at the initials engraved there. CVS. Coralie Van Syle. She formed the syllables slowly, letting them rest for an instant on her tongue and lips before releasing them. She thought: *I am Coralie Van Syle and in a strange land where I know no one and no one knows me. Nothing else matters.*

Her lips, from long force of habit, formed other practiced syllables: Popocatepetl, Ixtaccihuatl, the rocks of Acapulco, Chapultepec, Taxco, and the Causeway of the Sad Night. There had been, of course, those names upon the maps of the Orient and of Egypt in the circulars of the travel agencies. She regretted them. But time was short—so terribly, terribly short that she had hated each ugly little station in Texas that retarded her journey to the Rio Grande.

Upon the table lay a flat leather book and beside it a fountain pen. She reached over and took them into her hands. She wrote, tentatively, upon the fly leaf then turned the pages until she found the one she was seeking. The fingers which held the pen moved for a few minutes over the lines. She closed the book and laid it back upon the table. With a vestige of the old secrecy, for which there was no longer any need, she placed three brightly jacketed volumes on top of the book in which she had been writing.

Beside the books lay the little bunch of silly yellow wall-flowers which that impressionable young newspaperman had bought for her on that blistering hot railway platform. She hadn't bothered to put them in water and they were drooping now, their edges shriveling. Strange, the way that old Mexican woman had acted—as if she hadn't wanted to sell them. She had said something in Spanish which neither of them had understood. The young man had given her a *peso* for them.

She stared at the flowers, her eyes suddenly unseeing, and tried to remember more of his incoherent rattling talk about something which had happened up in the Pullman, among those boring ordinary people. With fierce satisfaction her lips formed the words: *boring ordinary people.*

Try as she might she could not fight off the queer sensation of uneasiness which was creeping over her again. It had been returning with increasing frequency throughout the day, tapping at the foundations of her resolve that nothing should mar the perfection of that flight into strange glorious space. What, she told herself desperately, was as important in all the world as this intoxicatingly sweet sense of freedom? That alone mattered now.

With perverse desire to taste again the mango-sweetness of guilt she drew the beaded hand bag from the place where it nestled beside her in the chair. She had tasted a mango for the first time that morning. *That,* she thought, *was exactly what it was like—the first bite into a ripe mango and the sudden revulsion from its sweetness.* She laid the bag upon her lap and carefully opened the clasp. With cautious fingers she took out an object and placed it upon the bag.

It lay there clean and sharp and evil-looking, against the tiny black and white beads. She looked at it for a long time before she could bring herself to touch it with a forefinger. She had seen them before in doctors' offices, associated in her mind with spotless white enamel and a pervading odor of disinfectants. But here, lying in her lap, it looked different somehow, and made her almost sick. The point of the needle looked so sharp and there remained in the glass tube a little of the thick liquid, almost as black as ink. Without wanting to, she pressed her finger against the end of the tube. The liquid welled up and she jerked away the finger. A shiver of coldness went through her.

The knocking at her door was very gentle and she did not realize for an instant that it was knocking. It came again, more insistently this time, and she thrust the syringe into the bag. She snapped the bag shut and rose. She was not aware until after she had called "Come in" and the door had opened that she was standing with her fingers tightly gripping the handle.

"Good afternoon." The man stood with one hand still upon the knob of the door and asked, "Am I disturbing you?"

She felt that his cool gray eyes were studying her and she cast a quick glance into the mirror of the door by his side. Its angle distorted her face but she saw only too plainly the hectic flush that had mounted to her cheeks. She knew, too, that she was breathing in gasps and that the hand which held the bag was trembling noticeably. She repressed the anger which flooded over her and said with an effort at composure: "You startled me." She laid the bag upon the top of the table and turned to him. "Come in, won't you?"

"Thank you." He closed the door and stepped forward.

She motioned toward a chair, said "Sit down" in a voice that she scarcely recognized as her own and sank again into the chair by the table.

He sat in the other chair and she thought, but could not be sure, that his eyes rested a moment too long on the beaded bag. His eyes were brown, she saw now, and merely flecked with gray. His dark brown hair was thin and touched with gray at the temples. She had seen him, without paying much attention to him, in the diner that noon, with the tall man who had stared so disconcertingly at her. And, she remembered now, that the newspaperman had introduced them at the steps of the Pullman.

"My name," be said in a soft pleasant voice, "is Rennert. I am one of the passengers back in the Pullman. Mr. Spahr introduced us on the platform at Saltillo, you may remember."

"Oh yes," she was getting her voice under control now, "I remember you very well." She groped desperately for something to go on with and found herself saying: "A warm trip we're having, isn't it?"

His eyes seemed to rest steadily, yet not rudely, upon her face. She thought that she detected a slight movement at the corners of his mouth as he agreed: "Yes, it's very warm today. We reached an elevation of about seventy-three hundred feet back at Carneros but are going down again now. By tonight it will be perceptibly cooler."

She crushed the stub of her cigarette into the tray and reached over to get another from her case. To do so she had to move the bag and again she thought that the man's eyes were fixed upon its beaded surface. Or maybe upon those yellow flowers, whose scent seemed all at once overpowering in its sweetness. She took out a cigarette, tapped it against the case and fixed it in the holder. He got up, struck a match and held it for her. She looked at the lapels of his blue serge suit, at the white soft collar of his shirt and at the unobtrusive blue-and-white tie which he wore. She smiled slightly and said: "Thank you so much." She watched him sit down and light a cigarette for himself.

Blue wisps of smoke stood between them, wavering in the current from the electric fan. She wondered what he found to interest him on the other side of the room behind her. There was nothing there except that battered old hatbox, whose lid wouldn't stay closed.

"My errand here is a bit delicate, I'm afraid, Miss Van Syle," he said, looking at her with a pleasant smile. "You've heard of the occurrence back in the Pullman this morning?"

She was breathing more regularly now and managed to put the correct intonation into her voice as she said: "You mean the man who died while we were passing through the tunnel? Mr.—what's his name, Spahr?—told me about it. Terribly unfortunate, wasn't it?"

"Very," he paused. "I hope that it will not entail any unpleasantness for the rest of us, however."

"Unpleasantness?"

"Yes. You see, when his body was taken off at Saltillo there remained some question as to how he died."

"But I thought Mr. Spahr said it was heart failure?"

"That's the natural supposition, of course. It's just possible, however, that the Mexican authorities may wish to make further inquiries into the matter. In case that happens I thought that it might be well for all the passengers to be ready to give any information which may be required. To avoid delay, you understand."

She said: "Oh yes" in what she knew was an inane manner and added quickly: "But I wasn't in the Pullman at all so there's no possible information which I can give them."

"No," he agreed readily, "there doubtless isn't, but I thought that I would see you anyway, just in case you might be able to throw some light on the man's movements last night. His name, it seems, was Eduardo Torner. He was a Mexican by blood but a citizen of the United States. The only Mexican on the Pullman.

He got on the train at San Antonio last night. I don't suppose you saw him there?"

"No, not that I remember, but then," she forced the words, "when I am traveling I seldom pay any attention to the people about me. It becomes so fatiguing, you know. That's why I always take a compartment."

Again she thought that there was an incipient movement of his lips and a little twinkle in his eyes. "You got on the train at San Antonio, too, I suppose?" he asked in the same conversational tone.

"Yes." She started to say something about having stopped to visit the Alamo and the Missions but decided not to.

"At what time, may I ask?"

She thought that this was going a little too far and put a distinct note of coolness in her voice as she replied: "I really do not remember exactly but it was soon after the Pullman was opened." *Remember? Would she ever forget a single second of that time as she had stood in straining expectancy, awaiting the opening of that door which was to be for her an escape into space?*

His insistence upon this point annoyed her. He asked: "You were upon the platform of the station before the car was opened?"

"Yes, for a few minutes."

"And you did not go back onto the platform after you got on the train?"

"No, of course not."

He leaned forward to deposit the ash from his cigarette into the tray and she thought that there vas a calculative look in his eyes, as if he were pondering something which she had said.

When he looked up he was smiling pleasantly again. "I'm really very sorry to have to bother you like this, Miss Van Syle, but there are two or three more things which I'd like to ask you. While you were standing on the platform in San Antonio, did anything unusual happen?"

"Anything unusual?" she frowned slightly. "What do you mean?"

"Just try to recall any incident, however insignificant, which attracted your attention."

She felt strangely flustered, helplessly aware that she was not carrying this situation through as successfully as she had expected. "I don't remember anything," she said, "except a man fainting. He had to be carried out of the Station."

She saw him lean forward slightly.

"Tell me," he said, "just what you saw of this incident."

She fixed her gaze on the firmly tied knot of the necktie below his firm square chin and said: "That, really, is about all there was to it. He was standing near a post, in the crowd waiting for the Pullman to be opened. There was another train waiting there at the same time. He sort of—well, crumpled up. There was quite a bit of excitement for a few minutes and that's all I saw until he was carried out."

"Could you describe him?"

She thought a moment then shook her head. "No, I only saw him from a distance. He looked fairly tall and had on a soft brimmed hat, I think. That's about all I can tell you about him."

"Miss Van Syle," there was something compelling about the directness of his gaze "I have another question. Did you see near this man at any time any of the passengers who are back in the Pullman now?"

She started as the ash from her cigarette dropped upon the skirt of her dress. She brushed it off and said: "I haven't seen all of the Pullman passengers yet but one man I have seen was on the platform at the time. I don't know his name but you were with him in the diner this morning. A sedate-looking little man with glasses. He was with his wife, I suppose it was. I happened to notice them because they were standing a little way in front of me and seemed to be having some kind of an argument. They both seemed nervous."

"His name," Rennert said thoughtfully, "is Mr. King. And he was standing there with his wife when the man fell?"

"No, she had left him by that time and gone back into the station. I remember seeing him kiss her good-by."

"This was before the man fell down?"

"Yes."

"And did you see Mr. King at the time the man fell?"

"No, I don't believe that I did see him at exactly that time. He had walked back a little way with his wife toward the gates of the station."

Rennert's smile was very very pleasant, she thought, as he leaned over and crushed his cigarette into a tray.

"One more question, Miss Van Syle, and I'll quit bothering you. It's about this morning while we were passing through that tunnel this side of Monterrey. Mr. Spahr was in the diner when the train started through, wasn't he?"

"Yes."

"Where was he sitting?"

"At the table across the aisle and behind me."

"Was he there when the train came out of the tunnel?"

"Yes, I remember looking out the window on the other side of the car. I saw him sitting there, though I didn't know who he was at the time."

"You're sure he didn't get up and leave the diner, then, while it was dark?"

She stared at him, puzzled. "Why, yes."

"But your back was turned to him, wasn't it?"

"Yes, of course."

Rennert got to his feet. "Thank you very much, Miss Van Syle. I trust that I haven't annoyed you too much by these questions. I'm sure, however, that you would prefer to have them asked by me rather than by the Mexican officials."

She laid her cigarette and holder aside and rose too. "Certainly." She glanced at herself covertly in the mirror, saw that she was standing with the proper poise. "I hope that I have been of assistance," she said graciously.

Rennert stood at the door and said: "Yes, Miss Van Syle, you have been of very great assistance indeed." He opened the door, said: "Good afternoon and thank you again," and was gone.

She stood for several seconds, staring at the chair in which he had sat. She felt her teeth pressing into the lower lip as she fought back a feeling of culpability. She thought: *I'm not sure! Really, I'm not sure at all! And, if I were sure, who but myself has a right to judge what I am doing?* Determination steeled her and she walked directly to the table, opened the hand-bag and took out the syringe. Without looking down at it she started toward the bathroom. She was a fool, she told herself, not to have disposed of it before. At the door she paused at the realization that the train had stopped.

She stood there for several moments, waiting, then walked back to the table, replaced the syringe in the bag and went to a window. She looked out at gleaming steel rails and hot gray dust and blank adobe walls over which no mountains were to be seen.

Chapter VIII
WIRES ARE DOWN!
(4:50 P.M.)

Vanegas lay flatly prostrate under the afternoon sun. An unnatural quietness seemed to weigh upon the usually noisy platform. Overalled railway employees stood in little groups conversing in low tones or moved about their tasks with grave-faced purposiveness. At a distance stood Indians, in gray-white pajama-like clothing, gazing at the train with contemplative eyes under straw *sombreros.* Even the vendors were few in number, merely a half dozen old women who stood beside baskets of fruit and *tacos* and brown jars of *pulque* and surveyed the windows with black eyes whose inveiled look did not conceal the hope that some belated purchaser might thrust out his head and require their wares.

Rennert had sought the comparative privacy of the first-class coach and sat now upon a green plush chair, staring thoughtfully across the parched gray soil at the splash of color which was a *pulquería.* Two telegrams lay spread out upon his lap. He brought his eyes back to the one which he had opened first, read it again.

It was from one of his associates in San Antonio, Texas, and ran:

> REPLYING YOUR TELEGRAM CONCERNING MAN WHO DIED STATION PLATFORM SAN ANTONIO LAST NIGHT FOLLOWING INFORMATION AVAILABLE STOP NAME EDGAR GRAVES OF BUREAU CRIMINAL INVESTIGATION STOP THOUGHT TO HAVE BEEN FOLLOWING SUSPECT IN MONTES KIDNAPPING CASE STOP GRAVES DIED FROM HYPODERMIC INJECTION NICOTINE POISON IN WRIST STOP NO INFORMATION AT PRESENT CONCERNING IDENTITY OF MURDERER STOP BELIEVED TO HAVE ESCAPED ON TRAIN PROBABLY ONE ON WHICH YOU NOW ARE STOP FURTHER DETAILS FROM YOU GREATLY DESIRED STOP WE ARE ASKING MEXICAN AUTHORITIES TO COOPERATE WITH YOU.

Rennert's interest in the affair was quickened by the information contained in this telegram. Throughout the day, as he had considered possible motives which might lie behind the murder of Torner in the tunnel, the thought of a connection with the Montes kidnapping case had never occurred to him. He ran over in his mind the details of this case, made familiar to newspaper readers throughout the Southwest by the hue and cry which had been raised.

Since the days when Texas was a stalwart and defiant young republic the name of Montes had been a household word along the lower reaches of the Rio Grande. A Montes had aided in establishing the freedom of Texas and had founded the dynasty of ranchers and cattlemen which had played an important part in the development of the new country. Sons and grandsons had intermarried with Anglo-American families and had kept the name of Montes alive as legislators and politicians. Today, if the financial and political power of the family had decayed slightly with the advent of industrialism to the Southwest, it still maintained its prestige unimpaired.

Two weeks before, the newspapers had screamed the news of the kidnapping from the family home outside San Antonio of the three-year-old son of Austin Montes. Days had passed while the police followed up clue after clue to no avail. Newspapers, particularly the influential chain controlled by Montes interests, demanded results in no uncertain terms. Old Miguel Montes, grandfather of the missing boy, had fulminated from the armchair where he sat in partial paralyzation and had offered enormous rewards. The State had followed suit (the gubernatorial eyes being fixed on reelection) and had thrown every effort into the investigation.

Three days after the abduction had come a brief note to the family assuring them of the boy's safety and telling them that instructions for the payment of the ransom money would be forthcoming as soon as the agitation had been calmed. The family had at once endeavored to stop the investigation until contact could be made with the kidnapers. They found themselves balked. Too much interest had been aroused and the magnitude of the rewards offered had spurred amateur investigators throughout the Southwest. Pleas from the Montes-controlled newspapers for abstinence from interference were in vain. The hue and cry went on. On the part of the kidnapers, ominous silence.

In time, however, the total absence of clues as to the identity of the kidnapers or to the whereabouts of the boy and unceasing pleas from the family began to have their effect. The case became relegated to the inside pages of the newspapers, where stories took on a monotonous sameness, despite the ingenuity of reporters. People began to turn their interest to the approaching political campaign and to forget the fiery gray-haired old man in the armchair and the grief-stricken parents with whom they had sympathized for so long.

And then had come the news which had catapulted the case back to the front pages. In a ditch near a little border town had been found an overturned and burning automobile. When the blaze was extinguished there had been taken from the ruins the partially consumed body of little Antonio Montes. Excitement had reached fever heat again and groups of self-appointed vigilantes had scoured the country along the Rio Grande, patrolling roads along which the driver of the car might have escaped. Suspect after suspect had been detained, questioned—and released. It became the consensus of opinion that the kidnaper had turned northward into Texas rather than attempt a flight into Mexico, as had been anticipated. The search began to lag.

Rennert had followed the case closely in the newspapers. He still retained memories of a weekend visit at the Montes mansion near San Antonio, the result of a case in which he had been of some service to Austin Montes, and he recalled now the brown curls of the youngster who had played about his grandfather's chair.

Throughout, what had struck him as peculiar was the absolute lack of any certainty as to the identity of the kidnaper or kidnapers. When the clues and rumors were sifted down there remained the unescapable fact that no one knew whether one or more than one person were involved, whether the kidnaper were a man or a woman, whether one familiar with the life of the Montes family or an absolute stranger.

And now this telegram and the increasing certainty that the federal operative had been close upon the trail of the abductor in

San Antonio; that the latter had been aware of the surveillance and had killed his pursuer in the throng upon the platform; that he had boarded the Mexico-bound train; that the man Eduardo Torner had either been aware of his identity or had witnessed the hypodermic injection of the poison, had followed him onto the train and threatened him with blackmail; that the tracked man had passed Monterrey without meeting the demands of the blackmailer and had made use of the same hypodermic needle to put the latter out of the way.

And yet, Rennert admitted, there was as yet no certainty that the death of Torner was murder or that it had any connection with the Montes case. It might, after all, have been due to heart failure or other natural causes. If murder, it might have been linked with the strike which was agitating the workers and the railroad officials. Despite his conviction that such was not the case, Rennert could not deny thc possibility. The connecting link, of course, would be the discovery that Torner had died from an injection of nicotine. And the telegram from the authorities at Saltillo, which had been handed to Rennert at Vanegas, had reported the doctor's inability to determine the cause of the man's death. He had at once wired them suggesting a search for the presence of nicotine. He expected a reply to be in his hands at San Luis Potosí, which the train would reach that night.

If this telegram reported that the death of Torner had been due to nicotine poisoning, as he was confident would be the case, he was resolved to seek the aid of the Mexican authorities in enforcing a search of the passengers back in the Pullman. He knew the perfunctoriness of the examination of Pullman passengers at the border and, while he felt doubtful whether the criminal would have kept the incriminating hypodermic needle about his person or effects, he felt the importance of at least making the search.

And of these passengers, to which one did the evidence of guilt most strongly point? There was the testimony of Jeanes that he had felt upon his hand the touch of some material that might have been the corduroy of Searcey's trousers or the plaited bag of Miss Talcott. There was Jeanes himself and the undeniable fact that of all of them he had had the best opportunity of plunging the needle into the arm of the man who had sat in the seat in front of him. His mention of the fact that someone had bent over Torner in the darkness might have been invented for the purpose of throwing suspicion away from himself. On the other hand, there was Mr. King's corroboration of this. Mr. King——

And what, Rennert demanded thoughtfully of himself, about Mr. King? Of all the men in the Pullman probably the one least likely to attract attention, he had from the beginning been obtruding in such a fashion that significance must be attached to the question. His conversation with Rennert upon the observation platform that morning, whatever might have been its purpose, had been the first alarming note to presage the death which had followed so soon. His recollection of an event which occurred in the station at San Antonio had been responsible for Rennert's theory that Torner's death was an outcome of that event and for his discovery that the whole affair was doubtless linked with the Montes kidnaping. Had the man's purpose throughout been to effect this very end?

If so, what about the melodramatic message of warning which King claimed to have been given him by a man in Saltillo who might be as apocryphal as the wife who had listened to a conversation upon the train the night before? It might well have been a none too subtle method of directing attention toward another of the passengers.

Yet, at the present state of his knowledge, Rennert had to admit that it would not do to take this assumption for granted. The message might have been intended for one of the passengers who was unknown to the bearer of the message. King might have given inadvertently some signal which the watcher had interpreted as the prearranged one. There were the limes upon the crossed sticks. Rennert's eyes narrowed thoughtfully. Once before that day the thought had come to him, as he had studied one of the passengers, that there might possibly be another factor involved in this matter—a factor which offered rather alarming possibilities. Again a feeling of distinct uneasiness came over Rennert. Ahead of them stretched the barren sparsely inhabited plains of San Luis Potosí, rimmed by mountains, and the wild upland districts of Guanajuato and Querétaro to be traversed before they arrived the next morning in Mexico City. He thought of Mexico City as a goal, clear in the light of morning, toward which they would speed through the black reaches of the night. . . .

He thrust the telegrams into a pocket and looked at his watch.

It was five minutes past five. They had been in Vanegas for fifteen minutes, when the time-table called for only a ten-minute stop. And they were now forty-seven minutes behind their schedule.

He got up and walked back through the diner.

Coralie Van Syle and Spahr sat at the table which they had occupied at noon. Spahr was enjoying himself hugely, Rennert surmised as he glanced at the small whisky and cognac bottles which stood empty before him. His fingers were twisting a half-empty glass around and around as he talked in a too-loud voice. "Course the newspaper don't pay for my drinks while I'm down here but I saved up a little money for this trip. Thought I might as well have a good time while I was about it." A suppressed hiccough. "Come on, Miss Van Syle, drink that an' we'll have another one." Miss Van Syle, looking cool and distant, sat across from him and smoked another cigarette. Crushed particles of paper and tobacco covered the bottom of the tray before her. She was gazing down at the wineglass with a faintly amused smile upon her red lips. Her eyes rose as Rennert passed and he felt them fixed upon his face. He turned his head, nodded and passed on.

He glanced into the smoker. Searcey sat by the lowered shade of the window. His jaws were moving slightly, as if they were just finishing the act of mastication, and his fingers were tamping tobacco into the bowl of a worn black briar pipe. He looked up as Rennert stood in the doorway.

"Have a match?" he asked.

Rennert tendered a packet of safety matches and watched Searcey light his pipe.

"Thanks," the other started to hand them back, then paused. "Do you have any more of these?" he asked.

Rennert felt in his pockets. "No, I don't," he answered.

Searcey returned the packet. "I thought if you did I'd borrow some. They seem to have run out back here." He paused and drew contentedly upon the pipe. "What in the hell's the matter now?" he asked. "Why don't we pull out of this god-forsaken place?"

"Probably changing engines," Rennert explained. "A new one from San Luis Potosí was to have met us here."

"We'll hope it's better than the old one we had. Judging from the map in the time-table there's nothing at all between here and San Luis but desert—and lots of that. It'd be a hell of a place to get stalled."

"Yes," Rennert agreed soberly, "it would." He wondered if this man knew just what a dangerous and unpleasant kind of hell it might turn out to be for all of them.

From up front came a frantic clanging of the engine.

"Well," Searcey laughed, "that sounds just like the bell of the old one."

"Yes," Rennert smiled. "I think I'll go back in the Pullman, if you'll excuse me."

He let the curtains fall to behind him and glanced in the direction of the door, outside of which the conductor had appeared.

"About to start again, are we?" Rennert called to him.

"Yes," the man adjusted his lips in a smile.

"With the new engine from San Luis we won't be long in making up our lost time, I suppose?"

"I am sorry, Señor Rennert," there was helplessness in the voice, "but there is no new engine."

"No?"

"It did not meet us here as we had hoped."

"What was the explanation from San Luis?"

"There was no explanation from San Luis."

"But you wired, did you not?"

"Yes, señor, we wired," he shrugged helplessly, "but there has come no answer. The wires—" he checked himself and stared out into the sunlight.

"What's the matter with the wires?" Rennert demanded quickly.

The conductor said in a voice as flat as the desert that

stretched before his eyes: "The wires are down, señor, between here and San Luis. They do not know, here in Vanegas, what the trouble is but there comes from San Luis no answer." He started to move toward the front of the train, paused and said with the same distortion of a smile: "It will be nothing, nothing at all. These things happen often. The wires will be repaired within a few hours."

"We can reach San Luis with the engine as it is?"

"But surely, señor, but surely. It will delay us but we can reach San Luis. *Con permiso.*"

Rennert stood for a moment, thoughtfully regarding his disappearing back. He told himself: *If I were sure which one is guilty I would notify the soldiers on this train to detain him and warn the others not to continue straight into danger.* He turned his head at the sound of footsteps on gravel and watched the Mexican soldier approach the steps. He knew that the only possibility of preventing the escape of the guilty person lay in keeping this group within the confines of the Pullman until identification was certain. And it was not yet certain. . . .

The soldier mounted the steps with heavy deliberate tread and stood before Rennert, regarding him with expressionless face.

"You watched the telegraph office?" Rennert asked.

"Si, señor."

"And did this man, this Mr. King, send a telegram from Vanegas?"

"No, señor, he walked to the office but he did not send a telegram."

"Did any of the passengers send telegrams?"

"No. Another, the one of the gray hair, walked upon the

platform and looked at the scenery but the others did not leave the car."

"This man who walked upon the platform—what were his actions?"

The Mexican shrugged. "He did nothing, señor, but walked up and down. He stopped by the end of the car, below the observation platform, and made some marks in the dust with a stick."

"Did anyone go near him?"

"I did not see anyone, señor, but I was watching this other man, as you told me."

"Very well," Rennert said abstractedly, "thank you."

When the man had gone he stood for a moment longer. King, then, had not dispatched the telegram to the wife who he claimed had remained in Laredo but had merely pretended to do so. And Jeanes had stood beside the train and made marks in the dust with a stick.

His face set in lines of concentration, Rennert made his way down the passage, stepping aside to avoid the debris which the porter was sweeping out of the smoker. The Pullman was quiet save for the sound of the electric fans. King sat with a time-table in front of him. He was slowly moving a finger up its lines.

Rennert stopped beside him. "Did you send the telegram to your wife as I asked?"

King looked up as if in surprise at Rennert's approach and attempted a smile. "Why, yes," he said pleasantly enough, "I sent it." He glanced back at the time-table.

"You asked her to send the answer to San Luis Potosí?"

"Yes, yes," King's voice sounded a bit gruff as if his thoughts were on the folded booklet in his hands.

"Thank you," Rennert said evenly. "I shall be looking for the reply at San Luis Potosí."

King did not answer.

Rennert walked on down the aisle and paused at the seat where Radcott sat staring out the window and drumming upon the sill with the tips of pudgy fingers.

"Another question about last night," he said pleasantly. "Did you see this man Torner after he got on the Pullman?"

There was something almost vacuous about Radcott's stare. "Yes," he said, "I saw him in his seat and later in the smoker, after the train had pulled out of the station."

"Could you tell me if he was wearing this in his tie?" Rennert held out the pin.

Radcott looked at it with suddenly narrowed eyes. He took it in his hand and examined it.

"No," he shook his head decidedly as he returned it, "he wasn't wearing that."

"You're sure?"

"Positive," Radcott moved restlessly in his seat.

Rennert thrust the pin into his lapel again. "Have you seen that pin before, Mr. Radcott?"

Radcott drew out his handkerchief and passed it quickly across his face. "No," he said firmly, "no, I never saw it before."

"None of the other passengers were wearing it—or one like it?"

"No, I'm sure not."

Rennert studied him for a moment. "Thanks," was all he said as he walked on. He was positive that Radcott had recognized that pin and had been more than a little startled by the sight.

He passed Miss Talcott, who was reading and did not look

up at his approach, and continued on to the door of the observation platform.

At the corner of the station an old woman squatted behind a basket of withered peaches. A dingy blue *rebozo* shielded her face from the sun and from beneath its folds she gazed at the train with eyes that held no expression whatever. Before her the sunlight slanted across the slate-gray dust.

On one side of the track stood Jeanes. His head was bare and raised slightly so that his hair was a brush of burnished silver in the sun. His eyes were fixed upon the horizon where mountains were blue-gray shadows, heat-obscured, and upon his face was a rapt look. His lips were moving and words came indistinctly to Rennert's ears.

"Quand je marche dans la vallée de l'ombre de la mort, je ne crains aucun mal, car tu es aveç moi: Ta houlette et ton baton . . ."

At his feet a faint breeze from the mountains rippled torn fragments of paper in the dust.

"When I walk through the valley of the shadow of Death . . ."

Chapter IX
SUNSET
(6:23 P.M.)

The Tropic of Cancer was past, the slim white stela that marks its location lost to sight in the darkness that was gathering upon the desert. As if mocking its alien whiteness cacti thrust huge dark fingers out of the soil.

The tiny crystals set in the old-fashioned celluloid comb sparkled in the light as Miss Talcott bent her head to peer along the floor of the Pullman. She came to the forward seat where Rennert sat, paused and said: "Do people who lose things annoy you, Mr. Rennert?"

Rennert had been staring thoughtfully out the window, his thoughts far from pleasant as he watched the sun melt the jagged peak of a mountain to the west. The extra edition of the San Antonio newspaper was spread upon his lap.

He looked around and said: "One's own shortcomings are always more annoying in others."

She laughed. "Yes and it's worse when one has an excellent memory like mine. It isn't a question of forgetting where I put it, I'm sure. Why, this is the first time I've lost anything since the night the report came that the *zapatistas* were going to raid

Coyoacan and everyone had to move into Mexico City before daylight. I lost a Chinese shawl in the confusion that night."

"And what is it that you've lost now?"

"My paper knife. I was using it this afternoon to cut the pages of a book but can't find it anywhere now."

Rennert frowned. "Do you remember when you had it last?" he asked gravely.

"Yes, it was while we were in Saltillo. I had been reading Manuel Azuela's last novel and while we were waiting there I finished cutting the pages and laid the knife on the seat beside me. Mr. Jeanes came along then to talk to me and I put the book down. I remember marking my place with the knife. When I picked the book up again the knife was gone. I thought that it must have fallen to the floor but I couldn't find it. The porter says that he has seen nothing of it. I'd rather hate to lose it. It's an old piece of Chinese bronze that I picked up in Acapulco, a relic, I like to think, of the days of the Spanish galleons."

"Did you ask Mr. Jeanes if he had seen it?"

"No," she shrugged slightly, "I didn't. I scarcely felt like getting started in another conversation with the young man."

Rennert indicated the seat opposite him. "Won't you sit down, Miss Talcott?"

"Yes," she cast a glance in the direction of the door, "I will. I've been wanting to talk to you all day and this seems a good opportunity while the others are in the diner." She sat down and smoothed out black taffeta with careful fingers. She smiled as she looked down at something which she held in her right hand. "Someone else has been losing things too," she said, "that's some consolation." She held out her hand.

In its palm rested a small band of tawdry brass set with three bright red pieces of glass. Rennert looked at it curiously and took it in his fingers. It was an exceedingly cheap and ugly ring.

"Where did you find this?" he asked.

"In the aisle back there, by one of the vacant berths. It looks like a child's ring, the kind we used to get as prizes at county fairs."

"Yes," Rennert was studying it. He looked up suddenly. "Do you mind, Miss Talcott, if I keep this? Not for its intrinsic value, I assure you."

She looked at him oddly. "Why, of course not," she said with an abstracted laugh. "You'll try to find the owner, I suppose?" a bantering note crept into her voice.

"Yes," Rennert's face was serious, "I shall try my best to find the owner of this ring." He slipped it into a pocket of his coat. "And now, Miss Talcott, would it be an impertinence to ask why you don't feel like starting another conversation with Mr. Jeanes?"

"Not at all," she lifted her eyes to look at him. Her hands were clasped placidly in her lap. "Mr. Jeanes is, I'm sure, a very very admirable young man. I'm sure he has all the virtues which a good young man should possess. He is exceedingly zealous. He has his own life running in a satisfactory groove, all his own thoughts and actions and emotions so tabulated that he feels sure that anyone, even God, looking at them with a careful and scrutinizing eye, would pronounce approval upon them. This done, he feels rather at a loss for an outlet for his excess energy. So he convinces himself that it's his duty to arrange other people's lives, whether they wish it or not. He doesn't approve of me or rather of the way I've arranged my life."

"So I judged," Rennert smiled.

"Understand," she said hastily, "I'm not blaming him in the slightest. I can see why doctrinaires don't approve of me.

Usually, I could sit and talk to him—or rather let him do the talking—and be mildly amused. Now," her smile faded from her lips and Rennert thought that a shadow of weariness darkened her face for an instant, "I am too tired. I've had too much contact lately with his kind, I've had to keep my face fixed in the correct beatific smile for so long that it's becoming an impossibility to keep it up much longer. Now I only want to get back to my house in Coyoacan and be by myself."

For a few moments there was silence.

"You have been in the States for long?" Rennert asked.

"No, only two weeks, but it seems two years."

The disc of the sun was invisible now and the jagged mountains were turning a deep black flanged with orange flame along the upper crests. Between them and the train stretched a dark level sea that became sand and cactus and rock only when one concentrated his gaze upon its surface.

"This has been an interesting day, hasn't it?" Miss Talcott remarked absently.

"Yes, though possibly not in the way you mean."

She considered this unhurriedly then smiled. "Yes, I think we mean the same thing, Mr. Rennert. The reaction of human beings to death?"

"Yes," he studied her face.

"Of course," she said after a moment, "our interest is slightly different, I imagine. To me that man who died this morning is an abstraction. What interests me is the way the people who were about him have been reacting to his death during the day."

"I should be interested, Miss Talcott, in hearing your observations, if you care to give them to me."

"Certainly," her voice quickened, "it has made the day rather interesting for me. I've been pretending to read but really I've not been much engrossed in my book. Mr. Spahr and Mr. Radcott have been trying to fight off thoughts of the man's death, one of them with liquor and the other with romantic notions about Mexico, its beauty and all that. Both of them are succeeding very well. Mr. Searcey is older and more calloused, but I imagine that he is doing much the same thing, emphasizing his callousness as a defense. Mr. King——" she paused.

"I'm interested," Rennert said quietly, "in knowing just what you think about Mr. King."

She laughed. "I was trying to think of some simile. He's like a lost and frightened child who can't see any familiar landmarks. Back in Fort Worth or wherever he comes from he would probably be cool and collected, arranging resolutions of regret to the dead man's family and protests to the railway company for not lighting their tunnels. Mr. Jeanes is concerned only with the man's soul and is happy with this concern. Interesting, isn't it?"

Rennert asked quietly: "And I?"

Their eyes met.

"You," she said, "are thinking mostly of who murdered him."

Outside the window the gathering night was a silence made up of the myriad muted noises of a Mexican countryside. The train had paused momentarily at one of the little groups of adobe huts that huddle about the railway tracks as if for security against the pitiless desert that hems them in. Scarcely worthy of names, they leave the map undotted and the time-table uncluttered save for an occasional condescending asterisk.

As the train drew out with a swish of steam and grinding of metal Rennert said: "You know that it was murder then?"

"Of course," her voice was matter-of-fact. "Wasn't it?"

"Yes, Miss Talcott, it was murder."

Her hands were unclasped now and the fingers of the left

were toying with the diamond ring. "I suppose you, too, look at it more or less abstractly, don't you?" she asked thoughtfully. "As a problem to be worked out—by formula or by the trial and error method?"

"Yes, I suppose so, although I try to disguise my interest in the puzzle by telling myself that my desire for justice demands its working."

Her laugh was spontaneous. "And now that we're both being frank, tell me what I can do to help you work it out."

"You can tell me, Miss Talcott, exactly what happened in this car while we were passing through that tunnel."

"I've thought about it quite a bit today," her manner became more serious, "but I can't think of a thing that would help. Anyone who was sitting in the car might have gotten up, slipped down the aisle and killed that man—" she paused. "By the way, have you found out how he was killed?"

"He was killed, I am sure, by nicotine poison injected by a hypodermic needle."

"I see," she looked at him thoughtfully, "easily done. Mr. Jeanes, Mr. Searcey, and Mr. King were all sitting close enough to him to have done it."

"You were not aware of anyone being in the aisle?"

"No, but I was sitting so far back that I couldn't have known it if one of them had been." He thought that her eyes narrowed a trifle behind her glasses. "I suppose you're checking up on Mr. Radcott?"

"Yes, he would have had to pass your seat if he had come into the Pullman."

"I think," she said slowly, "that you can leave him out of your calculations. I feel sure that he didn't go down the aisle. He's rather large, you know, and I think that I would have known it if he had done so, even in the darkness." She thought for a moment. "I'm afraid that's all the help I can give you. I know it sounds very stupid not to be able to tell exactly what happened in that tunnel but I doubt whether you yourself could have done any better, if you hadn't happened to be noticing particularly."

"I'm sure, Miss Talcott, that I could not have done any better." Rennert paused and said evenly: "Do you know that you yourself are included among the suspects?"

Her start was imperceptible, manifested only by a slight contraction of her fingers and a tightening of her lips. "I?" she laughed. "That's interesting. You mean because I was in the car too?"

"Yes, and because Mr. Jeanes is not sure now that what he felt against his hand was Mr. Searcey's corduroy trousers. He admits the possibility of it being your fiber bag."

He sensed rather than saw a slow tautening of her body.

"My bag?" she stared at him, her eyes guarded. "That's too foolish——" she checked herself and turned her face to the window. For several seconds she stared steadily into the darkness. Then she turned to him and said with a smile: "No, it's not foolish, I suppose, when you come to think of it. I imagine that my bag would feel much like corduroy if it touched the back of a person's hand. I remember now that Mr. Jeanes was rather startled when he touched it back on my seat though I didn't know at the time what was the matter with him." Her gaze was meeting his squarely, without wavering. "Would you like to see the bag in question, to feel it?"

"Yes, Miss Talcott, I would."

"Very well," her voice was unruffled.

She got up and led the way down the aisle, her shoulders straight. The starched white collar seemed unaffected by the day's heat and lent a stiffness to her carriage. When they came to her seat she picked the bag from its surface and held it out to him.

"It *does* feel like corduroy," she ran a hand over its side. "Mr. Jeanes is right about that."

Rennert took it and did the same. "A little rougher, of course, but I can see how a person might confuse it with corduroy at a sudden contact with it in the dark," he said as he held it out to her.

She made no motion to take it. "Don't you want to examine it?" she asked quietly. "The murderer, you know, might still have the needle concealed."

"I feel sure that he has probably disposed of it by this time, Miss Talcott—unless he thinks that he might have occasion to use it again."

"To use it again?" her eyes searched his face. "In that case I want you to look in the bag to make sure that I don't have it," she said steadily.

"All right," Rennert said with sudden determination, "I will."

He opened the bag and glanced through its contents. It contained a small coin purse, a gold pencil and memorandum book, a folded letter, a handkerchief, a photograph in a worn folding frame which Rennert did not open and a pasteboard box labeled "Veronal."

"Thank you, Miss Talcott. I'm grateful to you."

She let the bag fall upon the seat. "Not at all," her smile was pleasant again. "It interested me to realize that I could take this matter so objectively until it concerned me and that then I became perturbed. I'm a sublime egotist, I suppose."

"All of us are, more or less."

She was standing with one hand resting upon the back of the

seat in front of her. She looked toward the other end of the car and said: "Even Mr. Jeanes."

Rennert turned his head. Jeanes had walked into the car, his face looking pale and haggard in the electric light. He sank into his seat without a glance in their direction.

"I wonder what has become of that hatbox?" Miss Talcott said suddenly.

"Hatbox?" Rennert turned to her.

"Yes, I noticed that it was missing a few minutes ago when I was walking down the aisle looking for my paper knife. The owner must have claimed it."

"I'm afraid, Miss Talcott, that I don't know what hatbox you're talking about."

"Oh," she laughed, "I must get out of that habit of talking as if to myself. It comes from living too much alone, I suppose. You see, there was a hatbox there in the aisle this morning at breakfast time, a rather shabby-looking one. I remember wondering why someone didn't move it instead of always. . .stumbling over it. Now it's gone."

"The porter stopped to place it on one of the vacant seats when I called him upon discovering the dead man this morning," Rennert said reflectively. "I supposed that it belonged to you."

"No, he asked me last night if it was mine. It had, I believe, the initials O. W. stamped on it and wasn't fastened very securely. In fact it was bulging open slightly."

She lurched forward and had to grasp the back of the seat with the other hand as the train came to a sudden stop.

Rennert regained his balance and glanced quickly out the window.

The desert seemed cloaked in palpable blackness and the mountain peaks still stained with orange looked immeasurably far away, suspended in the vast dark reaches of interstellar space.

He turned to meet Miss Talcott's questioning gaze.

"Why are we stopping?" she asked. "There's no station here."

Chapter X
THE EYES OF TEXAS
(6:45 P.M.)

SPAHR WAS becoming slightly maudlin and during the increasingly frequent lulls in the conversation kept humming "The Eyes of Texas."

"The eyes of Texas are upon you
All the livelong day!
The eyes of Texas are upon you,
You cannot get away!"

Coralie Van Syle sat across the table from him, her fingers tightening upon the jade holder from which the cigarette emitted an upcoiling curl of smoke. She knew that she had about reached the limit of her endurance. Her face felt tight and drawn and the muscles about her mouth and eyes ached with the effort to keep them from twitching.

She glanced around the diner again, to see how much attention Spahr was attracting.

Mr. Searcey sat at the rear, at the last table on the other side. She looked at him over Spahr's shoulder and saw that he didn't seem to be paying any attention to anyone else but sat smoking his pipe. The electric lights lent a blank masklike expression to his face.

Across the aisle sat Mr. King and Mr. Radcott. The former was finishing a frugal meal of aguacate salad, toast and tea and glancing with slight distaste at the steak which his companion was consuming complacently. Conversation between them seemed at a standstill and King sat for the most part gazing out the window with an uneasy expression on his face.

"Lonesome-looking country, isn't it?" he remarked. "Desert and mountains, cactus and rattlesnakes and bandits. I'd hate to be lost out there."

Radcott laid down his fork and chewed for a moment, as his half-closed eyes followed the direction of King's gaze.

"I don't know," he spoke after a while, "sometimes I get a crazy notion that I'd like to ride off into mountains like those, away from everything, see what's in them, what's on the other side——" he did not conclude but sat staring out the window with a faraway look upon his face.

King caught at the edge of the table. "'What's the matter?" he asked, looking about him in alarm. "The train's stopped!"

"I don't know," Radcott peered out the window, "I don't see any station here."

The waiter hurried in with another bottle of wine and set it upon the table before Spahr.

"What's the matter?" Radcott asked him. "Why are we stopping here?"

The man shrugged and said deferentially: "I do not know, sir. It will be but a short time, I think. They are having trouble with the engine." He bowed and turned toward the kitchen, passing the conductor in the aisle.

Spahr had poured out the wine and was pushing a glass toward her and saying: "Have some more wine, Miss Van Syle. We might as well make a night of it, hadn't we?"

He picked up the bottle and held it over his glass. The wine gurgled and splashed up to the rim and over.

"Do not think you can escape them
From night 'til early in the morn,"

he was beginning again as he cocked a quizzical eye at the glass.

She felt a sudden tightening of the muscles in her throat and a queer sense of desolation surged over her. Outside the windows the mountains were vague heaped shadows upon the horizon. She reached up and pulled down the blind. She sipped red Rioja wine and waited for its reassuring warmth to spread over her tired body. For some reason there was no response. She waited, then drank again, emptying the glass.

"The eyes of Texas are upon you
'Til Gabriel blows his horn!"

Spahr concluded in a louder happier voice.

It was too much. Her hand shook as she set the glass upon the table and it fell over, the remaining drops of the wine staining the white cloth. She let her cigarette holder drop into the tray. She let her arms rest on the table and buried her face in them. She did what she had been wanting to do for hours and hours, it seemed. She cried, silently and without trying to control the hot tears that touched her arms.

How long she remained thus she did not know—nor care. She looked up at last, was vaguely aware of a solicitous expression on Spahr's flushed face. She got to her feet and said as steadily as she could: "Excuse me, please. I don't feel well. I think I'll go lie down."

"Let me help you," Spahr made a motion to rise.

"No, no," she gestured him back to his seat and fled down the aisle, without looking to right or left, without knowing whether there were other diners in the car or not.

Outside, she paused on the platform between the cars and went to the door. She pressed one hand against the coolness of the glass and gazed out into the darkness. She stood for a moment, conscious of utter weariness, then walked slowly to her compartment. It had become all at once a haven, a little compact private world with barriers that would shut out the universe.

She met no one in the passage. She closed the door and stood for a moment with her back to it, letting its quiet ordered air of security fill her as she had hoped the wine would do.

She put out a hand to turn on the light.

"If I were you, Miss Van Syle, I wouldn't do that."

The voice was soft yet sharp admonition barbed it.

In the silence that followed she heard very distinctly the gentle dispassionate ticking of the watch upon her wrist. The muscles of her throat tightened again into paralyzing knots and she would not have recognized her own voice as she spoke.

"Who is it?"

"That doesn't matter, Miss Van Syle. You will walk straight ahead to the other side of the room. Quietly, if you please."

It was the violation of her sanctuary that angered her, that sent hot surges of resentment over her body and made the blood pound through her heart. A slight breeze from the window bore to her nostrils the too-sweet, almost fetid odor of the withering yellow flowers upon the table.

"What are you doing in my room?" her fingers groped for and found the button of the light.

"I must ask you to lower your voice," impatience underscored the words. "I've finished here and as soon as you walk to the other side I'm ready to leave. You will say nothing to anyone about my visit here. If you're foolish enough to do so you will suffer the consequences. Now, move forward please."

She tried to recognize the voice, to identify it as one of the voices which she had heard that day. She thought, but could not be sure, that she knew to whom it belonged. . . .

Her middle finger found the light button and pressed it as she felt her wrist gripped by a hand that felt like steel encased by flesh.

She stared into the face before her while a kind of numbness came over her. "Oh," she heard herself say, "it's you!"

"I warned you not to turn on that light, Miss Van Syle," there was now a patient regret in the voice. "I'm sorry——"

She stared down at the upraised right hand and saw it move steadily toward her wrist. Her scream was merely a choking noise that stuck in her throat. At the sight of the clean bright needle that protruded from between the fingers of the hand nausea overwhelmed her and she did not feel the pain as the needle bit into her flesh. . . .

PART TWO

Chapter XI
WINGS IN THE DARKNESS
(7:00 P.M.)

STARS GLITTERED, faceting the sky over the top of the train. To the west the mountains reared ungainly humps cloaked in flame-crested purple against the horizon. The smell of the desert was acrid in the nostrils and a faint coolness was beginning to creep upward from the dry sands.

Voices and sharp metallic sounds from the forward part of the train reverberated with odd distinctness in the heavy stillness that seemed to be pushing in upon them.

A revolver cracked with a splintering sound. Laughter echoed after it eerily.

At his back Rennert heard a tiny clatter against the rail. He turned.

At the edge of the observation platform, he could make out the white jacket of the porter. He walked back.

The man was leaning over the railing, gazing toward the front of the train. "That shot," he queried quickly, "what was it?"

"One of the soldiers up front, I believe," Rennert told him.

The Mexican was silent, his dark face a part of the obscurity which surrounded him. His fingers seemed to be busied with something at his throat.

Rennert stood near the railing and said: "I understand that there was an unclaimed hatbox in the Pullman this morning?"

The other seemed not to understand and Rennert repeated his words.

"Yes," the answer was smothered by the stillness, "there was a hatbox."

"What became of it?"

"I took it back to the lady in the compartment. It belonged to her."

"Why wasn't it put into her compartment last night in San Antonio?"

Rennert could see the porter's shoulders rise in a shrug.

"But I did not know that it was hers, sir!" he protested. "She did not tell me and it did not have the same initials as the rest of her luggage."

"And she didn't inquire about it until this morning?"

"At noon, sir, she told me that it was hers and asked me to take it to her compartment while the others were in the diner."

Rennert's foot found and pressed against an object lying in the gravel close beside the rail. He stooped and picked it up.

"Was the hatbox locked?" he asked as he held his hand up to the light from the doorway.

"No, sir," the porter was staring down at him, "it was not locked. It was full—very full—and the lid would not close. I thought that it would come open while I was carrying it."

Rennert lifted his hand. In it he held a small tin whistle.

"You dropped this?" he asked quietly, as his eyes sought to penetrate the darkness to the man's face.

"Yes," the monosyllable was flat. He moved his head a trifle so that his face was concealed.

Rennert's eyes went for a moment to the barely discernible horizon and nearer to the swiftly in-crowding night.

"You were going to blow this whistle?"

"Yes, sir."

"Why?" (Was it his imagination, rendered receptive by the brooding silence of the desert, or was there a rustling sound, as of softly moving wings, close by the telegraph pole that rose in gallows-like isolation out of the dark ground?)

A tremor ran through the porter's voice, speaking unaccustomed English: "I but wanted to hear the noise, sir."

"The noise?"

"Yes. Everything is so quiet out here in the desert that a noise—I thought it would be good."

Rennert watched the lantern of the conductor approaching from the front of the train. He was trying to force himself into self-recrimination. A natural desire, to want noise to combat the fears engendered by the night. A small boy whistles while going along a lonely road. He knew many people who kept a night-lamp burning for the same reason, although they would not have admitted it. And yet—this abrupt unexpected stop in the desert and a shrill whistle that might pass unheeded in the train but which would carry far into the darkness. . . .

He asked: "Where did you get this whistle?"

"I found it, sir."

"On the train?"

"Yes, sir, on the train."

"In what part?"

"In the smoker, sir, while I was sweeping it."

"You swept it this afternoon?"

"Yes, sir, late this afternoon, before we left Vanegas."

"Thank you," Rennert said abstractedly as he turned away. "I shall keep this whistle for the present."

There was no response from the man upon the platform. Rennert walked forward to meet the conductor.

The man's face, lit from below by the swaying flame of the lantern, looked as if it had been slashed from dark granite out of which stared bright round crystals. He paused by Rennert's side at the foot of the steps and said with a muffled laugh: "Do not be alarmed, señor. It was but the soldiers shooting at a rabbit." He started to move forward.

"What has caused the stop here?" Rennert asked.

"The engine again, señor. It has stopped. They are going to have to send to San Luis Potosí for another."

The lights of the train were suddenly extinguished and for an instant the hulks of the cars were but black shapes looming against the sky. Then the lights flashed on again.

"No word has been received from San Luis?"

"No, señor, no word." The conductor seemed restive, disinclined to talk.

"How far are we from San Luis?"

"About sixty kilometers, the delay will not be great. *Con permiso.*" He stepped past Rennert and swung himself up the steps. His shadow loomed distorted for an instant against the sands.

They lay, these sands, like a heavy silent sea, motionless yet restless with contained movement, stretching away to become fused with the mountains and darkness.

Rennert, standing alone before them, felt a singular alertness of the senses, as if his body were tautened by the heavy silence that was crowding in upon the steel sides and brightly lighted windows of the train. He thought of the train as a projectile suddenly deprived of movement in its journey through space and poised stationary in unfamiliar elements. He found himself listening, for sounds that were not the sounds from the engine; these had receded now into a special category of their own. He thought, as his ears sought to sort out the tiny night sounds: *This is the eventuality which I have feared more or less consciously all day. Its implications make insignificant the danger from the individual on this train who has struck today like the desert rattler and like the rattler withdrawn his fangs until danger threatens him again. . . .*

"What's the trouble now?" King's voice was high pitched with alarm.

"The engine again," Rennert watched him descend the steps. "They're having to send on to San Luis Potosí for another—the one which failed to meet us at Vanegas," he added, knowing that he was underscoring the words.

King stepped to the ground beside him and glanced nervously in the direction of the front of the train. "What was that shot I heard a minute ago?"

"Merely one of the soldiers shooting at a rabbit."

"Are you sure that's all?"

"Yes," Rennert studied the man.

His whole manner bespoke his nervousness. The fingers that held a cigar to his mouth were trembling. He turned to stare out into the desert and shivered visibly.

"I just wondered," he said, drawing his coat together to button it, "if there's any danger from—well, from bandits? One hears so many stories about things that happen down here in Mexico. Miss Talcott was telling this afternoon about an experience of hers when a troop of bandits piled logs on the track and raided the train she was on. She says that only a few years ago trains kept their blinds pulled down when going through this country for fear of shots."

"There's always the possibility, of course," Rennert admitted, "but I'm sure it's very remote nowadays. Mexico is as safe today for traveling as many parts of our own country. Miss Talcott is speaking of the days of the Revolution. As for the shots from out of the darkness——" he checked himself at the realization that he was talking more to reassure himself than the little man before him.

"Well?" King queried.

Rennert laughed. "A Mexican with a gun in his hand is often like a boy with a slingshot. Didn't you ever have a temptation to aim a stone at a plate glass window?"

"Not that I remember. But what's that got to do with it?"

"That," Rennert said with a grim smile, "explains the shots that used to be fired at train windows while trains were still a novelty." He knew better than to try to explain the peculiar inverted psychology of a people who would appreciate the humor of being a target—like a plate glass window.

King drew upon his cigar so that it illuminated his gray face. "I wish," he said, "that I were back in Texas. From the minute I entered the station at San Antonio and heard about the strike down here I haven't had a minute's peace."

"Speaking of San Antonio," Rennert studied King's face, "there is a question which I've been intending to ask you, something else about the man whom you saw fall there."

"Yes?" King asked sharply. "Still on that subject?"

"Yes, Mr. King, I am still on that subject. Did both you and your wife see the man fall?"

King stared out into the desert and his fingers twitched at

his necktie. "Well, no, she didn't see him fall. She had gone back into the station for something."

"And you didn't accompany her?"

King cleared his throat. "Only as far as the gate," he said.

"And you waited there for her?"

"Yes."

"And then both of you got on the train?"

"Yes, yes, as soon as it was open."

Rennert was becoming increasingly certain that he understood Jackson Saul King much better than the latter thought he did. He wanted to tell him that he saw through the pitifully weak and despicable little fiction which he had tried to build up around himself. He decided, however, to wait until they reached San Luis Potosí. There was always the chance, of course, that he was mistaken.

He asked instead: "Your errand in Mexico must be very important, then, since you came on in spite of the strike?"

"Yes," Rennert noticed the relief that crept into the man's voice at the change in subject. "As I told you, I'm with the King & Dysart Cotton Mills of Fort Worth. The depression has hit us pretty bad and I'm going down to try to open up a market in Mexico. We believe that we can put out inexpensive cotton clothing such as the Mexican peon wears much cheaper than the Mexican mills. There's the tariff question, of course, to be considered. That's why I'm going down—to find out what the attitude of the new government is likely to be on that."

There was an interval of silence.

King looked toward the lighted windows of the train. "Think I'll go back to the smoker," he said. "Electric lights look good to me right now."

"Thank you, Mr. King, for your information," Rennert said evenly.

"Perfectly all right, Mr. Rennert." King turned his back.

Rennert followed him up the steps. As he gained the top he saw him disappearing into the door of the Pullman.

Rennert stopped outside the door of Miss Van Syle's compartment, undecided. He was wondering if that hatbox were important. He couldn't get rid of the idea that it was. He remembered now that it had been old and battered, incongruous beside the new and shining luggage which he had seen in the compartment. And then there was the question of the initials. O. W., Miss Talcott had said they were. Innocently enough explained, of course—a borrowed piece of luggage—but in combination with all the rest . . .

He knocked lightly upon the door, waited a moment and knocked again. Still there came no response.

He walked away, glanced into the Pullman and saw Miss Talcott, King, and Jeanes in their seats. He went forward to the diner and found it empty. He realized afterwards that it was the feeling of apprehension which had been growing upon him all day that made him retrace his steps and knock again, more loudly, upon the door of Coralie Van Syle's compartment.

When no answer came he tried the door, found it unlocked, and pushed it open. He switched on the light and saw her.

Spahr choked, straightened himself from the stooped position in which he had been standing with his hands braced against his bent knees, and dried his lips with a handkerchief.

He thrust the handkerchief into his pocket and leaned against the closed door for a moment until the walls of the little room should steady themselves. The train had stopped, he knew that, yet the floor and the walls seemed to be pulsating with movement.

The air in the tiny inclosed space seemed all at once stifling and he felt sickness coming over him again. He stood away from the door, braced himself and opened it. He stepped into the smoker.

Two men were sitting upon the leather seat, facing him. They were Radcott and Searcey. Spahr thought that another man had been sitting with them when he had come bolting in but he couldn't be sure.

He made his way to the first lavatory and turned on the cold water faucet. He let the basin fill, then leaned over and splashed water over his face.

"Sick, fellow?" it was Searcey's voice that spoke through the stillness.

"Urn-huh," Spahr murmured through the folds of the towel. "A little."

He straightened up and dried his hands, tossed the towel into the receptacle below the lavatory. He surveyed himself in the mirror. His face was chalk-white and his eyes bloodshot.

As he pushed through the curtains he heard Searcey laugh and say to Radcott: "They always do it as soon as they get across the border—fill up on liquor."

Liquor! Spahr made his way down the passage, one hand running against the wall. The damn fool, talking so confidently about liquor making him sick. It hadn't been that. It had been the peculiar ungraceful way in which she had slumped forward onto the floor, on her knees, with her forehead resting upon the carpet, hands thrust out on either side of her like broken wings. . . .

He came to the door and walked unsteadily down the steps.

The night air struck his face with welcome coolness and he stood for a moment upon the lower step, breathing deeply. It helped to steady his vision, to diminish the alternate pounding from side to side in his head. He lit a cigarette and stepped to the ground. He walked forward a few steps and sank down upon the sand beside the tracks.

The windows of the train cast faint rectangles of illumination against the ground but on all sides of him was silence. A telegraph pole loomed in stark black outline against the horizon where the sun had sunk.

Spahr stared at this pole for a moment, startled.

Perched upon the crosspiece were three huge birds, gaunt and motionless, their naked heads craned slightly forward, as if their eyes were fixed upon him.

He picked up a stone and threw it with all his force. It crashed against the pole and the birds rose with a flapping of wings, hung in the air for a moment, then sailed off into the darkness.

Spahr drew in deeply upon his cigarette, letting its smoke trickle slowly through his nostrils as he tried to think. The apparitions upon the pole had startled him more than he realized.

What had possessed him to do as he had done—to yield to the sudden nausea which had come over him, to close the door behind him and hurry to the smoker? He hadn't even stopped to make sure that she was dead, he hadn't done anything except stare down at her in that strangely cramped position on the floor.

He should, he realized now, have called someone, have said that he had merely gone to her compartment and found her like that. No one would have suspected him if he had told a simple straightforward tale like that. But now——

Suppose he went back into the Pullman now and told them that Miss Van Syle was dead on the floor of her compartment. They would want to know why he had not said something sooner, why he had closed the door and left her, why he had come like this out into the night and smoked a cigarette. They would think (his right hand rubbed a groove into the dry hard ground) that he had come out to bury something, to throw something away. They would think, that meant, that he had killed her.

The only thing to do now was to keep still. They would find her sooner or later and there would be nothing to connect him with her death. Unless——

A sudden spate of panic swept over him as he stared into the utter loneliness of the desert.

——Unless they found his fingerprints upon the handle of her door.

Chapter XII
DEATH LEAVES YELLOW FLOWERS
(7:20 P.M.)

Rennert rose and pushed the door shut with his foot.

He let his eyes wander purposefully about the compartment upon whose floor Coralie Van Syle lay in a crumpled heap. They took in the ordered arrangement of everything that had belonged to the dead woman—the brightly jacketed books stacked in a neat pile upon the table; a few articles of clothing carefully folded; the two expensive-looking traveling bags of brown grained leather. Everything betraying a tidy methodical nature—everything except the three discordant notes: the battered hatbox that lay flat upon the floor, its contents strewn about it; the black and white beaded bag which yawned open upon the table; the withered yellow flowers that should have been put in water.

He walked across the room and knelt beside the hatbox. Upon the top, beside the handle, the initials O. W. were stamped in gilt that had begun to crack. He sorted out the contents with practiced fingers. Two facts struck him as significant: the box had been filled with the odds and ends of wearing apparel that always remain at the last minute of packing and—this apparel was *brand-new.* Half a dozen frothy lace handkerchiefs, evanescent underwear, a pair of silk mules, a comb, a bottle of bath salts, even (Rennert's eyes narrowed) a toothbrush in virgin cellophane. He felt of the lining of the box then closed it and got to his feet.

He turned his attention then to the contents of the beaded bag which had been poured recklessly upon the surface of the table. There were a few coins, an unopened package of English cigarettes, a fountain pen, a long manila envelope.

He picked up the envelope. It bore the imprint of the Mexican Consulate in San Antonio and was addressed to the Immigration officials at Nuevo Laredo. He opened it and took out the oblong card which it contained. This certified that Miss Ollie Wright, age 36, by profession a school teacher, of a small town near Fort Worth, was authorized to visit Mexico as a tourist for the period of six months. Rennert stared at the card thoughtfully for several minutes before replacing it in the envelope. He returned the contents to the bag, snapped it shut and laid it upon the table.

He cast a glance at the books. They were copies of recent fiction and popular biographies and looked as if they had never been opened. Beneath them was a slim leather volume. He pulled this out and opened it. It was a diary and upon the flyleaf was written in ink the name of Coralie Van Syle. The name had been copied, with flourishes, over the entire page. Rennert turned the pages of the book, read a line here and there. As he read, the lines of his lips grew a bit grim and there was an odd far-away look in his eyes as he closed the book. He held it in his hands for a moment, undecided. Then he slipped it into the pocket of his coat. (The next day, very deliberately, he burned it.)

He inspected next the two traveling bags, both of which

were stamped with the initials C. V. S. The clothing in them was also new and expensive and had been carefully arranged so as to conserve as much space as possible. No evidence here of hurried, last-minute packing.

He rang the bell for the porter and stood staring down at the body before the door. The jade cigarette holder lay beside it, empty. He felt a faint twinge of self-reproach at having let the woman lie there while he conducted his search of her belongings, but he thought: *She is fortunate that Mexico has taught me as much as it has of that calm acceptance of death which passes at first for callousness and which is far, far kinder to the dead than the futile squirmings nourished in my race by fear of oblivion.*

His hand rested upon Coralie Van Syle's diary and his eyes upon the withered yellow flowers as the porter knocked at the door.

Rennert opened the door with his handkerchief. (It would be upon the inside, not the outside handle that any traces of the murderer's fingerprints would remain, since his own grasp had doubtless destroyed those upon the latter.) He motioned the Mexican inside.

The little man's eyes riveted themselves immediately upon the body and remained fixed there as Rennert spoke to him. This time, however, there was a slow downward sagging of the muscles in his face and his brown fingers moved slowly back and forth like the legs of a spider. He kept his eyes averted from Rennert's face as he backed out of the door.

He returned in a few moments with the conductor and one of the soldiers.

They stood, a silent trio, as Rennert told them of his discovery of the body. A bulging seemed to be going on inside the head of the conductor; his eyes protruded behind the lenses of his glasses, his tongue looked as if it were about to force itself from his mouth and perspiration stood out upon his face. The soldier, who must have been a pureblooded Indian, stood motionless as his eyes rested without expression upon first one and then another of the little group.

When they had placed the body upon the berth, Rennert stooped and picked from the floor the jade cigarette holder.

"When was the last time you saw this woman?" he asked the conductor when the latter stood before him again.

The man swallowed and began to rub the palms of his hands upon the sides of his trousers. "In the diner, señor, after the train had stopped."

"How soon after?"

"But a minute. I passed through on my way to the steps and she was there."

"Were there others in the diner at the time?"

"I think——" the conductor stood in thought for a moment, "yes, there were four men in the diner. One at the table with her, two across the aisle and the other, I think, at a table by himself. All of them were passengers from the Pullman."

"And did you go back through the diner when you left me at the steps?"

"Yes, señor, but there was no one there then."

Rennert consulted his watch. The train must have stopped, he estimated, at six fifty-five or thereabouts. He had left Miss Talcott in the Pullman, descended the steps and stood for several minutes upon the ground alone, before engaging the porter in conversation. The conductor must have preceded him out of the car, walked forward to the engine and returned to meet him at the steps. After a few words the conductor had returned to the train. Rennert had talked then to King, had gone to the door of

Miss Van Syle's compartment, to the Pullman and to the diner before opening her door. Twenty minutes in all had probably been consumed. It was now seven thirty-five.

He looked at the porter. "Where were you when the train stopped?"

"On the observation platform, sir," was the ready response. "You saw me there."

Rennert studied his face, remembering the whistle which had fallen from his hand. "Why had you gone there?"

The sagging of the facial muscles had stopped now and his whole countenance seemed to have settled, as plaster settles in ever hardening forms.

"I was watching, señor."

"Watching what?"

The man's shoulders rose in a slight shrug. "The country on each side of the track. I do not like the desert."

"How long did you stay there after I talked to you?"

"But a moment. I went then through the Pullman and the diner to the kitchen."

"Who was in the diner then?"

"Two gentlemen—one at a table by the door, the other in the center."

"That will be all now," Rennert dismissed him. "Ask the waiter in the diner to come in here."

The porter turned toward the door and for an instant, as his eyes met Rennert's, the latter saw in them an unguarded look of fear.

Rennert turned to the soldier. "How many of you are there on this train?"

"Eight, señor."

"You received orders at Saltillo to assist me?"

"Yes, señor."

"Very well, then. I want one of you to remain posted on the observation platform of this car. He is to see that no one leaves the car. Another is to remain upon the ground by the steps as long as the train remains here. His duty is the same. One of you will search this compartment at once, the other the smoker. You are looking for a hypodermic needle." Rennert tried to read the other's expressionless face. "Do you know what that is?"

"No, señor."

Rennert explained. "As soon as your search is finished, come into the Pullman. You will search it then, the luggage of the passengers and the passengers themselves."

"Very well, señor." The man inclined his head slightly and marched stiffly from the room.

At the door he passed the waiter from the diner. The latter was able to maintain almost unruffled his obsequious demeanor. His nervousness betrayed itself only by a continuous passing of his right hand over his polished black hair.

"You recognize this woman?" Rennert asked him, with a motion toward the berth.

"Yes, señor," the fellow responded readily.

"When did you last see her?"

"In the diner."

"She was there when the train stopped?"

"Yes, señor."

"How long did she stay?"

"I do not know. I was in the kitchen when she left."

"When did you next come into the diner?"

"In about ten minutes, señor."

"Who was there then?"

"No one, señor."

"How many people had been in the diner when the train stopped?"

The man thought a moment. "Five, señor, I think. This woman and a young man at the table with her, two men at the table across the aisle and a man at the table by the door."

"Very well," Rennert said rather abstractedly, "that will be all."

The conductor had been standing to one side.

Rennert turned to him and said: "When these soldiers finish their examination of this compartment it is to be locked until we arrive at San Luis Potosí. The authorities there will then take charge."

"Very well, señor."

Rennert met the two soldiers at the door.

He left them to their task and stepped into the passage.

Radcott and Searcey stood in the doorway of the smoker, regarding him with questioning faces.

"What's all the excitement about?" Radcott queried.

"Something has happened," Rennert said, "which requires the presence of all of us in the Pullman. Will you gentlemen be kind enough to step in there?"

"Sure," Radcott stared at him, his round face suddenly serious.

He stepped forward, followed by Searcey. The latter glanced quickly at Rennert as he passed, seemed about to pause, then strode on toward the door of the Pullman.

Rennert stood in the doorway and glanced down the length of the car.

Mr. King sat next to the aisle, nervously tapping a folded timetable against his crossed knees. Jeanes turned his face slowly from his contemplation of the darkness outside the window and stared intently at Rennert's face. At the rear sat Miss Talcott. Her head rested against the back of her seat but her eyes looked down the car with a queer brightness in them.

Searcey and Radcott sat down side by side across from Jeanes.

"Where's Spahr?" Rennert asked, his eyes traveling about the group.

For a moment no one spoke. Radcott, who was sitting on the edge of his seat, shook his head.

"I believe," came Jeanes' quiet voice, "that the young man is out there beside the track."

Rennert turned and made his way down the passage to the steps. He made out the motionless figure of Spahr, sitting on the ground a few feet away. He called him.

Spahr turned his head, rose and walked slowly toward the train. "What's the matter?" he asked in an unsteady voice.

"I want you to come into the Pullman," Rennert said. He let the young man pass him, glanced at the figure of the soldier who stood at the foot of the steps, then returned to the Pullman.

Spahr awaited him at the door. "What do you want?" his bloodshot eyes met Rennert's.

"If you will sit down, Mr. Spahr," Rennert said in a voice that carried down the length of the car, "I have something to say to you—and to the others."

There was a spasmodic twitching of the muscles about Spahr's lips as he stared at Rennert. He dropped into the seat by the door.

A taut silence fell upon the car.

Rennert stood in the center of the aisle, facing them, and said: "What began as a pleasure or a business trip for most of us has turned unfortunately into an unpleasant and serious affair. I think the time has come for all of us to put aside our circumlocutions and acknowledge openly the fact that one of us in this car is a murderer."

Chapter XIII
ALIBI
(7:50 P.M.)

PAPER CREAKED as King's fingers twisted the timetable. The rest sat motionless and silent, staring at Rennert's face.

"When we passed through that tunnel this morning," he went on, "one of you plunged a hypodermic needle filled with nicotine poison into the body of the man who sat in this seat at my left. Tonight that same person plunged the same or another needle into the wrist of the woman who occupied the compartment behind me. Last night that person did the same with a man who stood upon the station platform at San Antonio. Three murders in twenty-four hours! I don't wish to alarm you unnecessarily but I see no reason to doubt that we stand in danger of a repetition if this murderer feels for any reason that his security is threatened. That, I am convinced, is why Miss Van Syle was killed."

He let his eyes travel from one face to another.

Miss Talcott rose quietly and slipped down the aisle to the next seat in front. There was on her usually placid countenance an indefinable expression of eager interest. If her face had brightened, that of Jeanes had darkened, as if a shadow had clouded his line features. The eyes that met Rennert's might have been those of a man who is suffering pain in silence. Across from him, Searcey and Radcott sat listening. Searcey's small mouth was compressed into a straight grim line so that his face seemed longer and more grotesquely masklike. Radcott was perched upon the edge of his seat. His hands were held between his knees and were twisting and untwisting. The startled expression upon his round pink face might, in other circumstances, have been ludicrous. The color had drained entirely from King's face as he sat with his fingers tight upon the ends of the twisted timetable and stared at Rennert. Spahr was bent forward in his seat so that his countenance was invisible. One hand was buried in his rumpled hair.

"I am speaking to one of you alone now," Rennert's voice hardened, "the one of you who is guilty of these murders. I am asking you to confess. This car is guarded closely by Mexican soldiers, there is no escape. There will be no escape until we reach a place where the proper authorities can investigate this business. Your motive is known, your part in the Montes kidnapping case is known——"

At his side there was a sharp agonized intake of breath. Spahr had raised his head and was staring wide-eyed at Rennert's face. "Oh, my God!" came in a smothered undertone from his lips.

Rennert waited. No one spoke.

"Very well," he said after a full half minute had passed, "you have made your decision. To the rest of you I am appealing for assistance. The Mexican authorities are not going to let this matter pass without investigation. That will mean detention for all of us, endless inquiries and red tape. It would be much better if we settled it ourselves before it comes before them. There is also, I must remind you again, a personal danger involved for each of you unless the murderer is identified quickly. Now, does any one of you have any information, anything at all—however insignificant it may seem to you—to give?"

Radcott's rising was like a definite cracking of the strained silence that filled the car. He stood with both hands gripping the back of the seat in front of him and met Rennert's gaze squarely. A flush—half of self-consciousness, half of anger—had mounted to his cheeks.

"I hope, Mr. Rennert, that you won't misunderstand me," he spoke in a strained voice which would have been unrecognizable as his own. "I'm just saying what I'm sure some of the others here must feel. What right have you got to put all of us in the class of suspects, to be questioned by you? Why is it that you don't come under suspicion yourself?"

Rennert saw the eyes of all of them go to Radcott's face, then come quickly back to his. The eyes of all of them, that is, except Miss Talcott. She gazed steadily at his face and he thought that a faint smile hovered for a fraction of a second upon her lips before she determinedly compressed them.

Searcey spoke in an even voice: "I think, Rennert, that you'll have to admit Radcott's question is one that you ought to answer, though I think you're perfectly right in saying that we ought to avoid any tangle with the Mexican authorities if we can."

Rennert smiled slightly. "Very true, Mr. Searcey. I have no objection at all to answering Mr. Radcott's question. I have no authority here beyond that given to me by the authorities at Saltillo until this train reaches Mexico City. There are soldiers here to act under my orders. This authority was given to me in my capacity as agent of the United States Treasury Department.

In this matter, however, I have of course no official standing. In case any of you feel a reluctance to answer any question or prefer to wait until we arrive at Mexico City, you undoubtedly have that right."

Radcott stood for a moment, as if uncertain. "Well," a rather forced smile creased his cheeks, "in that case I suppose I'll withdraw my objections. I'm ready to answer any questions you've got." He sat down.

"And you, Mr. Searcey?" Rennert looked at him. "Satisfied?"

"Sure!" Searcey's eyes seemed to narrow slightly behind the blank stare of his glasses. "I withdraw my objection. You ought to have told us at the beginning who you were."

"Is there anyone else," Rennert asked curtly, "who has any objections to this inquiry?"

King shook his head with determination, Spahr in a dazed manner. Jeanes sat motionless, without taking his eyes from Rennert's face. Some of the tortured look had gone from them now.

"Very well, then," Rennert went on, "let us go back to last night at the station in San Antonio when a man fell down in what was supposed at the time to be a faint. This happened a few minutes before nine o'clock, when the Pullman was opened. Mr. King here saw the man fall. Did anyone else witness this?"

There was no response. Out of the corner of his eye Rennert saw King pass a hand across his forehead.

"Did any of you, except Mr. King, arrive at the platform before the Pullman was opened?"

He waited. They sat like still wax figures. Even the ordinary bodily stirrings seemed devoid of their usual sounds.

"I take this as a statement, then, by each one of you that he did not stand upon that platform before nine o'clock. If it can be proven that one of you did so, it will constitute a definite prevarication by that person and will put him under suspicion." He turned to King. "Did you see any of these people upon the platform before the Pullman was opened?"

King started. Without turning around to face the others he shook his head. "No," he said in a small voice, "I don't remember having seen any of them."

Rennert felt a bit of grim satisfaction. He felt that he had scored one point at least. One of the silent people facing him had admitted having been upon that platform before nine o'clock and now denied it. He wondered if this person remembered the admission made earlier in the day.

"And now we come to this morning," he said, "and the tunnel. You, Miss Talcott, were sitting in the seat back of the one which you now occupy. You, too, Mr. Searcey. The rest of you occupy the same seats as you did then. Is that correct?"

Miss Talcott nodded. Her mild and slightly absent expression did not change but the brightness of her eyes and certain quick birdlike little movements of her body testified to her interest. (Rennert thought: *She is exactly like a spectator at a play, interested not in the actors but in the parts they represent.*)

"Let me recapitulate your statements made this morning. Miss Talcott, Mr. Searcey, Mr. Jeanes, and Mr. King did not move from their seats while we were going through the tunnel. Mr. King and Mr. Jeanes both saw someone bending over the man who sat in the chair to my left. Mr. Jeanes felt some kind of material brush against his hand at the time. Mr. Radcott was upon the observation platform when the train started through the tunnel but came inside the door at once, remaining in the passage. Mr. Spahr was in the diner, the entire time. Does anyone wish to make any change in that statement of his own position or in that of others?"

Searcey got to his feet, his large figure towering over the others. A pallor seemed to have come over his face, succeeded now by a flush which mounted angrily to his cheeks. The effect beneath the sunburnt skin was ghastly under the naked glow of the electric lights.

"See here," his soft even voice was edged with steel, "we've been over this once before. Let's get it settled. You've eliminated, it seems, everyone except Miss Talcott and myself. My good friend Mr. Jeanes," there was no mistaking the bitterness in the tone, "says that he felt my corduroy trousers against his hand. That——"

"I beg your pardon, Mr. Searcey," Miss Talcott spoke for the first time, "but Mr. Jeanes is not so sure now that it was your trousers which he felt. He admits the possibility that it was this fiber bag of mine." She smiled slightly as she held it up.

Searcey stared at the bag. His mouth tightened. He turned to Rennert. "Is that so?"

Rennert nodded.

Searcey's eyes flicked the side of Jeanes' face. "Still," he spoke out of one corner of his mouth, "that leaves me in about the same position. I'm sure, Miss Talcott," exaggerated gallantry was in his voice, "that you are not under suspicion." He looked squarely at Rennert. "What I was getting at is this. I've said that I did not leave my seat while we were going through that tunnel. I could have done so, though. Radcott here and Spahr say that they did not come into this car. They could have done so, though. You are taking their word for it?"

"Unless we have evidence to the contrary, Mr. Searcey."

"Yet you admit that it's possible that either one of them did come in here?"

"Yes."

There was a frantic look in Spahr's eyes as he turned his head. "But the waiter back in the diner will swear that I didn't leave it while we were in the tunnel!" He looked at Rennert. "Isn't that so?"

"Unfortunately, Mr. Spahr, the waiter cannot swear to that. All that he can say is that he did not see you leave. While the train was in the tunnel and for several minutes after he was in the kitchen."

Spahr stared at him as the little remaining blood drained slowly from his cheeks. He reached into his pocket and drew out a package of cigarettes with a hand that trembled.

"But," he exclaimed suddenly, "Miss Van Syle was in there all the time. She——" he stopped and let the cigarette which he held fall to the floor.

"Unfortunately, Mr. Spahr, Miss Van Syle cannot verify your story," Rennert said quietly.

Spahr leaned forward again and buried his head in his hands.

Rennert's eyes met Searcey's. "So, you see, Mr. Searcey, suspicion does not rest upon you alone."

Searcey shrugged his shoulders and sank back onto his seat. "That's all I wanted to know," he said quietly.

Rennert was conscious of the tension which filled the car. Now that the accustomed noises of the rain had ceased it was as if each person there were a tautened wire which vibrated to the least movement on the part of another. The steady monotony of the electric fans was becoming unendurable.

Rennert waited a moment, watching the faces before him.

"And now," he went on in an unhurried voice, "we come to

the death tonight of Miss Van Syle, who occupied the compartment behind my back. She was seen alive in the diner a minute or so after the train stopped. I am going to ask each one of you to reconstruct his actions from that time until we gathered here. I don't need to impress upon you the importance of being as exact and as truthful as possible." He paused. "Shall we begin with you, Miss Talcott?"

She drew herself up and smiled. "Certainly. I was sitting here with you, you remember, when the train came to a stop. I did not leave my seat until a moment ago when I moved one seat forward."

"Was anyone else in this car during that entire time?"

"No," she shook her head meditatively, "not the entire time. Mr. Jeanes was in here most of the time, however."

"Most of the time?"

"Yes, about twenty minutes after you left he got up, too, and walked toward the rear of the car—to the observation platform, I suppose. He stayed only a few minutes—probably not more than three or four—then came back and sat down. Mr. King had come in and sat down before he went out."

Rennert turned to Jeanes. "That is true, Mr. Jeanes?"

The man met his gaze steadily. "Yes, that is true, I went, as Miss Talcott has suggested, to the observation platform. I remained there for not more than three minutes. I came back into this car at once."

"And may I ask why you went to the observation platform?"

"Certainly," Jeanes smiled slightly, "I was curious as to the reason for the stopping of the train."

Rennert kept his gaze on Jeanes' face. There was something too fixed, too pleasant and beneficent about that smile.

"Did you have any particular reason in your mind to account

for the stopping of the train?"

Jeanes' expression did not change but Rennert had the feeling that for a barely perceptible instant the weak blue eyes had held a cold, sharply speculative look.

"No," the man said evenly, "I had no particular reason in mind. I had supposed that we had stopped at a station but the unusual delay struck me. I thought that I would step to the platform. I could, of course, see no lights and so returned to this car."

Rennert was worried more than he would have admitted by the man's manner. He thought: *He is lying. The stopping of this train upon this barren desert, miles from any station, was not to him an unexpected eventuality. He had anticipated it, rather, and has been waiting for something to happen. He is still waiting.*

He turned to King and said: "That brings us to you, Mr. King. What were your actions after the stopping of the train?"

King passed a tongue over dry tight lips and said in a quick precise voice: "I was in the diner with Mr. Radcott when the train stopped. We both got up and went into the smoker. Mr. Searcey joined us there a few minutes later. I was rather—well, nervous—about the train stopping, so I left them and went down the steps. I talked to you a few minutes, you'll remember, then came back here to the Pullman." He cleared his throat. "That's all."

"Who was in the diner when you and Mr. Radcott left?"

"Mr. Searcey, Mr. Spahr and—and Miss Van Syle." He looked up. "Is that what you said her name was?"

"Yes, Mr. King, that was her name." He thought a moment. "And how long was it between the time the train stopped and the time you and Mr. Radcott left the diner?"

King considered. "Not more than four minutes, I should say."

"And how long after that did Mr. Searcey join you in the smoker?"

"Not more than ten minutes, I should judge. Probably less than that."

"Did anyone else come into the smoker while you were there?"

"Oh, yes," King sat up straighter in his seat, "I had forgotten. Mr. Spahr came in two or three minutes after Mr. Searcey did."

"He remained there how long?"

"I don't know. He went into the lavatory and was still there when I left."

"You went directly from the smoker to the steps?"

"Yes, I met the conductor at the top of the steps. He had just come up. I stopped and tried to talk to him, to ask him why the train had stopped but he didn't seem to want to talk, so I went on down and joined you."

"And after you left me and came back into the Pullman whom did you find here?"

"Miss Talcott and Mr. Jeanes. As she has said, he went toward the rear of the car and stayed a short time."

Rennert stood for a moment, cataloguing these details in his mind. He was searching, too, the faces before him for an indication that one of them was aware of a misstatement in the testimony of another. The time had been so short and they had been so closely confined within the two cars that it seemed impossible that anyone could have an alibi for the time spent in the compartment.

He looked next at Radcott, who was sitting with a frown of concentration upon his face, as if in preparation for questioning.

He seemed rather startled, notwithstanding, by Rennert's attention.

"I really don't have much more to say. It was just as Mr. King has told you—I went to the smoker with him and talked with him and then with Searcey until you asked us to come in here."

"You agree with Mr. King's estimate of the time that elapsed between your entering the smoker and Searcey's joining you there?"

Radcott pursed his lips. "I suppose so, though I'd say it was less than ten minutes, considerably. I really don't remember exactly."

"And what did Mr. Spahr do after Mr. King left?"

"He came out—he was, well, rather sick—washed his face and went out."

"That's the last you saw of him?"

"Yes."

"And you didn't leave the smoker?"

Radcott shook his head decidedly.

Rennert looked at Searcey, who was next to Radcott. He was sitting forward in his seat, resting one hand on the back of the seat in front of him while with the other he slowly stroked his long chin.

"As you know, I was in the diner when the train stopped," he said thoughtfully. "King and Radcott were there, at one table, and Spahr and the young woman at another. King and Radcott left, about three or four minutes after the train came to a stop, as they've said. The woman got sick, I think, or began crying about something and left." He met Rennert's gaze squarely. "I know you're going to want to know the time she left so I've been trying to get it straightened out in my mind. I should say that it was about five minutes after King and Radcott. I stayed about three minutes longer then left at the same time Spahr did. I went to the smoker, where I found King and Radcott. I didn't leave it until you came in."

"And where," Rennert put the question quietly, "did you leave Mr. Spahr? According to Mr. King and Mr. Radcott he did not come into the smoker until several minutes after you."

Searcey's face was as expressionless as the blank surfaces of his glasses.

"I left him at the door of the smoker," he said. "He started to come in with me but changed his mind."

"Where did he go?"

"I don't know," the words fell flatly into the stillness of the car.

Rennert saw the eyes of all of them travel from Searcey's face to the seat where Spahr was sitting.

The young man's eyes were half closed and there was a drawn expression on his face, as if he were holding his face immobile by an effort of the will alone.

"And now, Mr. Spahr," he said evenly, "you're the last one. Are the statements which these men have made as to your movements correct?"

Spahr nodded dumbly, his teeth pressed against his lower lip.

"You left Mr. Searcey at the door of the smoker?"

Another nod.

"Where did you go then?"

Spahr kept his eyes averted and said in a thick voice: "I went back to the diner—I'd forgotten something."

"What, Mr. Spahr?"

"My cigarettes."

Rennert, glancing back, saw Searcey's gaze directed at the man who was speaking. There was a curious intentness on his face and his lips were two straight hard lines.

"You came back at once to the smoker?" he turned his attention back to Spahr.

"Yes."

"And were sick?"

"Yes," a perceptible pause, "I'd taken another drink of wine back in the diner."

Rennert regarded him thoughtfully for a moment. "Did you see anyone in the diner, the waiter for instance, who can testify to your presence there?"

Spahr stared at him. "No."

"Mr. Searcey has said that the young lady was ill or crying. Is that true?"

Spahr's eyes surveyed him blankly. "Yes, that's true, she was crying about something. I don't know what about. She wouldn't tell me."

Rennert watched him for a moment, then looked slowly over the faces of the others.

"Do any of you find any inconsistency or false statement in what anyone has just said? If so, I should advise you to speak out at once, since it is to your own interest to do so."

A long interval of silence.

Rennert was conscious of a feeling of disappointment as he sought vainly for an expression upon some face which would indicate that someone had slipped up upon some detail, however trivial. He saw nothing. Spahr sat with one hand shading his eyes. The eyes of the others met his without wavering.

Rennert brought out of his pocket the piece of paper which King had given to him outside Saltillo.

"That brings us," he said, "to another matter, which may or may not be connected with the deaths which have occurred on this train. I have here a paper which was given to one of the passengers on this car by mistake at Saltillo. It bears a message meant for another of you. For whom was this message meant?"

Searching their faces he saw in the eyes of one of them confirmation of his suspicions.

"It is in Spanish," he said, "translated it reads: 'Our friends in San Antonio warn that danger hovers over your train. You are being watched. Take care!' Does that have any meaning for any one of you?"

One pair of eyes froze and the lips beneath them moved silently, as if in prayer.

No one spoke.

In the stillness which lay upon the car Rennert could hear very distinctly King's stertorous breathing at his side. At the rear Miss Talcott was leaning forward in her chair, an intent look upon her face. Her eyes were calculative, fixed on his face. He waited but she said nothing and after a moment sank back onto the seat while her eyes sought a point above his head.

Rennert looked down at Jeanes' white face and said: "Under the circumstances, Mr. Jeanes, I am going to have to ask you to tell us the contents of the message which you received and tore into pieces at the station at Vanegas."

Chapter XIV
SEARCH
(8:17 P.M.)

JEANES' EYES closed as if involuntarily, at a threatened blow. When he opened them they were cold and clear. When he spoke his voice was not raised yet seemed to ring out in the stillness.

"The message which I received in Vanegas had no connection with anything which has happened upon this train."

"I'm afraid, Mr. Jeanes, that we cannot take your word for that."

Jeanes' thin shoulders rose in a suggestion of a shrug. "I have told the truth. I can say no more."

"This message in my hand," Rennert extended it, "was it intended for you?"

"I cannot say."

There was, Rennert felt, an air of granite-like resolve about the man as he sat with straightened shoulders and upraised chin. It was not defiance so much as the calm acceptance of impregnability.

"I think," Rennert said, "that you are making a grave mistake, Mr. Jeanes, by maintaining that attitude. Remember that as soon as we arrive in Mexico City in the morning the Mexican authorities will take over this investigation. They may not be disposed to be lenient with your silence."

If the man was conscious that his face was the cynosure of their eyes he did not betray it by the movement of a muscle. The wraith of a smile that hovered about his delicately chiseled lips was but the reflection of his own thoughts.

Watching him, the thought struck Rennert rather forcibly: *He is not concerned by my insistence upon what will happen in Mexico City in the morning because he does not expect to reach Mexico City!*

When King got to his feet it was as if a tautened wire had snapped.

King's face was gray and his eyes looked as if they had sunk into hollows. He kept his hands buried in the pockets of his coat and his shoulders braced. He looked at Rennert and then at the others.

His voice was brittle: "My friends, I'm going to speak frankly. I don't like the way things stand now. Remember we're not in the United States but in a foreign country. I'm convinced, as Mr. Rennert has said, that there's a cold-blooded murderer on this car. Personally, I don't look forward to spending the night in the same car with him, without knowing who he is. What assurance have we that he hasn't kept the hypodermic needle with which he has killed three people already?" He paused and swallowed hard. "I'm going to suggest that everyone on this car submit to a search, both of his person and of his luggage. Then, if no trace is found of the needle or of another weapon, we can at least spend the night with some feeling of security."

He sank into his seat as if exhausted by the effort of

speaking, felt in his pocket for a handkerchief and passed it over his face.

For several seconds after he had concluded there was silence.

Rennert waited.

It was Radcott who spoke up at last, rather uncertainly.

"I agree with Mr. King, of course," he said, "although I rather dislike the idea of being searched. Still, if I thought it would do any good in finding out which one of us is the murderer, I'd be glad to submit to it. But do you think, Mr. Rennert, that this person will have kept the needle? Won't he have thrown it away?"

"Miss Van Syle was killed after the train stopped," Rennert reminded him. "The needle, therefore, is either on this car or cannot have been thrown very far."

"Oh!" Radcott stared at him. "That's right. In that case I second Mr. King's suggestion," he said feebly, dropping into his seat.

King looked back over the car.

"If Miss Talcott will be kind enough to retire to the ladies' room we can go through with it right now," he suggested.

Rennert watched their faces. He was rather taken aback by King's suggestion and by the ready acquiescence of the others. He had been determined to enforce this search in case the needle were not found elsewhere in the train but he had expected to meet with considerable remonstrance. He had the feeling now that the needle would not be found upon any of them, that if it were found at all it would be in a position which would implicate no one. Still, the search might bring something else to light. If it accomplished nothing else, it had at least added to his knowledge of Mr. King.

Miss Talcott had risen and was standing in the aisle, smoothing out the cuffs of her dress.

There was an abstracted smile on her face as she looked back at Rennert and said in a clear voice: "Wouldn't this be a good opportunity to find out if my paper-knife is still in this car?"

Rennert looked at her thoughtfully. "Yes, Miss Talcott, it is an excellent opportunity."

She started to turn away, paused and said: "But perhaps some of these people have seen it. Have you asked them?"

"No, I haven't."

King was sitting bolt upright in his seat, staring at Rennert. "What's this," he demanded, "about a knife?"

"Miss Talcott has lost a paper knife," Rennert told him evenly. "She suggests that I ask whether any of you have seen it."

It was a grim silence that held them for a moment.

King looked back at the woman. "Was it—" he faltered, "sharp?"

Rennert could see that she repressed a smile as she gazed at his agonized face. "Yes, Mr. King," she spoke very distinctly with, he felt, a certain sardonic humor, "it was sharp—very sharp." She watched him for an instant then looked up at Rennert. "I'll retire now if you wish. You may search my luggage, too, if you like. It's unlocked."

She walked down the aisle toward the rear of the car.

Rennert turned and entered the passage. He spoke briefly to the two soldiers who stood there. The needle, he learned, had not been found in the compartment which they had searched nor in the smoker. He gave them directions as to what was to be done in the Pullman. They were to concentrate their energies, he told them, on finding the needle and the missing knife.

King was standing in the aisle with a worried look on his

face when Rennert returned. "I think," he said hesitantly, "that we would all prefer to be searched by you, Mr. Rennert, rather than by those Mexicans." He looked about him for support.

Radcott and Searcey nodded agreement. Spahr and Jeanes made no motion.

"Very well," Rennert said, "if you will all stand in the aisle I shall do so while these men are going through your luggage. When I have finished you can step into the smoker until we are through here."

They obeyed.

Afterwards, looking back upon that scene, Rennert realized the strain to which he as well as the rest of them had been subjected during that day. It manifested itself on his part by an almost irrepressible feeling of amusement as he passed down the aisle, searching each one with careful practiced fingers. It brought back to him memories of other days, at border ports and crossings, and of indignant, resignful, or panic-stricken tourists, most of them with trifling peccadilloes looming large upon their consciences. The highly respectable and law-abiding lady who he knew had a large and awkwardly-shaped bottle of French perfume concealed in her bosom and whom he hadn't been able to resist torturing with his knowledge. The terrified schoolteacher with the alcohol which really had been bought in Mexico for medicinal purposes . . . It brought back other, grimmer memories. . . .

They submitted without protest, emptying pockets and unbuttoning vests and coats. King, in grim earnest as he opened his billfold and held it out for inspection, even offering to unlace his shoes; Spahr, lethargic and, Rennert noticed as he ran his hands over his body, trembling with occasional spasmodic twitches; Jeanes, like a figure of stone, his eyes upraised martyr-like; Searcey, with a slight smile hovering upon his lips and a word or two of banter; Radcott, seemingly so anxious to show his readiness to help that his fat fingers kept getting in the way.

At last it was finished, the last of them had moved forward into the smoker and Rennert had found nothing suspicious. As he walked down the aisle, watching the two Mexican soldiers busy at their task, he told himself that this was exactly what he had expected—nothing.

He paused at the seat on his left where one of the soldiers was engaged upon a considerable quantity of luggage. Radcott, he knew, occupied the lower berth here and Searcey the upper. He recalled the fact that Radcott had said that he represented a novelty supply company as he watched the Mexican going through the contents of a large sample case. It contained a number of gaudily colored boxes of popcorn, candy, and other confections. Rennert picked one or two of them up, looked at them thoughtfully and put them down. At an afterthought, he picked one of them up again and opened it. Satisfied, he replaced its cover as best he could and returned it to the case. He stared down at it for several moments. The box which he had opened had contained, besides the molasses-coated popcorn, an ornamental and worthless watchchain which looked like (but wasn't) gold. The wrapping of each of the boxes proclaimed the fact that other hidden treasures were within, as premiums for purchase of the dainties. Rennert was thinking of the popcorn which he had found upon the floor between the seats where the man who had been murdered that morning and his unknown vis-à-vis of the night before had sat. There was the stickpin, too, and the child's ring which Miss Talcott had found. Rennert was wondering several things about the bland-faced Radcott and his popcorn.

So engrossed was he in his thoughts, in fact, that his eyes

almost missed an object in the battered yellow handbag which one of the soldiers was turning inside out. With a word to the man he took the bag and carried it across the aisle. The end of the label which had been pasted upon it at the border certified to the fact that it belonged to William Searcey. Rennert took the object in his hands and stared at it. It was a bottle of brown hair dye.

His face thoughtful, Rennert returned it to the bag and went through the rest of the contents. There was nothing else there, however, that any male, without too great a thought for his own comfort, might not have carried in his luggage. He closed the bag and returned it to its place under the seat. Searcey, it seemed, had no other equipment.

The soldier whom Rennert had interrupted had continued his search of the vacant seats to the rear. The other had concluded his search of Miss Talcott's luggage and the unoccupied seat behind it. Both of the men now stood facing Rennert, their black eyes fixed on his face.

"You found nothing?" he asked. "Neither the needle nor the knife?"

"*Nada, señor,*" they responded in unison.

Rennert then gave them directions for completing their search of the Pullman and of the diner as well. (The needle, of course, might have been tossed from the observation platform or a door but in the darkness search for it would in that case be practically futile.)

As he walked slowly back toward the smoker, Rennert was asking himself whether he should not have taken the time to search the luggage of each of the passengers as he had done that of Searcey and Radcott. Certainly, the results in those two instances had justified it. He decided to let the rest remain for a later time. That needle was, after all, the most important thing right now. The needle and the paper-knife of Miss Talcott's . . .

In the smoker he found an uncommunicative weary group.

He stood in the doorway and said: "I wish to thank you for your cooperation. You may go back to the Pullman now if you wish."

King asked eagerly: "Did you find the needle?"

"No," Rennert answered, "we did not find it."

"You didn't!" King stared at him. "That means it's not in the car then."

"The rest of the car is being searched, Mr. King. Unless the needle is found within a few minutes you can rest assured that the murderer has thrown it from the train."

"What about that knife Miss Talcott mentioned? Did you find that?" Radcott asked.

"No, I regret to say that it has not been found either."

Radcott bit his lip. "I suppose," he said, "that it has been thrown away too. Still," he paused, "what would have been the use of anyone taking it if he was going to throw it away?"

Rennert looked at him steadily. "Your answer to that question, Mr. Radcott, is as good as mine."

"Yes," Radcott said weakly, "I suppose so."

He walked straight for the door, pushed aside the curtains and went out. King followed him, a preoccupied frown on his face. Spahr had been sitting by the window, staring out into the night. He got up now and walked out.

Searcey and Jeanes remained. Each, Rennert thought, was waiting for the other to go.

At last Searcey moved forward, paused by the door and said gravely: "I don't like to say this, Mr. Rennert, but I suppose you realize that one person wasn't searched tonight?"

"You mean Miss Talcott?"

"Yes, someone mentioned the fact in here a few minutes ago. Of course, I don't suppose there's any reason to suspect her but I thought I'd call it to your attention. In fairness to the rest of us, you understand."

"Thank you, Mr. Searcey, I haven't forgotten the fact."

Searcey started to say something, evidently thought better of it, and turned away.

When the curtains had fallen to behind him Jeanes stood for several seconds in the center of the room, his shoulders thrown back and his hands clenched at his sides.

Rennert waited for him to speak.

His voice, when it came, was quick and marked with a slight sibilance which might have been the product of emotion. "I must speak to you, Mr. Rennert, at once!"

"Very well, shall we sit down?"

"No, no, there is no time for that." Jeanes began to pace up and down. "I have reached a decision. I must come to an understanding with you and there is no time to waste."

Rennert lit a cigarette and watched him.

His throat seemed to contract for an instant then he went on: "These people in the Pullman do not interest me. The question of these two deaths is important, yes, terribly important to them. But I have sworn that I know nothing of them. You must believe me!" his voice was raised in its intensity. "Other things, beside which these two deaths are insignificant, are at stake, Mr. Rennert! I am but an agent here, an implement in the hands of a power which counts me as one of the sands upon the seashore. But I too may render service! It is sometimes given to an individual, even a weak one such as I. I am in danger. If I alone were concerned I should keep silent. But for the Cause which I serve, Mr. Rennert, I am asking you to give me that message which you read, to let me destroy it. I am asking you to erase from your memory the words which it contained."

In the intensity of his emotion he thrust forward his right hand and held it, trembling slightly, before Rennert.

Rennert studied him for a moment. "You admit, then, that these messages were meant for you?"

"Yes, yes, of course," there was a note of impatience in the voice.

"And you persist in your refusal to reveal the meaning of them?"

"I cannot."

"As I told you back in the Pullman, Mr. Jeanes, I am convinced that you are making a grave mistake. I have no wish to pry into your private affairs. But my own safety and that of the other passengers on this train are concerned now. That being the case, I cannot conceal any matters which have come to my attention since this train left San Antonio."

"But I have told you that these messages have no connection with the deaths which have occurred on this train."

"You are sure of that, Mr. Jeanes?"

Again Rennert had the curious feeling that a shadow darkened for an instant the translucence of the face before him.

"I am sure," Jeanes said in a suddenly low voice, "that they have no connection."

"And are you sure that they have no connection with the delays which this train has suffered, with our stopping out here upon the desert?"

Jeanes' hand dropped slowly to his side and his eyes went to the window. They stared unseeingly into the darkness which it framed.

"It is possible," he said, "that they have."

"You expected this train to be stopped en route to Mexico City?" Rennert's voice hardened.

"Yes," Jeanes' voice was almost a whisper now, "I expected it."

"And yet what you expected to happen has not happened, even though the train has stopped?"

He stood for a moment in silent abstraction then looked suddenly at Rennert. His face was hard and frozen and his eyes glistened under the light.

"I see, Mr. Rennert, that I must talk to you in other terms." His right hand went to his coat pocket and brought out a thick billfold. He held it out. "I have here three thousand dollars in cash, American money." He leaned forward slightly and deliberately spaced his words. "It is yours if you give me the message which you have and if you forget that you ever saw it."

Rennert's gaze was steady. "Your folly, Jeanes, is increasing," he said evenly, "if you think I'd risk my life for three thousand dollars."

The muscles of Jeanes' throat stood out like tautened cords. His right hand traveled again to his pocket. He brought out a packet of travelers' checks, flipped them between his fingers.

"Here is more money, enough to make you rich, Mr. Rennert."

Rennert turned toward the door. "The Mexican officials," he said curtly, "may be more susceptible to bribery than I. I'd advise you to save it for them."

Jeanes swayed upon his feet, as if the train were moving.

"Then may God's mercy rest upon your soul!" he said.

Chapter XV
THE NEEDLE AND THE KNIFE
(9:10 P.M.)

THE NEEDLE lay in shattered fragments in the soldier's outstretched palm. His upraised lantern cast a wavering illumination on the bent point, the glass cylinder broken in the center, the loosened plunger.

"Yes," Rennert said as he held out a handkerchief, "it is the needle that we were looking for. Where did you find it?"

The soldier carefully turned his hand so that the pieces fell into the handkerchief. The lantern light slanted across his dark face, whose prominent cheek bones left his eyes two glittering imbedded flakes of light.

"Under the water cooler in the passage, señor, where the empty paper cups are thrown."

Rennert folded the handkerchief, knotted it and slipped it carefully into his pocket. *In the passage outside the door of the girl's compartment,* he thought, *where the murderer tossed it as he emerged.* Although the discovery of the needle told him nothing of the identity of this person he was conscious of a feeling of relief that at last the murderer was deprived of the little instrument of death which he had used three times with such effectiveness.

"And the bronze paper knife?" he asked. "You did not find it?"

"No, señor, we did not find it. We searched the Pullman, the diner, the smoker, the passages between them." He hesitated. "We searched all the places except one."

"And that one?"

"The room of the ladies, señor. Shall we search that, too?"

Rennert held an unlighted cigarette between his fingers and stared down at the whiteness of it.

"Yes," he said, "search it too."

"Bueno, señor. ¿Es todo?" the soldier started to turn away.

Rennert thought a moment. "Have the kindness to ask the conductor to come here," he said.

"Bueno."

Rennert stood and watched the man walk toward the steps, his heavy shoes crunching against the loose gravel. When he and his lantern had disappeared, he still stood and stared into the darkness.

When he had first stepped upon the ground the darkness had been complete, Stygian. Now, as his pupils contracted, he was aware of the cold faraway glitter of the stars that studded the sky and began to make out shadowy details of the landscape about him. The black columns of the telegraph poles stretching away to the right and left like ruins of an ancient roofless temple. . .undulations upon the desert floor that he knew were cacti and stunted trees.

At his back the train lay like a monstrous reptile whose flat back blotted out the stars. From apertures in its belly glowed faint rectangles of light.

Up front in the second-class coach someone was strumming at a guitar.

> *"No vale la pena*
> *el pensar tan hondo,*
> *el buscar el fondo*
> *de las cosas tristes,*
> *de las cosas bellas*
> *si siempre se esfuman*
> *como luz de las estrellas."*

The soft voice, singing in steady melancholic monotony of the futility of striving for things as ephemeral as starlight, emphasized the sense of isolation which Rennert felt. Between the singer and his listeners up front and the Pullman behind there lay a chasm as deep, as impassable as that between the passengers in the Pullman and the desert outside their windows. A chasm of language, of blood, of unspoken thoughts and long thought-filled silences across which their eyes must look uncomprehendingly. . . .

The shadow of the conductor wavered across the gravel. He descended the steps and advanced toward the spot where Rennert stood.

"¿Sí, señor?" he queried softly, his body motionless while his eyes darted into the darkness.

"There has been no news of the engine?" Rennert asked.

"No, señor, no news."

"It should be returning soon, should it not?"

"Yes, señor, soon now."

"I wanted to ask you," Rennert said, "about your actions

after the train stopped. After you left me here and returned to the car did you meet or see any of the passengers from the Pullman?"

The man seemed to drag his thoughts with difficulty from some recess of their own. "Yes," he said, "a man was coming out of the smoker as I came to the top of the steps. He asked me why the train had stopped. I tried to tell him but I do not think that he understood. He went down these steps then."

"He was a small man, with gray hair and glasses?"

"Yes."

Rennert nodded, satisfied on that point. "Thank you," he murmured abstractedly, "that is all."

When the conductor had gone he began to stroll slowly up and down the gravel beside the track, smoking a cigarette and letting the cool night air aid in the ordering of his thoughts.

He went over again and again the testimony to which he had listened back in the Pullman, trying to find flaws in it.

At last he had to give it up.

These accounts of time and place and movements had dovetailed too nicely together, formed too perfect a chain of connecting inter-supporting links. Even taking into consideration the unreliability of the average person's calculation of time, if each of the versions were true, or evenly fairly accurate, only one of the passengers had had time enough, between the stopping of the train and his discovery of Miss Van Syle's body, to ransack her compartment and murder her.

Jeanes had been in sight of Miss Talcott, of himself and of King during the entire time, except for the brief interval when he had walked back to the observation platform. If Miss Talcott's and King's estimate of time were correct there would have been an insufficient interval for him to leave the platform, proceed along the ground beside the train, enter by another door and gain the compartment before Rennert. He would have had to go far up the train to find a door through which he could enter unobserved and would have had to traverse the same route on his way back to the observation platform.

Miss Talcott had not left the Pullman. Her story was verified by himself, by Jeanes and by King, at least one of whom had been in the same car with her the entire time.

King's account of his actions was vouched for by Radcott, who had left the diner and entered the smoker with him; by Searcey, who had found them there; by the conductor, who had seen King emerge from the smoker and go down the steps; and finally by himself, who had seen him descend the steps and who had followed him back into the Pullman.

Radcott had quite as unshakable an alibi. He had not been alone for an instant from the time of leaving the diner with King. When the latter had left him, Searcey had been with him in the smoker. Both of them had been there when Rennert went to call them.

Searcey had been in the diner with at least one other person from the time the train stopped until Spahr went out. He had accompanied Spahr to the door of the smoker, and from then on had been in the company of either King or Radcott.

There remained only Spahr. No one had seen him during those minutes which had elapsed between his departure from Searcey at the door of the smoker and his entry into the smoker, sick. There would have been ample time for him to have gone to the compartment next the smoker, murder the girl and proceed about his search of her belongings.

For that morning, likewise, when the train had been passing through the tunnel, Spahr had no satisfactory alibi. He might easily have left the diner, gone back to the Pullman and returned before the train emerged from the darkness.

There remained still unexplained that confounded reference to an extra edition of a newspaper. Spahr was, by his own admission, a newspaperman.

Rennert tossed away his cigarette, watched with narrowed thoughtful eyes as it cut a wide spiral through the darkness to glow for an instant against the sands.

He felt, for some reason for which he was unable to account, a reluctance to admit Spahr's guilt but could see no alternative. There was, of course, the possibility of collusion throughout the affair, that two people had been involved in the Montes kidnapping business, that both had entered the Pullman in San Antonio. In that case each would have an alibi prepared for the other. He saw, however, no reason to consider that possibility seriously.

He watched the same soldier step to the ground and walk toward him.

The man held his right hand outstretched. Upon the handkerchief which was spread over his palm lay an object which gleamed dully in the lantern light.

"I have found it, señor," he said.

Rennert gazed down at it. It was a slender knife of bronze, profusely decorated with scrollwork. He took it, still swathed in the handkerchief, and put it into a pocket.

"Where did you find it?" he asked.

"In the room of the ladies, señor. It was wedged behind the cushion of the seat. It is the knife which you wanted?"

"Yes," abstraction was in Rennert's voice, "it is the knife. Thank you."

Two men sat in the smoker. For exactly three minutes neither had spoken. It was as if the blue haze which filled the little room stood like an impalpable barrier between them, a barrier through which nothing but trivialities could sift.

Jackson Saul King sat upright upon the leather seat, his hands resting very firmly upon his knees, as if for support. His tired shoulders ached with the effort to keep them from sagging. In the silence he heard very distinctly the dispassionate ticking of his watch. The blind beside him was pulled down full length against the darkness and the desert and the panic that would surge in upon him if for an instant he relaxed his pose, lost his contact with reassuring leather and wood and manmade metal. He resolutely kept his mind on San Antonio, far away on the other side of the Rio Grande, where his wife had stayed in safety, surrounded by streetlights and pavements and honking auto horns. He thought: *I am glad that she is not here because I couldn't hide from her, as I am doing from these others, the fact that I am afraid. She would be understanding and try to act as if she didn't know it. That would only make it worse.* That reminded him of the lie which he had told Rennert regarding Mrs. King. He frowned. If there should be further investigation . . .

Preston Radcott's right hand was buried in the pocket of his trousers. He felt reassured now and a peculiar sense of exhilaration, never before experienced, sent electric tingles through his body. He felt singularly wide-awake and cool after the heat and perspiration of the day. He contemplated going back into the diner and getting a drink but hesitated. He thought: *Something is going to happen soon and I had better stay in sight of the others.* He wanted someone to talk to, someone with whom he could share this glowing sensation of recklessness that made him impatient of the prolonged quietness which held them.

He felt a kind of relief when King raised one hand, took the cigar from the corner of his mouth, surveyed it speculatively and dropped the end into the cuspidor. The man's silence had begun to annoy him.

King looked at his watch and said: "We've been here two hours and twenty-five minutes now."

"Um-huh," Radcott pulled himself up in his seat, drew a package of cigarettes from his pocket and selected one. He searched for matches then turned to King. "What about a match? I seem to be out and there aren't any here in the smoker."

King extended a packet of safety matches. Radcott took one, lit his cigarette and tossed the extinguished match to the floor.

"Thanks," he handed the packet back to King. "Seems longer than that, doesn't it?"

"Yes," King agreed, "it does."

Radcott blew a smoke ring and watched with half-closed eyes as it dissolved in the current of the electric fan.

"What do you think of things?" he asked.

"Things?" King looked at him sharply. "What things?"

Radcott's eyes squinted as a little eddy of smoke was thrust back into his face.

"The situation on this car," he said.

"Oh," King removed his pince-nez and slowly polished the lenses with a piece of chamois skin. The lids of his eyes were heavy and dark circles were discernible beneath them. He finished polishing the glass and carefully adjusted the pince-nez upon his nose.

"I think," he said judiciously, "that we have been heading straight for trouble ever since we crossed the border."

"How's that?"

King glanced at him sideways. "I haven't told anybody yet but this fellow Rennert," he carefully lowered his voice, "about a conversation which my wife heard last night before we got to the border."

"Your wife?"

"Yes, she got off at Laredo. She was sitting in one of the berths which hadn't been made up and heard two people talking. One of them said: 'I'll get off with you at Monterrey and you can get the money. If you don't, I'll blast the train on this trip.' The man who was talking had a foreign voice, my wife said. You see the connection, don't you?"

Radcott uncrossed his legs and sat up still straighter. "I don't know whether I do or not. What do you mean?"

"Just this," King's voice sank lower, "the man my wife heard talking was this Jeanes, of course."

"It was?"

"Yes, I'm sure of it. He's evidently some kind of a foreigner, judging by his voice. I think it's all tied up with these labor troubles. I think that Jeanes is an agitator for the strikers and that he's on this train to pass the word along down the line when to blow up this train."

Radcott emitted a startled whistle. "Gosh!" he said softly. "Maybe that's why the train is stopped out here. It may all have been a frame-up and they're just waiting until they think it's safe to do something. Still, it doesn't look as if Jeanes would stay on this train if he knew anything was going to happen to it."

"He can't get away, can he, the way the car is guarded?"

"No, that's right. That may be the reason he's been acting so funny all day."

"You remember the message that Rennert read to you back in the Pullman?"

"Yes."

"That was handed to me by a Mexican back in Saltillo. He must have thought I was Jeanes. We've both got rather gray hair, you know, and he could easily have mistaken us. That was evidently a warning from some of his friends that the soldiers were watching him and that it wasn't safe to do anything yet."

Radcott's eyes remained for a moment on King's face. Then he looked away and stared straight in front of him.

"What does Rennert think about it?" he asked.

"I don't know for sure. I think he believes that Jeanes killed that fellow back in the tunnel and this Van Syle woman or whatever her name was. Judging from what he said to Jeanes about a message that he tore up at Vanegas, he must suspect him of being mixed up in this other business, too."

"Why doesn't he have Jeanes arrested then?"

"I don't know. I wish he would. I'd feel safer."

Radcott sat for a long time, a frown creasing his forehead. The cigarette burned unheeded toward his fingers.

"If Jeanes can't leave the train we can't either, can we?" he murmured as if to himself.

"That's exactly what's worrying me," King said.

When Radcott spoke again his voice was grim.

"I'm glad," he said, "that I've got a knife handy in case anything happens."

King did not say anything for a moment.

"A knife?" he repeated then, very carefully.

"Yes."

"But why didn't they find it when they searched you and your luggage?"

Radcott smiled slightly. "They'd never think of looking for it where I had it," he said.

King leaned toward him.

"You can get it——?" he started to ask, stopped abruptly, looked up and said: "Good evening, Mr. Rennert."

Chapter XVI
GUADALUPE, VIRGIN MOTHER, SHIELD FROM HARM!
(9:25 P.M.)

"Good evening."

Rennert let the curtains fall to behind him and stepped into the smoker. His eyes rested on King's face, then on Radcott's. They did not miss the slight perturbation on both faces. He wondered what they had been talking about in low voices when he had appeared at the doorway.

"I'm going to ask you men to help me," he said pleasantly.

"Help you?" Radcott spoke up readily, taking his hand from his pocket. "Sure!"

"It's the same question—the whereabouts of everyone at the time of Miss Van Syle's death."

Radcott said: "Oh" tonelessly.

"I've asked Mr. Spahr and Mr. Searcey to reenact their movements after the train stopped and I should appreciate it if you gentlemen would do the same."

"Of course, if you think it will accomplish anything," King said with drawn brows, "but I've told you everything that I know about what happened."

"This will just be a repetition of your actions, of course. I thought we might get the time element straightened out a little better if we repeated them rather than depend on our memories."

"All right," King got to his feet and, followed by Radcott, walked to the door.

Rennert followed them. "Up in the diner, if you please."

In the diner they found Spahr and Searcey. As they entered, Searcey sat at the first table on their right, Spahr at the center table on their left, his back to them.

"If you will be kind enough to take the seats which you occupied when the train stopped," Rennert suggested.

They filed down the aisle and sat at the table across from Spahr. King sat with his back to the door, Radcott facing him.

Rennert stood in the doorway, watching them.

"We shall suppose," he said, "that Miss Van Syle is sitting across from you, Mr. Spahr."

Spahr glanced back over his shoulder and nodded silently, as his fingers played with the silverware.

Rennert held his watch in his hand and said: "The train stops now. Will you, Mr. King and Mr. Radcott, remain in your seats as long as you estimate you stayed before."

He waited.

They all sat in an uneasy silence. Spahr stared steadily at the tablecloth. Searcey leaned back in his chair, arms crossed, and regarded the others with blank eyes and expressionless face. Radcott and King sat and glanced self-consciously now at each other, now at the tablecloth, now out the window.

Not quite two minutes had passed when King turned to Rennert. "About this time, I think, we got up and left the diner." He looked back at Radcott. "That right?"

Radcott nodded. "Yes, I think so."

"Very well," Rennert said, "will you go back to the smoker now, as you did." The slight discrepancy in time, he knew, was to be expected throughout this procedure.

They got up and walked down the aisle and out the door.

"And now," Rennert looked up from his watch, "will you gentlemen estimate the time that Miss Van Syle remained in here."

Searcey nodded. He had drawn his pipe from his pocket and was filling it with tobacco from a pouch. He tamped it down with a forefinger and returned the pouch to his hip pocket. He took a match from the stand in the center of the table, struck it and applied it to the bowl. He drew upon the pipe and leaned back in his chair, in relaxation. A slight gurgling sound from the pipe was the only noise to relieve the stillness.

Spahr's face, seen in profile, was deathly white and his fingers were twitching as they moved the silverware back and forth, back and forth.

Outside, upon the gravel at the foot of the steps, Guadalupe Serrano, the little porter, stood and smoked a surreptitious cigarette and watched one of the *señores* from the Pullman talking with the brakeman.

They were standing close beside the train, between the diner and the Pullman car, and the brakeman seemed to be explaining something to the tall gray-haired man in the dark suit who was peering forward intently as the other held up his lantern. The light brought out their faces distinctly against the darkness—like, Guadalupe thought, two masks upon a dark stage in a show of *títeres*. One mask white and clear-cut, with bright shining eyes; the other, of smooth dark wood whose outlines were lost in the darkness.

Guadalupe wondered what they were talking about and what this *americano* was so interested in. But they were all like this (his dark eyes were luminous as he drew upon the cigarette) always asking questions about things that were unimportant.

At first it had amused him but ever since that man had died in the Pullman and the other man—the one so *simpático* who seemed to have charge of everything—had kept asking so many questions about the night before he had felt a kind of coldness all over his body, even though the sun had been bright and hot.

The conductor had been staring up at the *zopilotes* all day, afraid that they were following the train because of the dead body on it. Worse than the eyes of the *zopilotes,* Guadalupe thought, had been the way one person back in the Pullman had kept watching him, as if afraid that he were going to tell something.

Guadalupe watched the *americano* take some object—a billfold, it was—from his pocket and hand the brakeman several bills.

He tossed away the stub of his cigarette and turned back to the steps. As he glanced out into the darkness of the desert his brown fingers sought and fondled reassuringly the little wax figure which he wore attached to a string about his neck. It was the image of his patroness, the dark-eyed Virgin of Guadalupe, whose shrine stood upon a far-away hill outside Mexico City.

"*Tonantzin,*" he murmured, applying to her the Indian name which she knows best, "*defiende del peligro!*"

Spahr turned around in his chair and looked at Rennert.

"I think," he said in a toneless voice, "that she left about this time."

Rennert glanced at Searcey. "That right?"

"I'd judge so," Searcey said without taking the pipe from his mouth.

"Very well. Will you tell me when you followed her out?'

Another interval of silence that seemed endless.

Spahr leaned forward, his elbows on the table and his hands tight about the handle and the blade of a knife. His knuckles stood out white as he slowly bent the blade back and forth, back and forth.

Searcey looked out the window, the outlines of his face lost in the smoke that coiled upward from his pipe. His hair looked sleek and glossy under the electric lights. (Too sleek and glossy altogether, Rennert told himself. Hair dye in itself was not suspicious in the case of middle-aged men such as Searcey. But taken in conjunction with the dark glasses it made him wonder.)

Spahr let the knife clatter upon the top of the table.

"I think," he turned around, "that this is about the time I went out."

"Very well," Rennert said quietly, "do so."

Spahr got to his feet and began to walk a bit unsteadily down the aisle.

As he passed his table, Searcey too rose.

"I got up and walked out with him," he explained to Rennert.

"Very well," Rennert paused. Standing as close to Spahr as he was he could observe the frantic look in the young man's eyes and the suspicious tightening of his jaw.

"Did you gentlemen pause for a conversation here or did you leave the diner at once?" he asked.

Spahr glanced first at Searcey and then at Rennert.

"No," he said hurriedly, "we didn't stop. He said something to me and I answered him. Then I——"

"What did he say to you, Spahr?" Rennert asked quietly.

Spahr stared at him, his mouth partially open. The last remaining vestige of color had drained from his face and he put out a hand to support himself against the side of the door. "I don't remember," he said weakly, "it didn't amount to anything."

Rennert looked at Searcey, who stood very still, one hand about the bowl of his pipe. The smoke rose in slow lazy spirals before his blank glasses behind which his eyes seemed to be regarding Spahr steadily.

Rennert said: "Very well, will both of you proceed to the smoker, as you did."

Spahr moved forward like an automaton. Searcey followed him more slowly, with a lithe swinging gait.

The three of them crossed the platform between the two cars and came to a stop at the door of the smoker.

Searcey turned. "This is where Spahr left me," he said. "I went into the smoker."

Rennert seemed to consider this for some time. "Are you sure," he asked Spahr suddenly, "that Mr. Searcey went into the smoker?"

Spahr nodded. "Yes, I saw him go through the curtains."

Rennert looked directly at the dead surfaces of Searcey's glasses. "You see, Mr. Searcey, I thought it possible, although not exactly probable, that he had turned away before you entered."

Searcey's smile was mirthless. "Are you convinced now? If

not I am sure that our friends inside will swear that they saw me come through the curtains."

Rennert's smile was frank. "I am convinced that you did enter the smoker immediately." He turned to Spahr. "And now if you will go back to the diner as you did and return here we will have finished."

Both of them stood and watched Spahr's back disappear into the doorway.

Rennert's hands were upon the curtains when Searcey asked bluntly: "Was that the reason for all this acting—just to find out whether or not Spahr saw me go through this door?"

"No," Rennert told him, "I wanted to be sure of something else."

"And are you?"

"Yes, Mr. Searcey, I am." He held aside the curtains. "Shall we join the gentlemen?"

King and Radcott sat against the wall, as they had been sitting when Rennert interrupted them earlier. Both looked up inquiringly as Rennert and Searcey entered.

"Is the time about right for Mr. Searcey's entrance?"

"Yes," Radcott answered, "although of course it seems longer sitting here waiting like we have been."

Rennert returned his watch to his pocket and faced them. His face was grave.

"I estimate," he said, "that the three of you remained in this room for about four minutes, or possibly three, before Spahr came in. I want each of you to think back over those minutes and tell me if anything—anything at all—happened, to fix the time in your mind."

There was silence for a moment.

Memory seemed to come to Searcey and to Radcott simultaneously. It was Searcey who spoke. "It was the lights," be said with a stir of interest in his usually even voice. "They went out for a second or two while we were in here."

"That's right!" from Radcott. "I remember that distinctly. We talked about the possibility of them going off again."

Rennert looked at King. "You remember that also?"

"Yes, I do."

"And how long, Mr. Searcey, was that after you left Spahr at the door?"

"Less than a minute, I should say."

"Good!" Rennert could not repress his satisfaction. "That will be all, gentlemen. I should like you to retire to the Pullman now, if you will."

King and Radcott got up and walked with Searcey to the door. Radcott stood aside to let them precede him. He turned back to Rennert.

"Have we been of any help?"

"Yes, Mr. Radcott," Rennert looked him straight in the face, "you have been of a great deal of help."

Rennert watched Radcott's broad back disappear through the curtains. Then he walked slowly across the room, sank onto the leather cushions and lit a cigarette. He was smoking when Spahr entered.

Rennert watched him as he stood just inside the door, his hands held straight down at his sides and doubled into fists.

"Sit down, Mr. Spahr," he said quietly.

Spahr moved forward as if jerked by a string and sat beside Rennert.

Rennert kept his eyes on the young man's face as he asked:

"You have gone through your actions exactly as you did earlier tonight?"

Spahr moved his head up and down: "Yes," he murmured through set teeth.

"Very well. Did the repetition of your actions recall to your mind anything which happened during those three minutes or so while you were in the diner or in the passage between the diner and the smoker? Anything to fix the time?"

Spahr stared at him and shook his head.

"Any incident," Rennert went on, "no matter how insignificant it may have seemed at the time?"

"No," Spahr moistened his lips, "the train had already stopped, of course."

"And the lights?"

"The lights?" there was a blank expression on Spahr's face.

"Yes. That doesn't recall anything to your mind?"

"No."

Rennert regarded him thoughtfully. "Mr. Spahr," he said, "there used to be a popular song whose title was something like 'Where were you when the lights went out?' My question cannot be better put than in the words of that song."

Rennert sensed rather than saw a slow tautening of the compact muscular body beside him. Spahr turned his head and riveted his gaze on Rennert's face.

"I don't know what you mean," he said with forced lightness.

"You don't remember the lights going out for a second or so?"

"No, I don't."

"It was a minute or so after you left Mr. Searcey at the door there,"

Spahr sat for a moment, motionless, then his eyes left Rennert's face and sought the opposite wall. They widened into a fixed stare and he sank back against the leather of the seat. His jaw tightened. "Oh, yes," he said, "I'd forgotten about the lights. It was while I was in the diner. I remember now."

"I'm sorry, Spahr," Rennert said quietly, "but I don't think that you do."

Spahr's fingers tightened about the baggy knees of his trousers. "But it's the truth!" he broke out. "I'll swear to God it's the truth!"

Rennert looked at him steadily. "Since your memory seems to be returning," he said coldly, "perhaps you can tell me the subject of your conversation with Searcey as you were leaving the diner."

Spahr closed and opened his eyes, as if the effort gave him pain, then stared straight in front of him again. "It wasn't important," he said in a strangled voice, "it didn't amount to anything."

"In that case, let's have it."

Rennert, watching closely, saw a subtle change come over Spahr's bloodless face. His mouth became immobile; his eyes narrowed slightly and became wary and calculative. His voice when he spoke was low and broken.

"Searcey said something to me about how much wine I'd been drinking. 'Feeling pretty good, aren't you?' I think he said. I said I felt fine." He swallowed hard. "That's all there was to it. We went out then."

Rennert got to his feet abruptly. "That's all we've got to say to each other, then, Spahr."

Spahr looked at him. "You don't believe that, do you?" he demanded.

"Unfortunately," Rennert said, "I am in the unfortunate position of not being able to believe anyone. I sincerely hope that by tomorrow morning I can say that I do believe you. The consequences of a lie would be decidedly disagreeable to you, I'm afraid."

"Tomorrow morning?" Spahr asked dully.

"Yes, when we arrive in Mexico City. And now, if you follow my advice, you will get some sleep as soon as possible. If, in the morning, you find that you have anything further to tell me I hope that you will do so."

A slight tremor passed over Spahr's shoulders. "Sleep?" he exclaimed. "After all this? While we're in the middle of the desert with a murderer in the same car with us?"

Rennert said as he turned to the door: "I think, Spahr, that you can rest easily tonight. Unless I am mistaken, the murderer to whom you refer has lost his last weapon."

"You never can tell," Spahr's hollow voice was in Rennert's ears as he let the curtains fall to behind him.

Chapter XVII
THE ALBATROSS
(9:47 P.M.)

THE PULLMAN was silent. Three people sat in it without speaking. It was as if each were withdrawn into a special silence of his or her own, wrapped cocoon-like in strands of thoughts and reticences and private fears that sealed the individual from the prying eyes of others.

Paul Xavier Jeanes thought as he stared into the night beyond the window: *The forces of Evil have always been present in this strange country of Mexico, watered though it has been by the blood of saints. More blood must be shed before the power of the Antichrist is overthrown.* Cold determination steeled him (it had passed now, that moment of heart-stopping panic when he had thought of the consequences of what he was about to do) and he went over again his conversation with the brakeman, rehearsing mentally every movement that his hands would have to make when the moment arrived. At the anticipation his muscles seemed fused with superhuman strength.

He watched Rennert enter the Pullman and walk down the aisle. . . .

The silence was compounded, for William Searcey, of many

incipient noises that died just before reaching his alert senses. He remembered a day in Brownsville, when word had been received that a tropical hurricane was sweeping in from the Gulf, and the tense unnatural stillness which had lain like a pall upon the town as they waited, windows and doors secured against the fury of the storm that delayed in coming. He felt something like that now—not fear but the alertness which comes from a prescience of approaching danger. For him this trip had been overshadowed from the beginning with disaster, ever since the impact of a trunk against the wall of an adjoining room in that San Antonio hotel had jarred his mirror from the wall as he was shaving. (He caressed them, a few of these superstitions, with a tenacity that became more pleasurable from being concealed.) That shattered mirror had omened all that had happened since on this trip. And now this unforeseen, inexplicable delay in the darkness, which was bccoming worsc than the previous blind plunging forward into hinted-at dangers. The strange message which that fellow Rennert had read aloud—it bothered him. He thought: *It had a meaning for someone on this car. Something is going on that none of us suspect.*

He wondered, as he watched Rennert coming down the aisle toward him, just how much knowledge he was concealing behind that mild face and pleasant smile.

"Howdy!" he said when Rennert paused. "Sit down." He removed a foot from the chair opposite.

Rennert sat down and said: "I know how a school teacher feels now."

"A school teacher?"

"Yes, with the pupils sitting in rows before him and watching as he comes down the aisle, each one afraid that he's going to stop by his desk."

That offhand manner of his doesn't fool me, Searcey thought, *he's just as worried about the stopping of this train as I am.* He said with a slight laugh: "And I'm the pupil who has been reading a dime novel behind his geography?"

"If so, I haven't caught you at it yet."

Searcey was aware that their eyes were holding each other's steadily, as if each were unwilling to be the first to waver. "Still trying?" he asked.

Rennert smiled. "To tell the truth, I was occupied in wondering how soon this train would start and we could all go to bed. I'm tired."

"Same here." *I wish he'd quit this sparring and say what he's here for,* Searcey thought. "No sight of the new engine yet?" he asked.

"No, it's taking an unusually long time to make the trip between here and San Luis Potosí."

"Just what I was thinking."

They sat in silence for a moment.

"Spahr told me what you two talked about as he was leaving the diner," Rennert spoke quietly.

Searcey knew that he kept any expression from his face. (He felt that the sunburn was somewhat of a help in this. It hurt so damnably when he moved a muscle of his face.) "He did?"

"Yes, I suppose his version was correct but I thought that I'd get you to confirm it."

Searcey waited a moment, thinking. "This sounds like the old police trick we read about," he smiled painfully. "I suppose you let him think that I had already told you."

"No, he doubtless knew that I would question you in case he didn't answer."

"Well," Searcey crossed his legs and relaxed a bit, "I probably wouldn't have said anything if he had kept still. I saw that your question back in the diner scared him pretty bad. I wouldn't like to get the young fellow in trouble and I'll admit this makes things look bad for him, unless he can explain about that cigarette holder."

Rennert's face took on a careful lack of expression. "Go ahead," he said quietly.

"Well," Searcey chose his words with care, "he had that woman's cigarette holder in his hand as he was going down the aisle. Must have picked it up from the table where she left it. I asked him if he was going in for fancy holders. He held it up in his hand—he was a little tight—and laughed and said something about not having a pansy in his lapel yet. We went on out then." His eyes probed into Rennert's. "Is that the same story he told you?"

"Not exactly."

Searcey was immediately on his guard. "He didn't tell you about the cigarette holder?" he frowned.

"No."

"I'm sorry, then, that I had to be the one to tell you. He must have been afraid to, afraid that it would be circumstantial evidence against him." He asked the question which he had been wanting to ask: "You don't think he killed the woman, do you?"

Rennert sat for a moment, as if lost in thought. "I'll be frank with you, Searcey. I don't know whether I think he did or not. What would be your idea?"

"I don't know," Searcey said carefully. "Ordinarily, I don't think Spahr would have nerve enough to kill anyone. He's still rather wet behind the ears, I should say."

"What do you mean by ordinarily?"

"When he wasn't drinking."

"He had been drinking considerably, hadn't he?"

"Yes, though he held his liquor pretty well."

"Did you notice how much he drank while he was in the diner?"

"No," Searcey couldn't tell whether the question was a random one or not, "I didn't notice particularly. I remember that he got a bottle of wine while the woman was still with him."

"Did she drink any of it?"

"A little, I think. At least enough to make her sick."

"She was sick?"

"Sick or sleepy, I don't know which. She put her head down on the table."

"And Spahr finished the wine?"

"I couldn't say."

"Was there an empty bottle on the table in front of him as well as this full one which he ordered?"

"I don't know."

"You couldn't see his face or the table in front of him very plainly then?"

"No, but I can't say that I paid any particular attention to him."

"Thanks," Rennert got to his feet, "that's all I wanted to know."

Searcey's frown deepened. "I'm still like a schoolboy. What's that bottle of wine got to do with this business?"

"It was merely a question," Rennert said, "of how much wine you saw Spahr drink."

Searcey's eyes were riveted on the side of Rennert's face. He was puzzled. . . .

Trescinda Talcott had been dozing. It was a habit she had

gotten into during the past few weeks, when real or feigned sleep had been the easiest way to cut unwelcome shackles and to drift into gentle unawareness of time's passing. It had become like a drug to her and she had sought it so often, letting her visions recede further into a past which she had not shared, that she knew she had been thought, toward the last, old and queer. She didn't care. There was a feeling of almost voluptuous warmth in her tired body now as she sat with half-closed eyes, releasing one by one, reluctantly, dreams of days which she had never lived. The dark brown curls that had rested, perhaps, as her head rested now, upon that pillow. The plump little fingers that had traced painstakingly the hieroglyphics upon the woodwork that still remained after all these years. The slow careful pencil marks that spelled out in the copy book the words: "The Lord is my shepherd." That, of course, had come later, but she remembered how they had told her that he had never been able to pronounce the letter R. Just like a little Mexican or a Chinaman, he had always said: "shepheld."

"Shepheld," unconsciously her lips formed the word and she stared up uncomprehendingly at the realization that a man was standing beside her chair, looking down at her.

She sat upright and brushed a hand across her eyes. The memories fled, leaving her body an empty shell.

She said: "Good evening, Mr. Rennert. I'm afraid I dropped off to sleep."

He smiled pleasantly and said as he sat on the seat opposite: "I suppose my welcome is not very hearty, then, since I disturbed you. I wouldn't have stopped but I thought you were awake." He paused and she thought that his voice sounded a bit queer. "I thought that your eyes were open."

"They were, I suppose," she relaxed against the back of the chair again, "I often sleep that way and," she hesitated, "I suppose I talk in my sleep sometimes."

"I believe you did say something." (It was, she decided, nothing but a very careful precision in his speech.)

"I wanted to tell you," he said, "that your paper-knife has been found."

She noticed for the first time that he had very clear and penetrating brown eyes. The gray that flecked them added a charm, she thought, which they might otherwise have lacked.

He took from his pocket the knife, wrapped in a handkerchief, and held it upon the palm of his hand.

"That is, I took it for granted that this is your knife."

She looked at it and said: "Yes, that's it. I had given up hopes of finding it. Where was it?"

She had the feeling that this was exactly the question for which he had been waiting.

"It was found wedged in behind the seat in the ladies' lounge," he said.

"Oh," she had to laugh, "of all the places! No wonder I couldn't find it." Very slowly she realized the implications of his words. "But I wonder how it got in there?" she met his eyes. "I'm sure I didn't carry it in."

"Are you positive, Miss Talcott?"

"Of course. I left it here upon this seat."

"Then someone else must have carried it in there and hidden it," he said quietly.

"Hidden it?" she had the curious feeling that she hadn't awakened completely.

"Yes, isn't that the only logical explanation?"

"I suppose so." All of a sudden, it seemed, her senses began to clear. "The person who hid it must have expected to have some use for it, then?" Resolutely she thrust forward, at one with herself again: "In other words, the person who murdered those three people with a needle wanted to have another weapon handy. Is that what you mean?"

"Yes, Miss Talcott, that is exactly what I do mean." He folded the handkerchief about the knife again. "Under the circumstances I think that you won't object if I keep this for the present?"

"Of course not. You mean because of fingerprints on it?"

"Possibly, also to prevent its disappearing again during the night."

"I see," she said calmly and asked: "Are you any further along with your investigation?"

"Yes, Miss Talcott, I believe so."

She laughed slightly. "I'm afraid I haven't shown much interest but I didn't know anything I could do to help." With a forefinger she pressed down a pleat in one of the starched white cuffs. "I've been wanting to ask you about one thing ever since you spoke to us after you had discovered that girl's body in her compartment. You said that her death and that of the Mexican this morning were connected with a kidnapping case. There's no doubt about that, I suppose?"

"No, there's little if any doubt in my mind that the kidnapper of the Montes boy—or at least someone involved in the business—is on this train, that he is the murderer of Miss Van Syle and of Torner."

"Montes?" she frowned slightly. "I don't believe that I recall that case. I so seldom read the newspapers."

Rennert glanced at her with some surprise, telling himself that she must indeed have been isolated from the world. He told her of the case briefly.

Her eyes did not leave his face. They brightened and then narrowed slightly. When he had concluded she sat for a time without speaking.

Her voice, when it came, had in it an unaccustomed note of harshness. "Kidnapping is a crime more unpardonable than murder, I've always thought. I believe that I could myself lower a person guilty of it inch by inch into boiling oil." She pressed her lips firmly together to check an incipient trembling. (It had been a mention of brown curls that had almost made her lose control of herself.) She said: "My attitude toward this business is not so indifferent now, Mr. Rennert, since you told me that. If there's anything I can do to help you I hope you'll let me know."

"You have been of some help, however."

"How is that?"

"About the hatbox."

"Oh, yes. I was curious about that. It belonged to the girl back in the compartment?"

"Yes, it had been put into the Pullman by mistake. The person who murdered Torner in the tunnel this morning slipped the needle into it while the car was still in darkness. It was unlocked and bulging open, you remember. The idea probably was to recover it later, when there was no danger of a personal search. In the meantime Miss Van Syle had the porter carry it into her compartment. She probably found the needle, I'm not sure. At any rate the murderer went to her compartment to recover it. It constituted, you see, the only proof we have that the man did not die a natural death."

"But why did he murder her?"

"Doubtless because she returned unexpectedly to the compartment and discovered her visitor."

"I had supposed the hatbox was hers, since she was the only other woman on the car. She probably borrowed it from someone. That would explain the difference in the initials."

Rennert's gaze was on the window as he said: "In one way, you're right. She did borrow the hatbox. She borrowed it from the Ollie Wright whom she left back in Texas."

"A friend?"

"Herself."

She studied his face for a moment. "I wonder if I know what you mean," she murmured.

He continued to gaze out the window.

"I didn't mean to be enigmatic," he said. "It was just that the appropriateness of your expression struck me. The story of Miss Van Syle is a common one, one that always makes me just a little bit rebellious at the suffering life works on so many of us."

"I know," she said without thinking. His tanned, rather rugged and homely features belied the slight huskiness which she thought that she detected in his voice. "I should like to hear her story, if you wish to tell me," she said.

"It goes something like this, I think. There was in a small town in Texas a girl by the name of Ollie Wright. She was a schoolteacher—the fourth grade—and would have been perfectly happy and contented had she not had dreams. She dreamed of being Coralie Van Syle, of the Long Island or something Van Syles, and of traveling about the world in a private compartment, of looking condescendingly at the Ollie Wrights of the world over a jade cigarette holder. Instead, however, of doing as most girls would have done, letting their dreams lose the sharpness of their outlines through apathy or putting them resolutely aside, Ollie Wright determined that for one summer, one brief glorious summer, she would be Coralie Van Syle. Whatever became of her afterwards, she would have that memory. When she boarded this train last night she was in every detail Coralie Van Syle, except for that hatbox, probably utilized at the last moment for clothing which would not be contained in Coralie Van Syle's expensive new luggage, for a passport made out in her real name and for a diary. She lived for one day as Coralie Van Syle."

Miss Talcott's eyes were vague as they too sought the window for an instant. "'One crowded hour of glorious life'" she murmured.

"I've been wondering," Rennert said, "if it was worth what it cost."

"Of course it was," her reply was firm. "I'm sure it was. She didn't, you see, have to come back to reality."

For a long time she didn't speak but sat staring out the window, through which crept vague night-sounds.

She turned her head, then, and had the same unruffled smile upon her lips as she said: "You see, I suppose, the only part of this girl's story that makes it at all interesting?"

"You mean the hatbox?"

"Yes," a bit of brightness came into her eyes as she looked at him, "Ollie Wright's hatbox. It was a remnant of her real life that she didn't succeed in discarding. It represented Ollie Wright. It killed Coralie Van Syle."

"The Albatross about her neck."

"Exactly. Posada could have made a sublime cartoon out of that, couldn't he? . . ."

Chapter XVIII
TIES UPON THE TRACK
(10:15 P.M.)

SPAHR RAISED dull red-rimmed eyes as Rennert stepped into the smoker. He was still sitting, lethargic, upon the leather cushions. He did not speak.

Rennert sat down beside him.

"You should have told me the truth about your conversation with Searcey back in the diner," he said quietly.

Spahr stared straight in front of him and clasped his hands more tightly together. "You've talked to Searcey?" he asked in a flat voice.

"Yes."

"He told you about the cigarette holder?" his lips were moving as if he were unconscious of their action.

"Yes. I think that you had better tell me exactly what happened."

Spahr's face was white and rigid as chalk. He sat for a moment without speaking.

"I suppose I'd better," he said at last. "I thought maybe you'd take my word for it and wouldn't talk to Searcey." He made a strangled sound in his throat. "Miss Van Syle left her cigarette holder in the diner. I had it in my hand when I went out, I was going to take it to her. Searcey saw it and made some crack about it. I answered him and we both went on out." He paused and went on with a quickened voice. "I left Searcey at the smoker and went to her compartment and knocked at the door. There wasn't any answer, so I went away—to the smoker."

"And the cigarette holder?" Rennert asked quietly.

"I don't know. I suppose I lost it somewhere. I don't know what became of it."

Rennert said evenly: "That cigarette holder was lying beside her body when I found her, Spahr."

The soft regular purr of the electric fan was a throbbing accentuation of the silence which lay heavy upon the little room.

Out of the distance, eerie in the profound stillness, came the shriek of a train's whistle.

Rennert drew a breath of relief. The engine at last and the resumption of movement toward their destination! He hadn't realized to what extent it had depressed him. This slow slow waiting . . .

Spahr's knuckles cracked loudly as he jerked apart his intertwined fingers and buried his head in his hands.

"There's only one explanation for that cigarette holder," Rennert told him. "You entered Miss Van Syle's compartment——"

With a frenzied movement Spahr ran his fingers through his hair. "But somebody could have planted it there," he interrupted, "to put the blame on me!"

"There was scarcely time for that, Spahr, and you forget the matter of the lights."

"The lights?" Spahr raised his head and stared at Rennert.

"Yes, the fact that you didn't remember when they were extinguished. That happened when you stood in the darkened compartment, before you turned on the lights—if you did turn them on."

The muscles about Spahr's eyes twitched convulsively. "Do you mind," he asked, "if I have a drink?"

"I believe," Rennert reached for the bell, "that a hair of the dog that bit you is recommended now."

"Thanks," Spahr said.

"Remember that we are going to be in San Luis Potosí soon and that this is going to be your last chance, probably, to tell the truth."

"Yes, I know," Spahr's voice was lifeless.

They sat in silence until the porter had come and taken the order.

Ahead the whistle shrilled nearer.

Spahr looked up. "That our engine?"

"Yes, I presume it is."

Spahr fumbled for a cigarette.

The porter came softly into the room with whisky and soda water. As he fixed Spahr's drink and handed it to him Rennert asked: "That's the new engine, I suppose?"

"Yes, sir," the man answered. "We will start in a few minutes." For a fraction of a second longer than necessary his black eyes rested on Rennert's, an unusual brightness glinting in them.

As Spahr drained his glass in gulps and set it on the floor beside him, Rennert said to the Mexican in Spanish: "You have something to tell me?" He hazarded the question, since there had been no expression in the eyes, only a reflection of something which might have been fear.

The little man glanced swiftly in Spahr's direction and said in a sibilant undertone: "When you have the time, señor, I wish to speak to you." There was an odd tenseness in his manner and his hand jerked toward the glass.

"Very well," Rennert regarded him curiously, "I shall see you in a few minutes."

"Before we get to San Luis Potosí, señor."

"Before?"

"Yes," the man turned away his eyes, "I am leaving the train in San Luis."

Rennert frowned.

Before he could say anything more Spahr broke in with: "What about bringing some matches in here? There haven't been any here all evening."

The porter stood in the doorway, inclined his head and said: "Very good, sir, I shall bring some." Without another glance at Rennert he was gone.

Rennert brought out a packet of matches and handed them to Spahr. He watched the latter light the cigarette which had been dangling from the side of his mouth.

Spahr handed the matches back, drew a lungful of smoke and expelled it without sound. "That's better!" he said with an almost normal voice.

"You're ready now to tell me what happened?"

"Yes." Spahr stared at the end of the cigarette and said slowly. "I *did* go into Miss Van Syle's compartment, you're right. She had been rather—well, agitated about something—back in the diner and had had a crying spell, so I was kind of worried about her. I opened the door—it was unlocked—and went in. I saw her there, lying on the floor. I don't remember exactly what I did then. I remember closing the door and feeling for the light. I turned it on and saw that she was dead. I must have dropped the cigarette holder then, I don't remember. The room was close and hot and I got sick. I went out and shut the door behind me. That was when I went to the smoker."

He leaned back in the seat, let his head rest upon the leather and looked straight into Rennert's eyes. "That's the truth, Mr. Rennert! I'll swear to God it is! She was already dead when I went in."

Rennert kept his eyes on Spahr's. "Her hatbox was open when you were there?"

"Her hatbox? I don't know, I didn't notice." Stark fear was in Spahr's eyes as he demanded hoarsely: "Do you believe what I've said?"

A bell jangled up front and the hissing of steam came faintly to their ears. A slight quivering went through the car, as if at an impact.

Rennert got to his feet. "You asked me that same question before, Spahr, and I answered it. My answer is the same now." He turned and left the room.

He walked to the steps and swung lightly to the ground. The conductor was standing, lantern in hand, and gazing toward the front of the train. He turned as Rennert approached and a smile broke the dark surface of his face.

"It is the engine from San Luis Potosí."

"Good." Rennert stood beside him and watched the flashing of lights at the front of the train. "Did you learn what caused the delay in bringing it?"

The man stared again straight in front of him, the smile gone. "There were ties piled upon the track," he spoke as if unwillingly, "between here and San Luis. It took time to remove them."

Ties upon the track! Rennert was immediately alert, as if cold water had douched his face. He experienced, at the same time, a feeling of something approaching relief. They were becoming tangible now—all these vague hints of danger that had come with such persistent repetition throughout the day. He admitted to himself now how much they had worried him, hovering as they had like invisible particles of dust about the train and making their presence known only by irritation of the senses.

He asked in a level voice: "What happened while they were removing the ties?"

The conductor's manner was odd. It was as if he had quietly retired into a private world of his own, bounded by horizons of impregnable reserve. He said: "Nothing happened, señor."

There it was again, the intangibility of the whole affair. It came edging in upon them again, like unseen mist out of the darkness. Nothing had happened. As if those ties had materialized out of the night to lie upon the track and delay still further the advance of this train that had been meeting delays with steady purposive monotony all day.

"There was no indication of the persons who put the ties there? Of their purpose?"

"No, there was nothing."

"There was no town near by?"

"No, it was between Moctezuma and Bocas."

"There were——" Rennert hesitated, then went ahead, "no shots fired at the crew?" Damn it, the man was already so terrified, unless he missed his guess, that there was no need to evade the issue. "No, señor, there were no shots," the answer came.

The train's warning whistle cut into the stillness.

"I think, señor, that we are ready to start now. *Con permiso.*" The conductor moved toward the steps and mounted them as with an effort.

Rennert followed, passed the man at the top of the steps and made his way toward the Pullman. Behind him he heard the door closed against the darkness and the silence and the vast immutability of the desert.

The porter was engaged in making up Rennert's berth. Beyond, green curtains masked the berths on either side of the aisle. From the rear came the low murmur of voices and he saw Radcott lean out of one of the seats and glance down the aisle.

Rennert stood beside the porter and said in a low voice: "When you finish, go back into the diner. I shall join you there."

"Muy bien, señor," it was a mere wisp of sound and the little man did not turn his head.

Rennert never knew whether those whispered words of his had been overheard or whether one person in that car, seeing the two of them engaged in speech, had guessed the import of his words. Probably the latter, since the fear that had stalked this person's mind all day must by this time have been verging on blind panic.

He walked toward the rear. There, on either side of the door, he found King and Radcott in one seat and Searcey on the other side of the aisle.

Radcott had removed his tie and was flipping it against his knee. "Off at last, are we?" he asked with unnatural gayety.

"At last. The engine has arrived from San Luis Potosí."

King consulted his watch. "Only three hours and fifty minutes late," he observed dryly.

Searcey looked worried. "With no more delays we ought to make up part of our lost time during the night, oughtn't we?"

"Yes——" Rennert felt a gentle tug at his elbow and turned.

It was the conductor, his face looking tired and haggard and dirt-streaked under the lights. His eyes met Rennert's with a look of inquiry. "You wished to see me, señor?"

"No," Rennert frowned, "it wasn't I."

The man seemed bothered. "But the gentleman in the diner said that it was you," he insisted.

As the lights were extinguished Rennert was looking into his suddenly fear-filled eyes.

The unmistakable sound of the train's gradual acceleration of speed was in Rennert's ears, the steady puffing crescendo and the click of wheels upon rails. Yet there was discernible no movement at all in the Pullman.

"What the hell?" Radcott's voice sounded muffled in the unrelieved darkness that enveloped them.

Rennert pushed past the conductor and sped down the aisle. Behind him he heard the man's labored breathing as he followed.

He came out from the passage and stood at the door, staring across empty space at the receding lights of the train. Dust whipped his face and tormented his eyes, yet he saw, with all the distinctness of a scene caught by a spotlight, the tall erect figure of Jeanes framed by the rectangle of the door of the last car.

Chapter XIX
MATCHES FLARE BRIEFLY
(10:40 P.M.)

OUT OF the darkness at Rennert's side came a startled choking exclamation from the throat of the conductor. His fingers caught Rennert's arm in a frantic grip.

The door of the diner had become now no more than a faint point of light and the rumble of the train came back to them faintly, muffled by the swiftly incrowding silence of the desert. Overhead the stars glittered in stark isolation, pin pricks in the thick enveloping mantle of the sky.

"This car——" the conductor's voice was a shell, "—it has been uncoupled." His fingers released Rennert's arm. "There has been a mistake!"

"No," Rennert's voice was cold and hard, "there has been no mistake."

Silence from the other while realization came. Then, *"Madre de dios!"* like a spate released from the dam of Anglo-Saxon reserve his blood flooded back to its meridionality. "We are lost!" his despairing cry echoed into the night.

"You saw the man who stood at the rear door of the train?" Rennert's level voice stemmed the flow of emotion.

"Yes."

"It was he who sent you back to see me?"

"Yes."

Rennert stood for a moment, staring into the utter blackness of the night which had engulfed the last vestige of man-made light. He thought:

It has come at last, the moment toward which this car of people has been moving so inevitably!

Resolutely he shook off the momentary feeling of helplessness that assailed him and turned back into the Pullman. He heard the conductor following, in silence.

In the passage he came upon a dim figure, standing at the door of the smoker. The faint glow of a low-burning cigarette stub illuminated the lower part of Spahr's chalk-white face.

"What's the matter?" the young man asked in an unsteady voice.

"Come back into the Pullman with me," Rennert said, and waited for him to precede him.

Spahr drew upon the cigarette, staring across it at Rennert's face. Without a word he moved forward.

Rennert stood in the aisle and felt in his pocket for matches. He brought out a packet and counted them with his fingers. Three remained. (*Three tiny ephemeral splinters of wax-coated wood confronting the vast dark world that had thrown its shroud over them!*)

Someone (King it was) struck a match and held it aloft. Its flame flickered, sank and rose to cast a weak momentary light over the narrow tomblike passage between the curtains.

In the center of the aisle, in front of King, stood Searcey and Radcott, their eyes fixed inquiringly on Rennert's face. Miss Talcott sat upon the edge of her berth. She had evidently been about to retire and wore a dark dressing gown and slippers. Spahr stood to the right of the aisle, one hand grasping the curtains of Rennert's berth. At the rear, just at the edge of the illumination, stood the Mexican soldier who had been stationed upon the observation platform.

It was a scene which Rennert was never to forget, a taut fear-clad moment in which eight dissimilar people faced one another, drawn together by the magnet of a common dread of what might lie beyond the light.

They seemed to be waiting for him to speak.

He tried to keep cool normalcy in his voice as he said: "This car has been uncoupled from the rest of the train, which has gone on without us. There is nothing we can do except wait until they miss us and come back."

A sharp intake of breath from King punctured the silence that greeted his words.

"For God's sake, man, what do you mean? Uncoupled?" the voice was hoarse and fear filled it, unrepressed.

"Just that, Mr. King, it was uncoupled while we were waiting for the new engine."

"That couldn't have been done by mistake," Searcey's quietly controlled voice cut across King's. He was standing with one hand buried in the pocket of his trousers, the other slowly stroking his chin. Near the cuff of the upraised sleeve the corduroy was darkened by what looked in the uncertain light like a stain.

Rennert's eyes met the dark panes of the glasses. He was thankful for the steadiness of the voice that had come from below them.

"No, Mr. Searcey," he said, "that is exactly it. It could not have been done by mistake."

"Who did it, then?" excitement pitched Radcott's voice high.

"One of the train crew? None of us would want to be left stranded out here—and we're all here."

Searcey's eyes had gone swiftly about the little group. Now they met Rennert's again. "Where's Jeanes?" he demanded sharply.

"Jeanes is on the train which has left us behind."

He saw Searcey's thin mouth tighten as King started and let the expiring match fall to the floor.

"That," Rennert said, "is the situation. The battery that supplies the lights in this car has run down—or more likely been deliberately short-circuited. It all resolves itself into a matter of waiting for a time in the darkness. In that connection it might be well to take stock of our means of illumination. Does anyone have a flashlight?"

No answer came out of the darkness.

Rennert turned to the conductor, who, he judged, still stood in the door. "Your lantern?" he asked. "Where is it?"

"In the train," came the disembodied voice. "I left it there when I came back here to find you."

Rennert's fingers ran over the smooth surface of the little packet which he held. It became increasingly apparent what Jeanes' procedure had been—to make sure that the conductor was in the Pullman so that the discovery that the car was missing might be delayed as long as possible. Except for the porter there was no one else likely to make that discovery at once. The porter. Where was he?

"It seems," Rennert turned to the others, "that we are reduced to matches." He smiled grimly. "Communism, I believe, becomes imperative under these circumstances. How many matches have we among us?"

"I haven't any, I know," Radcott said. "I've already looked through my pockets."

King's voice faltered. "I'm afraid I only have one left. There are some more back in the smoker, I suppose."

"No, there aren't," Spahr spoke up. "I noticed that there weren't any there and asked the porter to get some, but he didn't do it. I don't have a one." He let the butt of his cigarette fall to the floor and ground it under foot.

"Say, don't do that!" Searcey said sharply. "We could all have gotten lights from that."

"Oh," weakly from Spahr, "I never thought of that."

Searcey muttered something under his breath, then suggested: "Suppose we strike one more match and all get lights from it. We can keep them going, as long," he amended, "as our supply of tobacco lasts."

This matter of the matches worried Rennert. It was so fittingly a part of the strange inevitability which had held them in its grip all day, demolishing one by one the barriers that their civilization had sought to erect against the relentless realities of nature. He thought of Searcey's words, "as long as our supply of tobacco lasts," as he said in what he hoped was a lighthearted voice: "A good idea! Everyone get ready and I'll strike another match."

He could hear them moving about, feeling in pockets.

"All set?" he asked.

"Yes," someone murmured.

Rennert struck the match and applied to its flame the cigarette which he had put into his mouth. As soon as it was alight he turned to Spahr, holding the match in cupped hands.

Spahr held a cigarette to it and inhaled deeply. As Rennert

went on to the next one he noticed the young man staring curiously down at the palm of his right hand.

Rennert held the match over the bowl of Searcey's pipe.

As he did so Miss Talcott's laugh fell upon his ears. She had gotten up from the edge of her berth and her fingers were playing with the cord of the dressing gown.

"This reminds me of old times," she said, looking from one of them to another, "like the days back in the Revolution when you had to expect this every time you took a train trip. I always used to carry a flashlight then."

The flame touched Rennert's skin and he let it fall. Over the glowing bowl of Searcey's pipe he saw Radcott's puckered mouth as he thrust forward a white tube.

"Since I haven't any matches to contribute to the cause," Miss Talcott said out of the darkness, "I think I'll retire, if you gentlemen will excuse me."

"Retire?" The exclamation came from King. "Do you mean to say that you can sleep in a situation like this?"

Her laugh was a pleasant note of genuine amusement. "Why, of course. Standing up in the aisle and striking matches won't accomplish anything, will it? If we're going to be raided we might as well get some rest to prepare ourselves for it."

"Raided?" King's voice was a blur. "What do you mean?"

"Of course," there was a slight note of seriousness in the woman's voice now, "I don't think there's any danger of it but there's no use in hiding from ourselves the fact that it's possible."

"You mean bandits?" Radcott asked. He pronounced the word with something approaching awe.

"No," Miss Talcott was on the edge of her berth again, "I don't think there's any danger of bandits in this part of the country any more. I was referring to the Cristeros."

“The Cristeros? What are they?”

“Bands of religious dissenters—fanatics, some people call them—which have sprung up since the Mexican government started enforcing the laws regulating the Church. Most of the stories one hears about their depredations are, I’m sure, exaggerated, although back in 1927 they did pillage several trains out in the western part of the country, near Guadalajara especially. The idea was to harass the government. They used to be rather active around San Luis Potosí, too, but I don’t know whether they are any longer or not. If a group of them should attack this car,” her voice took on a peremptory, steel-like quality, “don’t be so foolish as to make any resistance. When they discover that we are Americans I doubt whether they will do more than perhaps take a few of our belongings. We’re probably safer than the rest of the train.” She paused and said thoughtfully: “That may even be why we were left here.”

In the silence that followed someone’s breath came and went quickly.

There was a quick movement and another match flared. King was holding it, cupped between his hands. He was staring toward the rear of the car, where the Mexican soldier was still planted. From the stolidity of his expression none could have divined his thoughts.

“But what about him? Won’t they fire when they see him on this car?”

Miss Talcott was sitting with one hand on each curtain. She had removed her spectacles and her eyes looked dark, sunken into her face.

“I wouldn’t give much for his chance,” she said quietly, “in case an attack does occur.” She got into the berth and drew the curtains together. "And incidentally, Mr. King, you used your last match then," she said with what sounded like a laugh as one white hand stood out for an instant against the dark folds.

King's fingers, holding the match, trembled.

"Why don't we go back in the smoker?" Radcott suggested nervously. "We'll feel more—well, more together there. And we won't bother Miss Talcott then."

"Good," Searcey said briefly. He started toward the rear, Radcott following.

"Hold that match just a second longer, will you?" Spahr said to King as he stepped forward. "My cigarette's gone out."

He held the cigarette in his mouth and with the fingers of his right hand steadied its end to meet the wavering match.

King stared down fixedly. "What's that you've got on your hand?" he demanded.

"Don't know," Spahr straightened up, "looks like red paint."

King's hand jerked spasmodically as the flame touched his fingers. He let the match fall. "I think I'll go back in the smoker too," he said hoarsely.

He groped his way down the aisle, Spahr and Rennert following silently.

The smoker was close, heavy with stagnant tobacco-impregnated air now that the fan had stopped. Searcey and Radcott were sitting upon the leather cushions.

King began to pace up and down, the end of his cigar glowing and fading, glowing and fading.

Water splashed into the basin at the side of the room.

"What are you doing?" King asked in a strained voice.

Spahr stood with his back to them, bending over the lavatory. He turned off the faucet and, as he dashed his hands through the water, said: "Getting this stuff off my hands, it feels sticky."

Radcott held a doubled arm up to the end of his cigarette. "I must have gotten some of it on me too," he peered down at his sleeve, "at least it looks like it."

Spahr had turned and was drying his hands. He held the towel up and stared down at it for a long moment. He crumpled it suddenly and tossed it down.

"I think," he said in a small voice, "that I'll get some fresh air." He started to the door.

Rennert stepped aside to let him pass. "I wouldn't leave the car if I were you," he said.

"I won't," Spahr pushed through the curtains as if blindly, "I'll go back on the observation platform."

The silence began to grow oppressive.

"Anybody know any new stories?" Radcott asked lightly.

Rennert stepped into the passage and moved toward the barely discernible bulk in the doorway.

The conductor was standing and staring out into the darkness over the rails ahead. In the glow of Rennert's cigarette his face was a chiseled block of granite.

"A cigarette?" Rennert asked.

"Yes," the voice was eager. He took one from the package which Rennert proffered.

"Do you have any matches?"

"No. I do not smoke—ordinarily, but this waiting——" the man left the sentence suspended.

Rennert held out his cigarette and watched him hold his to its end, draw upon it gratefully.

He asked quietly: "Do you know what has become of the porter?"

"The porter?" the voice was flat. "No, I do not know."

"Did you see him in the train when you came into this car?"

"No, I think that he was in here, in the Pullman." Rennert felt the man's eyes fixed on his face. "He is not here? Now?"

"I am afraid not. He was making up the berths when the train pulled out and left us in the darkness. He may have had time to get off and catch the train but I doubt it."

Behind them, in the smoker, voices were a murmur.

Rennert asked very carefully: "Do you know why he wished to see me?"

Ash fell unheeded from the conductor's cigarette. The lips that held the cigarette said slowly: "He had something which he wished to tell you—before he got off at San Luis Potosí."

"Do you know what it was?"

The Mexican's voice was so low as to be almost inaudible. "It was about last night, señor Rennert. You asked him if he saw anyone talking with the man who died this morning. It was about this that he wanted to talk to you."

"He saw someone with this man Torner then?"

"I do not know, señor, but I think that he did. It was late at night and he was carrying a ladder to one of the passengers who had rung. He said that he saw this Torner then, sitting in the last seat at the back of the car."

"He didn't say who was with him?"

"No, he did not say. He had fear, I think, and was going to tell you just before he got off at San Luis." The pause became prolonged. "He did not tell you?"

"No," Rennert's voice sounded curiously faraway. "He did not tell me."

Their cigarettes were motionless, two fireflies suspended in the darkness. Coolness crept upward from the sands, touching and fastening itself to their feet and legs like strangely dry fog. The sky was close over their heads, pressing down upon them its heavy impenetrable pall.

The shot that cracked behind them was a knife slicing the stillness.

Chapter XX
BLOOD IN THE NIGHT
(11:14 P.M.)

SINGULARLY, RENNERT's thoughts, as he rounded the corner of the passage and went through the Pullman, were on matches. They had become for him things of immense importance, safeguards, weak and diminutive though they were, against utter helplessness. And he knew, as he heard heavy feet pounding ahead of him, that one of that group had lied. For held in the cupped hands of one of them (he couldn't for the moment distinguish which one) was a lighted match.

Upon the observation platform he found a weird tableau set against the night.

King stood in the doorway, holding up a lighted match. Searcey and Radcott were on either side of him. All were staring at the two figures outside.

Spahr was leaning against the railing, his face white. The soldier stood erect, his eyes averted as he slid the heavy revolver into the holster at his side.

"I don't know what he shot at," Spahr was saying through tight lips. "We were just standing here when all of a sudden he pulled out his gun——"

"¿Que Paso?" Rennert addressed the soldier. The black eyes flitted to his face as the hands made a quick upward gesture. "I am sorry, señor, but I thought that I saw something moving out there," he glanced sideways into the darkness. "I fired."

Very young the soldier looked now, as he stood in his ill-fitting uniform, staring with eyes bright with alarm into the desert night, whose palpable blackness had provided a dark breeding ground for the phantoms of the imagination of his ancestors long before rails had been laid across these dusty stretches.

Rennert turned to the others. "It was nothing. He merely fired at an imaginary object out there."

Spahr said haltingly: "I don't think it was an imaginary object."

"You don't?" King stared at him. "What was it?"

"I think it was those buzzards still out there."

"Buzzards?" King said sharply. "What buzzards?"

"Three of them were perched on a telegraph post out there while I was sitting on the ground. I tried to scare 'em away but I suppose they came back."

Searcey watched King flick the end of the match over the railing. "By the way," he said, "I thought you said you didn't have any more matches?"

King's face was indiscernible. "I was mistaken," he said shortly. "I did have one left."

"No more?"

"No more."

Searcey stepped forward beside Spahr. The bulk of his tall body loomed against the sky, blotting out the stars. "I don't suppose," he said over his shoulder, "that there's any danger of that soldier running away and leaving us, is there?"

"I think," Rennert said, "that he's probably as glad as we are to keep to the shelter—such as it is—of this car."

Silence fell upon them. They were all, Rennert knew, staring out into the impenetrable obscurity which hemmed them in. A faint breeze from the desert floor slid under the railing and was gentle on their faces.

"Going back into the smoker?" Radcott asked.

"Let's do," Spahr said quickly.

King murmured assent.

"I think," Searcey said, "that I'll stay out here with Rennert for a moment." There was purposive firmness in his voice.

As the footsteps of the others died away in the passage Searcey turned to face Rennert. He knocked the bowl of his pipe against the railing and slowly filled it with tobacco from his pouch. "Let me get a light from that cigarette before you throw it away," he asked.

Rennert handed him the cigarette, which had burned down almost to his fingers. Searcey took it and pressed the end against the tobacco in the bowl. For a few seconds the only sound to disturb the silence was the regurgitation of the pipe.

When it was going satisfactorily he tossed the butt of Rennert's cigarette over his shoulder and said: "That's better" through teeth that must have been clamped tightly upon the stem.

Rennert leaned against the side of the car, opposite the soldier.

There was a faint clicking sound as Searcey moved his pipe from one corner of his mouth to the other. "What about telling me," he said quietly, "exactly how things stand?"

"Very stationary, I should say, on the desert."

"I don't mean that—about this car being left behind. I mean about Jeanes. Did he have anything to do with this?"

"I feel sure that he did."

"Uncoupled this car?"

"Yes, or had it done."

"Any idea why?"

"Yes," Rennert answered after a moment, "I have several ideas."

"Care to tell them?"

"I see no reason why I shouldn't. Jeanes was anxious to escape our company and saw no other way to do it."

Searcey smoked for a moment in silence. "You don't think, then, that his real object was to leave the car stranded out here so that it could be robbed?"

"Frankly, I don't, although it's possible. If that had been his purpose I think that an attack would have been made before now."

"Maybe he'll get off at San Luis Potosí and come back—with others."

"That's possible, of course."

"But you don't think so," Searcey's voice was a probe.

"No, I don't. I have the feeling that we've seen the last of Mr. Jeanes, unless the Mexican soldiers who are on the train miss us and prevent his getting off."

Searcey's body seemed absolutely motionless. Rennert wondered if he imagined that there was a tenseness about it, as of tightly coiled springs ready to whirl into action at the touch. There had been, he realized now, something of this effect of coiled springs about the man throughout the day. It became more noticeable now, here in the darkness where one could not observe the masked directness of his gaze and the enforced steadiness of his nerves. Only his voice, steady and cool and persistent, coming from a black bulk.

This voice asked: "Did Jeanes kill these two people on this train?"

Rennert watched the steady glow of the pipe. "The evidence is certainly against him," he said.

Searcey said very evenly: "That's not an answer."

"I'm afraid that it's the only answer I can give right now."

"Did you know that he had a knife?"

"No," Rennert said slowly, "I didn't know that."

"Well, he did. I saw it a few minutes before the train left us, after you'd gone back into the smoker."

"What kind of a knife was it?"

"A small ordinary knife with a celluloid handle. I saw him take it out of his trousers pocket and put it in his coat pocket."

"Why didn't you tell me sooner?"

"This is the first chance I've had." Searcey was silent for a moment. "It struck me that that was rather conclusive proof."

"Of what?"

"That he committed these murders."

"Not necessarily."

Searcey stood up. "That means that you don't think he did commit them," he said.

"I'm not sure that he did, Searcey."

"And it means that you suspect one of us who are left?"

"I'm not satisfied as to the innocence of a single person on this car."

"Including myself?"

"Yes, including yourself."

Corduroy brushed against corduroy as Searcey moved a step closer.

"Want to explain that statement a bit, Rennert?" his voice was soft, dangerously so.

"The explanation is up to you," Rennert said evenly.

"To me?"

"Yes, the explanation of that blood stain on your coat sleeve."

Searcey stood stockstill. Only the bowl of his pipe began to glow a bit brighter. Above it his glasses were oval panes of reflected light.

"What blood stain?" for the first time Rennert heard his voice falter.

"On the cuff of the right sleeve."

Rennert could make out that Searcey had raised his right arm and was staring down at it.

"It does look like blood," his voice seemed to come from a distance.

Whistling, low but determined, echoed down the passage.

Searcey stepped back and let his right hand fall to his side.

A cigar glowed in the doorway and King's nervous voice sifted through the stillness which held them. "Who's out there?"

Rennert answered him.

King stepped upon the platform. "Everything all right?" he asked with forced cheerfulness.

"Everything is all right, Mr. King."

King seemed to hesitate. "I was just wondering about Miss Talcott," he said.

"About Miss Talcott?"

"Yes, doesn't it seem strange to you that she didn't come out of her berth when that shot was fired?"

"Really," Rennert admitted, "I didn't give a thought to Miss Talcott. She didn't come out then?"

"No, I haven't seen anything of her. I stopped in front of her berth just now and could hear no movement. You don't suppose," King paused and went on desperately, "that anything has happened to her, do you?"

"I don't think so, but we might be sure." Rennert started toward the door. "Coming with us, Searcey?"

Searcey's voice was toneless: "I suppose so."

They walked down the corridor in silence. They came to a stop at the second berth on their right.

Rennert called softly. There was no response. Behind him he heard King's breath coming and going rapidly.

Rennert called again, more loudly, and put out a hand to unfasten the curtains.

"Yes?" a muffled voice came from within.

"Rennert, Miss Talcott. Are you all right?"

"All right?" there was a pause. "Why, of course."

"We were worried when you didn't come out when that shot was fired."

Again a pause. "Oh, yes, the shot. What was it?"

"The soldier on the observation platform merely got alarmed and fired out into the desert."

"I supposed that was it. I didn't see any need to get up."

Rennert smiled. "Very well, Miss Talcott, pardon us for disturbing you. I trust it won't happen again."

"I hope not," he thought he heard a laugh within. "Good night."

King laughed self-consciously. "Imagine," he murmured, "sleeping through all this!"

"Shall we go back to the smoker," Rennert suggested.

There was a pause. "If you don't mind," King said, "I'd like to talk to you a minute, Mr. Rennert."

Searcey's shoulder brushed against Rennert's. "I'll go back to the smoker and let you have your talk," he said.

Rennert drew King to the vacant seats across the aisle. They sat down.

"You'll probably think that I'm still imagining things," King seemed to be absorbed in contemplation of the end of his cigar, "but there's something that has me worried."

"Yes?"

"It's about those stains on Spahr's hands and on Radcott's sleeve."

"What about them?"

King cleared his throat and said: "I don't think it's red paint. I think it's blood," the words seemed to be thrust out of his mouth.

"The same thought, Mr. King, has occurred to me."

"It has!" shock was in the exclamation. (*He wanted,* Rennert thought, *reassurance against his fears and not confirmation of them.*)

"Yes, the decidedly unpleasant conclusion has been forced upon me that several of this group have blood upon their clothing."

King sat very still, his breathing all at once inaudible.

Then, as if at the snapping of a thread, the cigar fell from his mouth, he leaned forward blindly and rested his head in his hands.

"I'm afraid, Mr. Rennert, I don't mind admitting it," the words came brokenly from a throat that might have been held by a tight hand. "Today has been like a nightmare to me. One thing after another—and now this blood and we don't know where it comes from. There's something unnatural about all of this! It's insane, I tell you, insane!" His voice rose to a hysterical pitch and he reached out with one hand, caught Rennert's sleeve. "Why couldn't that be it—one of the men on this car is a madman, something's snapped in his brain and he's killing us one by one?"

Rennert reached forward and caught him by the shoulders. He shook him. "See here," he said sharply, "you've got to cut that out!"

King subsided a bit.

Rennert got up and made his way forward, ascertained with some difficulty which was his berth and pushed aside the curtains. He found his grip and opened it. He took out a bottle of whisky and carried it back to King's seat.

"Drink this," he ordered, "it will help you."

King groped for the bottle, found it and held it to his lips. For several seconds there was a gurgling choking sound. Then Rennert felt the bottle thrust again into his hands.

"Thanks!" King said in a mumble.

Rennert thrust the bottle into a hip pocket. "Feel better?" he asked after a moment.

"Yes," King's voice was still unsteady. "Sorry I acted like that, but I'd had about all I could stand."

"Shall we go back into the smoker then?" Rennert got to his feet.

"All right," King rose and they went down the aisle in silence.

In the passage King paused and caught Rennert's elbow. "I want to ask you a favor," he whispered.

"Yes?"

King laughed embarrassedly. "Don't ever say anything to anyone about that," his voice was urgent.

"Of course not," Rennert assured him. "The strain today has gotten us all rather keyed up."

"No, no, I don't mean that. I mean about the whisky."

"Well," Rennert was rather at a loss.

"You see," King went on in quick hushed tone, "that's the first drink I ever had in my life. I'm president of the Tarrant County Temperance League and if my wife or any of the organization were to learn of it——" he didn't finish.

Rennert said, just before he opened the curtains of the smoker: "I'll carry the secret to my grave, I assure you. But if your wife or any of your fellow members do hear of it, advise them to take a trip like this sometime."

The air of the smoker was stifling and reeking with smoke. Two points of light glowed against the wall.

"Who is it?" Radcott's voice came from below one of the points of light.

Rennert told him. He stood in the doorway and looked about him. "Shall we have roll call?" he suggested grimly.

"Here!" Radcott responded with a slight laugh.

"I'm here," Spahr spoke up beside him. There was a pause.

"And I am standing here," Searcey said in a level voice from across the room.

Rennert said: "I wanted you all together because it becomes necessary to inquire into a matter which seems to involve several of us. I am going to strike a match now. Radcott, I want you to step forward and hold up your left sleeve."

"What the hell?"

"Exactly that, Mr. Radcott."

"Well," Radcott got to his feet and came forward, "here it is."

Rennert struck a match (only one remained now) and held

it close to the extended arm. Extending from the elbow downward was an irregular dark smear that glistened slightly.

Rennert held the match before Radcott's face. The latter blinked. He was breathing heavily and his face looked moist and flushed.

"Are you aware," Rennert asked him, "that you have blood upon your sleeve?"

"Blood!" the eyes widened into a stare of horror. "Blood! Is that what it is?"

"That's what it is, Mr. Radcott. Can you account for it?"

"No," Radcott swallowed noisily. "I can't. I don't know where I got it."

Rennert felt the flame hot upon his skin. He said: "If you will turn around, I should like to see your clothing."

Radcott did so. Rennert moved the match quickly over his body. He could see no other trace of the ominous dark stain.

He was about to let the match fall when Radcott said sharply: "Give me a piece of paper, somebody! An envelope—anything."

Spahr took an envelope from his pocket and thrust it forward. Radcott snatched it and held it to the flame of Rennert's match. As it flared with what seemed dazzling brightness, Rennert let the match fall and turned to Spahr.

"I suppose," he said, "that you know by this time that what you washed off your hand in the basin was blood—not red paint?"

Spahr said weakly: "Yes."

"Can you account for that blood on your right hand?"

"No, I can't."

"I wonder if you're aware, Rennert," Radcott's voice was more incisive than he had ever heard it, "that you too are smeared with blood?"

A taut breathless silence followed his words.

"Good God, man, it's all over the shoulders and back of your coat! And yet you ask *us* where we got it on *us!*"

Rennert's fingers were very tight upon the little paper folder in which remained a single match. He felt an almost uncontrollable desire to laugh at the whole mad, utterly mad situation. For an instant, when the realization of the presence of blood stains upon three of these men had been thrust home to him, an idea of its explanation had crossed his mind. On second thought, it had not been as impossible as it had seemed at first. Why could not two or three or even more of them have been involved in the affair from the first, each protecting the others? And now he himself wore a coat which was stained with blood!

"If you'll take off your coat," Radcott held the burning paper and spoke in cold measured tones, "you'll see it."

Rennert did so. He held the coat of blue serge to the light. Both shoulders and the back between them were damp with blood.

He stared at the coat for a moment, as the truth darted into his mind.

He was putting on the coat again as Radcott tossed the expiring fragment into the basin.

Without a word he turned and pushed aside the curtains. He walked down the passage and into the Pullman. He stopped before his berth and deliberately struck his last match. He held it up.

Dark stains ran down the edges of the curtains from a point about halfway up.

He threw the curtains aside and held up the match.

On a level with his eyes the edge of the mattress of the unmade upper berth was dark and sodden with what could be nothing but blood. As he stared at it a tiny drop formed, hung for an instant like a dark stalactite and fell to the floor.

In the berth, grotesquely huddled, lay the body of the porter.

The flame of the match touched Rennert's skin. He let it fall and heard a faint sizzling sound as it expired upon the damp carpet.

Chapter XXI
RIDER OF A WHITE STEED
(11:50 P.M.)

The man was dead, Rennert ascertained when his fingers had groped to the pulse of the brown hand which lay outflung, claw-like, near the edge of the berth. The flame of the match, in its brief illumination, had shown clearly the handle of a knife protruding from the center of the damp blackness that soiled the back of the starched white jacket.

Rennert extracted the knife with a handkerchief-wrapped hand and examined it as best he could in the light from his cigarette. It was small, with a celluloid handle and a thin blade that looked (but had not been) inadequate for such a grim mission. There had been strength behind the blow and exact knowledge of where it should fall.

Rennert slipped the knife into his pocket. He let the curtains fall together and stood staring into the darkness that masked them. It helped, this unfathomable darkness, in giving his thoughts an unusual clarity, undisturbed by extraneous sights.

He visualized what had happened: the porter, hesitant to divulge whatever information he possessed yet betraying by his manner his hesitation; his sudden resolve when the engine had arrived and the normal routine of the train's journey toward San Luis Potosí was about to be resumed; someone watching him closely, aware of his knowledge and resolved to silence him at the first opportunity.

Rennert remembered the porter's words to him in the smoker, when he had been sitting with Spahr, and his own words to the man when the latter had stood where he was standing now, making up this berth. A brief interchange of words which had been overheard or noticed by the watcher. Then darkness in the car as the lights were extinguished and in the darkness this knife thrust dexterously into the back of the man who stood here. The body caught as it fell and tossed into the upper berth, whence the blood had dripped. . . .

In the darkness again. There was something uncanny, terrifying about this murderer's ability to strike in an element which left others helpless. . . .

The aisle was a vault, muffled by the thick enveloping curtains, and voices were hushed and confined in the narrow space.

"What is it?" Radcott's voice was high-pitched in its excitement.

The glow of a cigarette lit indistinctly Spahr's white face, and behind and to one side of him the bowl of Searcey's pipe was a glowing coal.

"I've found the source of the blood," Rennert said to them with quiet emphasis, "the porter has been stabbed and his body put into an upper berth. Everyone who has brushed against the curtains has gotten some of the blood on his clothing."

"God!" the exclamation came hoarsely from Radcott's lips.

"Stabbed, you say?" sharp terror was in King's voice.

"Yes, Mr. King, stabbed."

"What with?"

"A knife."

"A knife," King said in an oddly flat voice. He repeated it: "A knife."

None of them seemed to move for a long moment. The only sound was that of heavy labored breathing.

"Do you have any idea," King seemed to be moving forward, "what kind of a knife it was?"

"A small knife with a celluloid handle. Why do you ask that?"

King choked. "Because I know——"

A fist thudded dully on flesh and Rennert felt himself carried backward by the impact of a head upon his chest. He caught hold of the shoulders of the inert man and shoved him toward the berth. Awkwardly, he stretched him upon the mattress.

It was, he knew, King. He was breathing in long labored gasps and moaning slightly. His nose was bleeding.

Satisfied that he was not seriously injured, Rennert drew another cigarette from his pocket and applied it to the end of the one which he held in his lips. He inhaled with quick puffs as his fingers went deftly through King's pockets. He found two full packets of wax vestas and half a dozen wooden matches.

He straightened up, lit one and looked across its flame at the dimly outlined figures in the aisle.

Radcott stood in the center, his eyes bright as they stared at the match. Behind him stood Searcey and Spahr, their faces almost indistinguishable.

Rennert knew that his voice was vibrant with anger as he said: "I suppose there's no use asking who struck that blow?"

The silence became prolonged. He could see Spahr and Searcey looking at each other and at Radcott. Radcott stood very still and stared straight in front of him.

"I don't know," Searcey said evenly. "I didn't but I couldn't say which of these two men did."

"I didn't!" Spahr put in quickly. "I was standing back here behind both Searcey and Radcott. I couldn't have!"

Rennert looked at the man who stood in the center of the aisle. "And you, Radcott?"

"No," the monosyllable fell tonelessly from his lips.

"I wonder," Rennert said incisively, "if all of you realize exactly the situation in which you stand? You're as powerless here, as utterly cut off from escape, as if you were on a desert island. You might get away from this car, yes, but there would remain the desert. For miles on all sides of us there are nothing but a few huts, miserable little villages along the railroad. We're certain to be missed by the train crew before long. They will return for us. If one of you has left this car, you'll be found as soon as daylight comes. If not along the railroad, the soldiers will probably not bother searching for you. The desert will do their job for them."

He paused and looked from one vague outline of a man to another.

"Now, since that is clear, the one of you who is guilty should realize that by such acts as this he can only delay retribution. When a criminal begins to strike out to prevent discovery he's on the defensive and his time is short. To one of you I have only this to say—either confess now or quit making things worse for yourself. Unless you silence every person on this car, you cannot guard yourself. And even then, the fact that you remain will in itself condemn you."

"See here!" Spahr's voice held unusual firmness. "Why are you so sure that one of us three is guilty? It looks to me as if there were no doubt that Jeanes is the guilty man. He killed this porter, then uncoupled the car and got away. I don't know whether it was Searcey here or Radcott who hit King, but I don't think that's any proof that either one of them is guilty. Circumstantial evidence can point against anyone," he paused, "you know that yourself in my case, and I'd say that one of these two men didn't want King to say something that would incriminate him. But that's no proof of his guilt."

"Not necessarily a proof of his guilt, no, Spahr. The proof of that will lie now in his silence when he knows that King is going to recover in a few moments and will go ahead with what he started to say, unless——" Rennert's pause was momentary but Spahr supplied the ending.

"Unless he is silenced, you mean."

"Exactly."

"I see," Spahr said weakly. It was as if the sudden energy which he had displayed were vitiated now, its essence seeping out of an unexpected leak in the dike of his assurance.

The only sound to break the stillness was the soft steady gurgle of Searcey's pipe. The odor of his tobacco was strong and pungent in the confined space in which they stood.

From the berth beside them came a louder groan and a stirring. Rennert lit another match.

"All right!" Radcott's voice was a snapped wire. "I was the one who hit him."

He moved to the berth opposite that in which King lay and sank onto it. He rested an elbow upon his knee and propped his chin against the palm of a hand.

"I suppose I was a damn fool to do it," he went on in a

strained voice, "but I didn't stop to think. The only thing that came into my mind was that I didn't want him to tell about the knife. I was afraid that you'd think——"

"Suppose," Rennert cut in, "that you tell us about this knife, Radcott."

Radcott nodded and drew in his breath. He expelled it noisily and said: "I suppose it was the knife the porter was killed with, I don't know. It was a small one, a cheap one. It was in one of the boxes of popcorn that I had in my sample case. The company I work for puts things like that in as premiums, you know. The soldiers didn't open any of the boxes when they searched my things and I didn't say anything about having a knife in one of them. Later, I got it out and put it in my pocket. I said something to King about having it, thought I could trust him to keep his mouth shut." He shot an angry glance in the direction of the berth.

Rennert brought out the knife and held the match close to it. "That the knife, Radcott?"

The other looked down. "Yes," he murmured.

"And what became of this knife?"

"I don't know! I lost it somewhere. It slipped through a hole in my pocket, I suppose. I felt for it a while ago and found that it was gone."

"When was that?"

"After the train had pulled out and left us."

"Did anyone but King know that you had this knife?"

"No, I don't think so. I didn't tell anybody else about it. Of course, someone may have seen me get it out of the box and anybody could have picked it up off the floor after it fell out of my pocket."

Rennert turned to Searcey. "Is this the knife that Jeanes had?"

Searcey bent over and peered down at Rennert's palm. "Yes," he said, "I think it is."

A hoarse choking sound came from the berth and King thrust his feet over the edge. He sat up and for a moment or two held his head in his hands.

He raised his eyes then and looked across the aisle at Radcott. His hands fell quickly and his voice rose high and shrill: "You know who killed the porter, then, do you? You know who killed these others? He's the one!"

"Shut up, you damn fool!" Radcott snapped at him. "Don't pull that stuff!"

"You know it now, don't you?" King got unsteadily to his feet and stood before Rennert. "He had a knife and when the lights went out in his car he got up and went down the aisle toward the place where the porter was standing. I know because I was sitting next to him."

"I got up, yes, but so did the rest of you. You did yourself." Radcott's voice hardened. "And since you're so damned free with your remarks about me what about yourself? You're the only one who knew I had the knife. How do we know you didn't pick it up when it fell?"

He leaned forward and deliberately spaced his words: "And what about your alibi for the time when that woman was killed? We both said we stayed in the smoker after we left the diner, but we didn't say anything about my going to the lavatory, did we? How do I know you stayed in the smoker during that time? You could have gone out and come back and I wouldn't have known anything about it." He got to his feet. "What have you got to say about that, you damn sniveling old hypocrite?"

Rennert hastily struck another match. In the increased light he observed as best he could King's face.

The man stood as if paralyzed, staring at Radcott. His face was working convulsively, he opened and closed his mouth but no sound came from it.

Faintly, out of the distance, came the scream of a train's whistle.

PART THREE

TIME-TABLE OF NATIONAL RAILWAYS OF MEXICO

*Tropic of Cancer			
Laguna Seca	*Lv.*	*5:52*	*P.M.*
Charcos	"	*6:10*	"
Venado	"	*6:32*	"
Moctezuma	"	*6:52*	"
Bocas	"	*7:23*	"
San Luis Potosí	*Ar.*	*8:15*	"
San Luis Potosí	*Lv.*	*8:35*	"
Jesús María	"	*9:08*	"
Chirimoya	"	*9:53*	"
Obregón	"	*10:34*	"
Rio Laja	"	*11:11*	"
S. Miguel Allende	"	*12:03*	*A.M.*
Emp. Escobedo	*Ar.*	*12:45*	"
Emp. Escobedo	*Lv.*	*1:05*	"
Mariscala	"	*1:40*	"
Querétaro	*Ar.*	*2:00*	"
Querétaro	*Lv.*	*2:10*	"
Huichapan	"	*4:44*	"
Apaxco	"	*7:00*	"
Lechería	"	*8:02*	"
Emp. Tacuba	"	*8:30*	"
Mexico City (*Colonia Station*)	*Ar.*	*8:45*	"

*Non-agency, flag station.

Chapter XXII
WITH DRAWN BLINDS
(12:10 A.M.)

"¡Señor! ¡Señor!" the conductor's excited voice shrilled down the passage. *"¡Es el tren!"*

Rennert felt relief surge over him in recurrent waves. He was all at once desperately tired and his eyes felt heavy with sleep.

He looked into the obscurity before him where four men stood. "Your last chance," he said, "for a confession before the Mexican authorities take charge. We arrive in San Luis Potosí within an hour. Does anyone have anything to say?"

No one spoke. No one, it seemed, so much as moved.

Rennert waited a moment. Then he said: "Very well" curtly, and walked between them down the aisle. He had the curious feeling that heavy breathless silence was closing in behind him, like waves in the backwash of a ship.

He found the conductor standing on the front platform of the car, his gaze fixed eagerly on the rear lights of the train, approaching at what seemed a snail's pace over the desert.

"They have missed us at last and come back," the aftermath of relief seemed to rob the man's voice of inflection.

They stood in silence, then, and watched the lights approach. Soon uniformed men could be seen grouped about the rear doorway. Then voices clear and loud over the rails between them. Someone called out to the conductor. He shouted back a response. The train slowed down still more, the space between the cars narrowed, there was a shock as they touched.

Spanish flowed in staccato waves.

Rennert stood to one side during the confusion which their getting under way again entailed. He watched the excited interview between the conductor and several trainmen, he saw the overalled brakeman gesticulating wildly and heard his vehement protestations: "*¡Pues, no sabía yo, no sabía yo!*"

Lights flashed on in the Pullman.

The train whistle shrilled again, steam surged out in waves of hissing sound, a creaking strain passed like a tremor through the car and they moved forward.

Ten minutes later, Rennert sat in the diner, the sound of wheels against rails becoming again an accustomed pleasant monotony in his ears.

Across from him sat the voluble excited Sergeant Estancio. Sergeant Estancio was repeating, as he leaned over the table and gesticulated with a hand which held a cigarette cupped between thumb and forefinger:

"We were almost to San Luis Potosí when I saw that the Pullman was missing from the train. I had the train stopped at once." (Rennert did not miss the emphasis on the first person.) "We came back, señor, at once and found you here. The brakeman says that it was not his fault, he says that it was this man—this *americano*—who uncoupled the cars. He says that he talked to him while we were waiting for the new engine, that he asked him how one uncoupled the cars. This brakeman," a slight expressive shrug, "is not too intelligent, señor. He explained how it was done. He says that this man uncoupled the cars—not he." A pause. "As for myself, I do not know. There will be inquiries. Yes, there will be inquiries."

Rennert said thoughtfully: "This *americano* is still on the train?"

"*Cómo no, señor.* He is up in the first-class coach. He is being guarded. It is thought," the sergeant glanced about him quickly and lowered his voice, "that he is a labor agitator from the United States and that he comes to Mexico to help the cause of these strikers."

"Was there any disturbance up the line?"

"Disturbance?" the man's quick black eyes darted to Rennert's face. "There was a shot or two fired at the train, yes. Close to the place where the ties had been piled upon the track when the engine passed on its way to San Luis Potosí. No harm was done."

Rennert asked: "Is it permitted to talk to this *americano* whom you have under guard?"

"Yes, señor, my instructions from Saltillo are that I am to allow you to act as you will until we arrive at San Luis Potosí. There the authorities will take charge." The sergeant rose with alacrity. "You wish to have this man brought here?"

"Yes, if you will be so kind."

"Very well." He turned and walked quickly toward the rear.

Rennert sat and gazed thoughtfully at the carefully drawn blinds over the windows until the Sergeant returned, preceded by Jeanes.

Rennert made a motion to the prisoner to be seated. He obeyed like a man in a daze. The sergeant sat across the aisle.

Jeanes' eyes seemed to have sunk far into hollows in his face, where they glowed brightly, like reflections of the fierce consuming heat of inner fires. His face had the pallor of death. He laid his hands upon the tablecloth and clasped them together so tightly that the knuckles stood out sharply against the skin.

He did not speak but Rennert detected in his whole manner a definite exaltation that bothered him more than he would have admitted. He thought: *He acts as if he had succeeded, not failed, in some enterprise.*

"And so, Mr. Jeanes, we meet again."

Jeanes' lips were tightly pressed together, bloodless. He sat as if unconscious of his surroundings.

"You realize as well as I the situation in which you find yourself," Rennert went on quietly. He leaned forward and lowered his voice still more. "May I say that I am very sorry indeed that circumstances have been such that I have had to play a part in bringing it to pass?"

Jeanes looked up at him and his lips parted in a kindly smile. "I forgive you," he said in a low vibrant voice, "you knew not what you did."

"I think, Mr. Jeanes, that I have known all along. At least, I know now. But I feel that you yourself are to blame. In your zeal for a cause, however worthy that cause may be, you have become blinded to everything else. Even human life has lost in value for you."

"No, my friend," the voice was gentle and patient, "human life has taken on for me its greatest value, that of sacrifice."

Rennert knew the futility of argument. He felt a tinge of pity for this man, going so willingly, so eagerly even, to what could be nothing but death that he had already tasted of the cup of self-immolation and found pleasure in its bitterness.

He said: "By your action in uncoupling that car you put yourself into the hands of the Mexican authorities. If I can, however, I shall be glad to help you out of the results of your folly. You are a citizen of the United States?"

For a long time Jeanes did not answer. A glow in his deep-set eyes and a slow tensing of the muscles of his interlocked lingers alone testified to the struggle which was going on within him.

He said in a clear high voice: "I am a citizen of France."

There was in it, Rennert felt, nothing of the heroic. It was the calm statement of the pride in nationality that clings to man even in his flight to the stars.

"In that case," he said, "I am afraid that I can do little for you."

He brought out of his pocket the knife with which the porter had been stabbed and the paper which had come into King's possession at Saltillo.

"In return for an answer to a question and an assurance from you with regard to one matter I am willing to make no mention of this paper to the authorities." He paused. "The question is—has this knife ever been in your hands?"

Jeanes' burning eyes had fixed themselves immediately upon the paper. He took them away from it as with an effort and looked at the knife.

"No," he said, "that knife has never been in my hands."

"Have you seen it before?"

"Yes," Jeanes spoke as if his thoughts were elsewhere, "I have seen it."

"Where?"

"In the Pullman. One of the passengers—Mr. Radcott, I believe his name is—took it from a box of confections."

"Did anyone else see him take it out?"

"I do not know."

"Was there anyone else in the Pullman at the time?"

"Only Miss Talcott. She, I believe, was reading at the time."

Rennert said after a moment: "The assurance which I want is that there is no further danger to this train or to its passengers. Will you give that to me?"

Jeanes was silent for a long time, his eyes again upon the paper which Rennert held.

"I cannot assure you of that," the words fell at last, like icy particles, from his lips.

Rennert's eyes narrowed. The feeling of pity which he had experienced left him at the realization of what this man's words implied.

"You're willing then," his voice hardened as he returned the knife and the paper to his pocket, "to let a train full of innocent people run straight ahead into destruction?"

Jeanes' smile gave a ghastly effect to his white face. "I too am on this train," he reminded gently.

Rennert stared at him as the realization of his own impotence broke upon him. That was it—the ties had been heaped upon the rails in order to allow this man an opportunity to escape. The plan had fallen through, the engine alone had been stopped, and Jeanes was being carried along with the rest of them—to what predestined holocaust none but he knew.

Rennert glanced at his watch, noticing as he did so that Jeanes' eyes fixed themselves quickly on its face. He gestured to the sergeant and looked straight into Jeanes' eyes.

"In case we do not meet again," he said, "may your soul find the mercy you wished for mine."

Jeanes' face still retained its set gentle smile. "I thank you, my friend," he murmured as he rose to face the soldier.

He turned down the aisle and walked with shoulders erect toward the door.

Rennert sat for a long time, deep in thought, and did not realize at first that the train was slackening its speed. He watched the sergeant come back into the diner and glance quickly up and down the sides of the car, making sure that the blinds were still drawn.

The man stopped beside his table and said in an expressionless voice: "It was here, señor, that the ties were piled upon the track."

Rennert nodded absently. "Will you ask the conductor to come here?" he said.

"Cómo no, señor."

When the conductor came Rennert motioned him to be seated. He spoke to him in a low voice for several minutes. When he was sure that the man understood what he was to do he got up and said: "Just before we stop at San Luis Potosí, remember. I shall be with him in the Pullman."

"Yes, señor."

Rennert walked back into the other car, upon which the hush of exhaustion seemed to have settled.

Radcott, Searcey, and Spahr sat in the smoker, without speaking. Radcott was slumped down upon the seat, his eyes fixed in a steady stare at the floor. His face was damp chalk. Searcey's teeth were clamped upon the stem of his empty pipe and there was a noticeable slackness about his mouth.

He took the pipe from his mouth and said grimly: "Well, what's the news from the front?"

"The front is San Luis Potosí," Rennert said. "We shall be there in a few minutes now."

Spahr looked up from the corner by the window, where he sat smoking a cigarette with quick nervous puffs. "Is it my imagination," he demanded, "or is the train beginning to slow down again?"

"It was at this point," Rennert told him, "that the engine crew found ties piled upon the track when it was on its way back to San Luis."

"Oh," Spahr said flatly, "they're watching the track now, is that it?"

"Yes."

"And these blinds," he gestured toward the window, "have been pulled down in case of shooting?"

"Yes."

Searcey's blank eyes swept Rennert's face. "Did Jeanes get away?" he asked.

"No, he is still on the train, up front."

Searcey slid the pipe back into his mouth, his teeth clicked against the stem. "In custody?"

"Yes, in custody."

"Under suspicion of what?" Searcey's lips tightened.

"Under suspicion of being a labor agitator."

Spahr drew a lungful of smoke and expelled it without sound. "They don't think he committed these murders, then?" he asked in a small voice.

"I can't answer that question, Spahr, until we get to San Luis."

"Will we have to get off the train?"

"I can't say."

"Well," the young man grinned feebly, "I'm ready for bed. Before long it's going to take the whole Mexican army to keep me awake."

There was a lightness about Spahr's manner that might have been due to relief or to high nervous tension, Rennert reflected as he left the smoker and walked toward the Pullman.

In the doorway at the rear stood the same alert-eyed Mexican soldier.

In the seat to Rennert's right sat King, staring straight ahead of him without expression in his tired eyes. Rennert, as he approached, observed the change which had come over the man during the day. He looked now immeasurably older, as if these experiences had ravaged his face of a veneer of complacency, leaving it a clay mask upon which so many emotions had left their stamp that it was now a mere blur. He looked up at Rennert but did not speak.

Rennert rested upon the arm of the chair opposite him and said: "We're getting into San Luis Potosí in a few minutes. You haven't forgotten that you are to receive an answer to that telegram to your wife here?"

"No, I haven't forgotten," King's lips twitched convulsively. "Do you think we'll be held here?" he asked after a pause.

"I hope not, at least for long. Of course there are several matters which the Mexican authorities will want to settle before they allow anyone to go on."

King leaned forward. "Tell me, Mr. Rennert," he said desperately, "whether you think there's going to be any suspicion of me in this awful business. After what Radcott said, I mean."

Rennert regarded him steadily. "It's true, is it, that you were alone in the smoker for a few minutes?"

"Yes, it's true, but I'll swear I didn't leave it!"

"Did you by any chance tell anyone about this knife of Radcott's?"

Again there was the twitching of the muscles about King's

lips. He said in an almost inaudible voice: "Yes, I did tell one person."

"Who?"

King sat as if incapable of speech.

"Of all the stupidities which you could commit now the greatest would be to conceal any kind of information," Rennert said sternly.

"Yes, I suppose so," King swallowed. "I told Miss Talcott about the knife."

Rennert, engaged now in tightening the strands of evidence about the person who he felt sure was guilty, couldn't repress entirely his start of surprise. "When did you tell her?" he asked.

"After the train had stopped and I went back to the Pullman. I went back to where she was sitting and stopped to talk to her a few minutes." He hesitated. "She seemed so calm and unruffled about everything that it was rather reassuring to talk to her. She just joked about the whole business, said it was better than reading a novel, and I—well, I suppose I got into the same mood. She said something about wishing she had her paper knife to protect herself in case the worst came to the worst and I told her about Radcott having a knife. It was all in a joke, though. I really felt better after having talked to her."

Rennert asked quietly: "What comment did Miss Talcott make when you told her about the knife?"

King thought for a moment, a frown creasing his forehead.

"She said something I didn't quite understand. She said that if anybody was killed with that knife he could at least have the consolation that he had drawn the grand prize."

The train emitted two prolonged whistles.

Rennert sat with a thoughtful expression upon his face. Then his lips parted in a grim smile. "She knew that the knife had been a premium in a box of popcorn?" he asked.

"Yes, I told her that. That's what seemed to amuse her so."

Rennert's lips retained their smile. "The grand prize to which Miss Talcott referred," he said, "was death."

King looked bewildered. "What a gruesome idea!" he shivered a bit. "I can't understand that woman," he went on reflectively. "She's so calm and self-possessed about everything that it's rather comforting to be around her. And then, all of a sudden, she'll make some peculiar remark that almost makes my blood run cold. And some of the stories she tells!"

He sat for a moment in thought. "Like that one about the five poplar trees opposite her house near Mexico City. She said that during the Revolution some army occupied the town. There was a lot of shooting and disturbance during the night and in the morning she woke to find a body hanging from each of those five trees. There were signs stuck on each body telling why the man had been executed. Four of the signs said: 'For looting.' On the fifth body the sign said simply: 'A mistake.'" He winced. "I wonder," he ventured, "whether her mind isn't a little unbalanced after so many of these harrowing experiences."

Rennert's smile died and his lips adjusted themselves into contemplative lines. "No, Mr. King," he said, "Miss Talcott's mind isn't unbalanced. I should say that it's adjusted to a nicety with her surroundings by the dust of Mexico which has settled on it without her knowing it."

The engine wailed again into the night.

The conductor passed along the aisle. His eyes met Rennert's in a quick understanding glance.

"Are we getting into San Luis Potosí?" King asked, shifting uneasily in his seat.

"Yes," Rennert did not move from his perch upon the arm of the seat. He thrust a hand into his pocket and said: "By the way, I suppose I'd better return to you these matches which I took the liberty of taking from your pocket while you were unconscious." He held them out.

King took them without looking up. "I don't suppose," he said as his fingers crushed them, "that there's any need to say anything about my having told you that I didn't have any more?"

"No, I don't think there's any need to say anything about what you did. In times of economic stress it's called, I believe, hoarding."

Silence stood between them for a moment.

"I'll get off with you at Monterrey and you can get the money. If you don't, this will be the last train trip you take not wearing handcuffs. Don't forget extradition."

King started from his seat, his face bloodless, as the words, carefully enunciated behind him, cut across the sounds of the train's passage.

Rennert watched him.

He turned his head to stare down the aisle, empty except for the figure of the conductor, who was standing facing them, his eyes on Rennert's face.

"I thought——" he brought his gaze back to Rennert's and swallowed hard. "Who was that?"

"The speech which the conductor has just repeated at my request, Mr. King, is my reconstruction of the words which you overheard in the Pullman here last night and the latter part of which you interpreted as 'blast the train on this trip,' 'earrings and cuffs' and 'extra edition.' "

King sat as if stunned and incapable of speech.

"You have only a few minutes," Rennert said to him quietly, "to tell me why you invented that story of your wife having been on this train last night."

Chapter XXIII
FIVE POPLAR TREES
(1:30 A.M.)

THE CONDUCTOR moved along the aisle again. Rennert looked up, nodded and murmured: *"Gracias."*

King still sat staring straight in front of him. "What do you mean?" he asked weakly.

Rennert was beginning to lose patience. "Exactly what I said, King. I know that your wife entered the station at San Antonio with you but did not get on this train. You yourself heard a Spanish-speaking person talking English in one of the seats behind you. You tried to lead me to believe that it was your wife who had listened to his words. Why?"

King took out a handkerchief and passed it over his face. "It's hard to explain," he said in an undertone.

The train was slowing to a stop.

Rennert got to his feet. "Not so hard to explain, King. You were alarmed, to put it mildly. You wanted to take someone into your confidence but didn't want to let it be known that you were too nervous to sleep as the train was approaching the Mexican border. Hence the story of your wife who got off at Laredo. Isn't that correct?"

King didn't look up. "Yes, that was it. I didn't want you to know how frightened I really was. You see, I'm used to Fort Worth——"

Rennert walked down the aisle and left him.

The stop at San Luis Potosí, ancient treasure-house of Spain, was brief, unconfused and, in view of the tension-charged atmosphere and this very lack of confusion, vaguely disquieting. A hush pervaded the dimly illuminated platform and the few people who stood there had the appearance of being huddled in silent groups. Here and there electric lights glinted upon the steel of naked bayonets in front of stolid dark faces.

The army officer who boarded the train conducted his inquiries with expedition and efficiency. A few words to the overawed Sergeant Estancio and to the conductor and a formal introduction of himself to Rennert, to whom he handed a telegram with a request to accompany him into the diner.

As he walked forward Rennert tore open the envelope. The message was from the officials at Saltillo and informed him that an autopsy had revealed traces of nicotine poisoning in the body of Torner. Information, Rennert reflected as he stepped into the diner, which he had taken for granted but which was essential in order to unite satisfactorily the various strands of the case.

The officer did not sit down but stood stiffly in the center of the aisle, his alert black eyes probing into Rennert's. His voice was quick, staccato, as he requested an account of the events of the day, particularly since the train had left Saltillo.

Rennert summarized them concisely, though a bit wearily. He realized with a little annoyance that the man was paying but perfunctory attention to most of what he said.

At mention of the message which had been given to King

at Vanegas, however, his interest visibly quickened and some of the impassivity left his oval, sharply featured face. He took the piece of paper from Rennert and his eyes grew sharp and calculative as he read it. He folded it and slipped it into a pocket of his uniform.

"You have been vouched for by the authorities in Mexico City, Señor Rennert," he spoke in a voice which had metallic undertones. "It is their order that this train, with all the passengers in the Pullman, continue on to Mexico City without delay. There the authorities will take charge. Their instructions are that no arrest is to be made until Mexico City is reached. I am to accompany you there."

"They are not aware that two more deaths have occurred on this train since it left Saltillo?"

"No, I shall wire them from here." As if a veil had been drawn across them his eyes became all at once guarded. "I think that it is, in their opinion, a case where international complications are to be feared. In the present state of affairs there is a wish to avoid this if possible."

"You have learned that there was an attempt made tonight to stop this train? That ties were found piled upon the track?"

"Yes," the answer came in a quick low voice. "An armored car with machine guns will precede this train into Mexico City to avoid any further obstruction." He hesitated and said delicately: "It was feared that a demonstration might be made in San Luis Potosí. It is for that reason that it was thought best not to make the arrest of anyone here."

"The arrest?" Rennert queried. "Of the person who has committed these murders on the Pullman?"

Reserve was stamped upon the man's entire manner. He said: "No, Señor Rennert, that matter is to the authorities of less importance than another. It is a question of one who crossed the border on this Pullman, one whose presence in Mexico will cause," he paused and chose the word with care, "embarrassment to the Government."

"The identity of this person is known?"

"Yes, the immigration authorities had suspicions and sent a description to Mexico City. There is no doubt as to the identity." The obsidian surfaces of his eyes clouded and cleared again. "If this person should also prove to be guilty of these murders," he said tentatively, "things will simplify themselves, will they not?"

"Yes, but I am sure that is not the case."

The officer's shrug was a masterpiece of tact. "That," he said without expression, "is regrettable, is it not?"

Rennert felt unattuned to the air of dynamic tension which seemed to pervade the situation. He was conscious of increasing weariness and felt an almost irresistible desire to yawn. He asked: "The bodies of this woman and of the porter will be removed here, I suppose?"

Concentration lay heavy upon the features of the other. "There were no instructions about these bodies," he said at last, "since it was not known about them at Mexico City. I think, however, that it will be the wish of the authorities that they be not removed in view of the situation here at San Luis Potosí."

Rennert frowned. "You realize, of course, the fact that one of these bodies has been lying in a compartment for several hours—in rather warm weather?"

The man permitted himself another shrug of neatly uniformed shoulders. "Of course, Señor Rennert. But they could not be removed without observation. Rumors would spread. The newspapers would learn of it."

Rennert said grimly: "One of these bodies is lying in the

berth above mine. I'm not particularly squeamish but I can't say that I relish the idea of spending the night below it."

The smile was a gracious teeth-revealing one. "But, of course, Señor Rennert! It will be removed. It can be put into the compartment with the other body, can it not?"

"Yes," Rennert knew that his smile was a feeble effort compared to the Mexican's. He added: "It is fortunate that I am not addicted to nightmares."

"Nightmares," the officer became very serious, "are caused by overeating late at night." He seemed to grasp eagerly at a chance to divert the conversation to safer channels. "Cheese is very bad. You have not been eating cheese?" solicitude was in his voice.

"No," Rennert bit his lip, "I haven't indulged in any cheese lately."

"Very well, then," the brown hands came upward, palms thrust out, "you will not have the nightmare."

Fifteen minutes later Rennert looked up and down the silent curtain-shrouded aisle, at each end of which a soldier stood in the doorway. He let his head fall wearily upon the pillow and stretched his legs between the cool sheets. As he reached for the light his eyes rested for an instant upon the dark stains that ran along the edge of the curtains masking his berth.

The train hurtled on.

He never got over the feeling that the dream which he had that night was oddly premonitory. He saw, straight and slim and distinct against a Mexican morning sky, five poplar trees. From four of them hung grotesque scarecrow figures that swayed drunkenly in the breeze. The fifth tree was as yet unadorned.

Chapter XXIV
THE RIM OF THE VALLEY
(7:30 A.M.)

CLOUDS FROTHED milky-white below the train and sent long tentacles along the rocky ground to touch the rails. Here and there the rays of the sun had cut a swathe through the white foam to reveal vertiginous depths of black volcanic stone and impudent pine trees clinging to barren slopes beyond and below which lay other depths of thick white foam.

Rennert lay in his berth and looked out upon the scene.

The train was laboring along a runway fashioned of moist dark earth studded with stones, the edge of which fell away with breathtaking abruptness to the sky above the earth where men lived. He always thought, as he viewed the rim of the Valley of Mexico by the light of early morning, of Jules Verne's projectile-encased men who had stared for a fleeting moment at the unseen surface of the moon, uncertain whether the dark mysterious world of vast seas of water and forested hills that came and went in the lightning space of time were or were not an illusion.

He got up reluctantly and began to dress. He walked down the silent aisle to the deserted smoker. When he had finished his ablutions he glanced once more out the window.

A *maguey* lifted cruel gray-green claws from the ground. Along a crumbling adobe wall a small white goat was running, pursued by a barefooted boy in white pajama-like clothing. For an instant, through an opening in the gray wall bougainvillea-splashed tiles were visible.

The train was slowing down.

Rennert walked toward the rear and stepped upon the observation platform. He was grateful for this interval of solitude before the others had risen.

The morning coolness of Mexico tingled in his nostrils and filled his lungs.

"Good morning, Mr. Rennert."

Miss Talcott sat in a chair by the railing. She looked up at him and smiled.

"Good morning, Miss Talcott. You're up early."

"Yes." She breathed deeply, sensuously, her eyes half closed, and said: "I'm just a bit drunk, Mr. Rennert, with the smell of the Valley about me again. I've been aching to get back to it—the smell of the dark moist earth, the 'dobe walls, the flowers," she paused and laughed happily, "even the goats. It feels like home again."

"When the dust of Mexico has settled upon a human heart," Rennert quoted, "that heart can find rest in no other land."

"Yes," she rested her right hand upon the rail and let her eyes wander along the low wall of gray adobe that paralleled the track. "The Mexicans are right about that. I shall never try to leave Mexico again," she said it very quietly and decisively, as if the words marked a period to some current of thought.

Vitality seemed to have flowed into her suddenly, Rennert reflected. Her cheeks were slightly flushed and her eyes bright and eager. Her hand moved restlessly upon the rail, its fingers tapping impatiently so that the diamond upon the third finger glittered and danced with the rays of the sun.

"You have tried to leave it then?" he questioned quietly.

"Yes," she stared straight in front of her for a long time, her eyes all at once cloudy with vagueness. Her voice, when she spoke, seemed to come from far away. "Twenty-five years," she said, "they pass so quickly, don't they, in retrospect?"

Rennert knew that she was on the verge of confidences, the confidences that come so easily when one sees the end of a journey near and feels the tightening of bonds of intimacy with those whom one never expects to see again. He was silent.

"You've been in Taxco?" she asked.

"Yes."

"There's a little cantina there, among the rocks, called '*El Recuerdo del Porvenir.*' The Memory of Tomorrow. Do you know it?"

"Yes." *(Scarlet and magenta, ochre and rose and black, a little drinking-place and a tiled dome proclaiming the glories of God!)*

"I was thinking of that," she said, "and of the twenty-five years that have passed since I came down to Mexico to marry. He was an American engineer, interested in the mines down by Taxco. He had a house out at Coyoacan already furnished for me. He knew my tastes so well, you see. There was bougainvillea on the walls and a tiled fountain in the patio. La Casa de los Alamos, he called it, because of the poplar trees about it."

She was silent again, as if unaware of Rennert's presence, and her fingers tightened slightly upon the railing.

"Just before I got there, he died, of dysentery," she went on, speaking as if to herself. "I decided to live in his—in our house for a while and then go back to the States. I had no close relatives, you see, so it made no difference to anyone. Somehow, the time slipped by and I didn't leave the house. I began to realize that I was drifting into almost an unawareness of time. I tried to leave Mexico then. He had a mother living back in Vermont. I visited her—and came back to Mexico. I've visited her every year since—and come back. We would talk about him, about when he was a child."

The train had stopped but she seemed unaware of the cessation of motion.

"His mother died last winter," she went on, clearing her throat, "but I went back this spring anyway. It had gotten to be such a habit with me—something, you might say, to hinge my life on, like the change of seasons. Her friends have been kind to me but it wasn't the same. They all have their own children and their children's children to talk about and aren't really interested in him. I shan't go back again. I shall be satisfied with life now, I think—to live quietly in our house, La Casa de los Alamos, until the end." The fingers of her left hand were slowly turning the old-fashioned ring.

"His ring?" Rennert asked quietly.

"Yes, he sent it to me before he died."

Silence stood between them.

The gray adobe wall still ran beside the track. An opening in it gave a vista of a narrow unpaved street stretching away into the distance.

Against the wall stood a low straw-thatched hut, flanked by a fence of organ cactus. Battered oil cans symmetrically arranged on either side of the narrow doorway flowered into scarlet and magenta and blue blossoms against the gray adobe. A bare-armed full-breasted Indian woman in a shapeless white garment was watering the flowers with another oil can. She turned, looked at the train for a moment, then resumed her task. She bent over the flowers intently, as if counting the drops of water that fell on each flower.

From between the interstices of the cactus fence peered three or four children of various ages. Their interest seemed to be divided between the two people upon the observation platform and something that was happening toward the front of the train.

Rennert moved to the railing.

Heavy feet were approaching, rising and falling in steady regular beat. There was a faint creaking sound, as of metal or wood against leather.

The children drew back into the shelter of the cactus, where one had the feeling that they were standing, motionless and wary as animals.

A squad of Mexican soldiers came into view, their faces stolid and expressionless as so many fiber masks below their visors. Squat Yaquis from the mountains of the West, their lithe sinewy bodies seeming to move in a freedom that forgot the uniforms which clothed them. Their fixed bayonets glinted wickedly in the sunlight that flowed over the top of the wall.

In their midst walked Jeanes.

Every feature of his porcelain-white face was sharply limned by the sunlight, which the edge of the gray wall sliced off at the level of his erect shoulders. He did not look to either side of him but strode with quick light step, his gaze fixed just above the peaks of the mountains that rimmed the Valley. He was bareheaded and his hair was a nimbus of silver ruffled by the air.

A sharp word of command from the officer who walked in advance and the troop turned the corner into the opening in the wall.

In that atom of time when Jeanes turned his face full into the sun Rennert thought, but could not be sure, that there was a smile on his lips.

Another turn and the little body of men was gone. The sound of their feet lingered for an instant in the still air, then that too was gone.

There was a soft rustle at Rennert's side and he looked down at Miss Talcott.

Her fingers were going through the movements of the cross.

Her eyes met his and she quickly let her hands fall to her lap. Her smile was a wraith. "I don't know why I did that," she said in a small voice. "I'm not religious, you know. And goodness only knows I ought to be used to sights like that."

Rennert was silent. (Miss Talcott had met the need which he too felt.)

A little gurgling sound rippled through the stillness.

Both looked down.

In the dust beside the track, his bare brown body seeming to fuse with and grow out of it like some hardy desert plant, sat a plump infant who regarded them with round-eyed uncertainty. Behind him, white teeth displayed in a confident smile, stood a girl of perhaps six years, clothed in a one-piece dress of an indeterminate dark hue.

"*Dame cinco centavos,*" she said, as if stating some perfectly obvious fact which had just occurred to her.

Rennert felt as if he had stepped out of chill dawnlight into the pulsing warmth of the sun. He laughed out of pure gratefulness and put a hand into a pocket. He brought out a copper coin and tossed it to the ground.

The girl swooped upon it, then turned sparkling black eyes upon him. "*Gracias, señor.*" She stooped to pick up the baby, who waved fat arms in protest. His eyes were fixed on something upon the platform.

Miss Talcott's voice was stiff: "Now they ask for five *centavos* instead of one, as they used to do. That's what the tourists have done for this country." She stirred uneasily in her chair and moved her right hand over a bit. "It's a mistake to give money to beggars in Mexico!" she went on in a voice suddenly vehement. "It keeps them shiftless and prevents them from working. They're lazy enough anyway."

Rennert looked at her, analyzing the emotion which had shaken her usually unruffled voice. Her lips were held tightly compressed and her eyes stared without expression straight back over the rails.

There was another squeal, this time of unadulterated delight. The dust-brown baby was peering through the railing, supported by the arms of the girl. His black eyes regarded Miss Talcott's hand and his mouth made inarticulate sounds.

"*Quiere el anillo, señora*" ("He wants your ring") the girl explained proudly.

Miss Talcott looked down quickly, said "*Andale*" to the girl, in a sharp voice, and got to her feet. Her hands were folded against the black taffeta, their tapering fingers pressed tightly together. The diamond glowed with fire against the taut white skin.

"I think," she said to Rennert in a blurred voice, "that I'll see if the diner is open yet."

Chapter XXV
ALBINO
(8:45 A.M.)

RENNERT STOOD and watched Miss Talcott disappear into the passage.

Slowly he drew a cigarette from his pocket and lit it. His face was thoughtful and there was an abstracted look in his eyes as he let the smoke trickle through his nostrils to drift away over the railing. (He was thinking of the bed of an *arroyo* in the dry season, thirsty sand and hard unfeeling rock and stunted desert growth—yet underneath, betraying its presence only when man or nature had cut deep, the vital waters everpresent.)

He made his way into the Pullman, where morning activity was beginning to be manifested.

Radcott's curtains bulged and were thrust aside as he passed. The salesman sat upon the edge of his berth, sleepy-eyed, and suppressed a yawn.

"Must be getting close to Mexico City," he commented, groping for his shoes.

"Yes," Rennert paused and eyed him. He had put on a clean white shirt but wore the same trousers as the day before. "A final check-up on a few points," he said pleasantly. "May I see the pocket out of which your knife slipped last night?"

Radcott stared at him with dull eyes whose whites were shot with faint streaks of blood. "Still the sleuth?" he said with thinly veiled sarcasm.

Rennert smiled. "Yes, still the sleuth."

The other shrugged. With his right hand he pulled out the lining of his trousers pocket. It was empty and in the cloth had been worn a small hole.

Rennert nodded. "Thank you."

"Anything more?" Radcott shoved the lining back into place.

"Yes. There's the matter of the premiums in your boxes of popcorn. Is it possible that two of these boxes contained knives?"

Radcott pursed his lips. "No, it's not. I had one sample of each of the prizes which the company gives."

"You're positive of that?"

"Positive."

"Several of the boxes are missing, aren't they?"

Radcott glanced at him in surprise. "As a matter of fact," he admitted, "there are several of them missing. I suppose the porter took them."

Rennert held out in the palm of his hand the stickpin with the head fashioned as a white horse, the child's ring, and the tin whistle. "These were all in boxes of the popcorn, were they not?"

Radcott stared at them for a moment. "Yes," he said at last, warily, "they were." He raised his eyes. "What are they—evidence?"

"Yes," Rennert's voice was serious as he slipped the objects back into his pocket, "they are evidence, Mr. Radcott." He walked on.

At the door of the smoker he paused and pushed aside the curtains. He stared in astonishment at Searcey.

The man was standing in front of one of the basins. His face was still damp from the water and in his hands he held a crumpled towel. The dark glasses lay upon a ledge before him and he stared back at Rennert with eyes that were unshielded.

The eyes gave a startling incongruous effect, seen in contrast with that sunburned skin and dark lashes, brows and hair. The irises looked pink and the realization came to Rennert that he was looking into the eyes of an albino.

There flashed into his mind the explanation of several things which had bothered him about this man—the bottle of dye found in his luggage and the glossy unnatural aspect of his hair, the cruel action of the sun's rays on a skin sensitive to exposure, the short-sightedness and the eternal wearing of the dark concave-lensed glasses.

Searcey's eyes were drawn into a squint as he peered toward the doorway. He turned his head quickly and reached for the glasses. His hand brushed them from the ledge and they fell, shattering against the side of the basin.

He stood as if paralyzed, staring down at the broken fragments.

Rennert came into the room and leaned against another basin, gazing thoughtfully at the tip of his cigarette.

Searcey turned. "Well?" his lips curled and his voice was hard and brittle. "You looked at me as if I were a freak."

"Sorry," Rennert said, "I was merely surprised."

Searcey was jerking his tie into place with unsteady fingers. "At what?" he demanded.

"At the fact that you had disguised so successfully that you are an albino."

Searcey's jaw tightened. "It's no disgrace, is it?" he asked coldly.

"None at all. I was merely wondering why you did it."

The albino gave a final deliberate tug at the tie and let his hands fall to his sides.

"To avoid being looked at as you looked at me a minute ago," his voice was bitter. "To avoid being pointed out as a freak of nature—like a hunchback or a dwarf." He paused and stared past Rennert's head. "And to get a job," he concluded.

"A job?"

"Yes," Searcey was evidently struggling to get his voice under control. "Being an albino in the United States isn't so bad because lots of people have almost white hair. But have you got any idea what it would be like in Mexico, where everybody's dark? I've got a chance to get a job buying up mining leases from the natives if I get into Mexico City on time this morning. The company that offered it doesn't know that I'm an albino. What chance would I have if they did know it? Can you imagine me gaining the good will of a bunch of black-haired, black-eyed Mexicans? I've tried it. They all act as if I were the original sun god or something—but they won't do business with me."

Rennert studied his face for a moment then got up.

"What time is it?" Searcey asked.

Rennert looked at his watch. "Nine-ten."

Searcey's fists slowly clenched. "How late are we?"

"About two hours. The train made up some of the lost time during the night."

"We'll be delayed at the station, I suppose—on account of what's happened?"

Rennert said very quietly: "The murderer only, I hope."

"The murderer?" Searcey stared at him for a long moment. "You know who it is?"

"Yes."

"You're positive?"

"Positive."

"What gave him away?"

"The popcorn—and the knife."

Searcey's eyes were almost invisible, drawn into two narrow slits. He laughed mirthlessly. "Well, it won't make any difference to me if we are delayed. Those broken glasses mean that I won't get the job, I suppose."

"The glasses?"

"Yes, I've got another pair in my grip, of course, but it's bad luck—worse than breaking a mirror."

Rennert, watching him, saw that his lips had almost disappeared, so tightly were they compressed. As he started toward the door the man stopped him.

His voice was uneven: "I'm going to ask a favor of you, Rennert."

"Yes?"

The eyes looked into his in a long searching gaze. "I'm broke," he said, "flat broke. I've got to have a cup of coffee."

Rennert's emotions were mixed as he took out a silver peso and handed it to him.

Searcey held it in his hand for a moment, staring down at it, then slipped it into a pocket. "Thanks," he said in a voice that was again soft and even. "If I get into the City in time to get that job we'll call this breakfast a celebration. If I don't," he shrugged, "it'll be the prisoner's last meal." He looked up. "What was it that the Roman gladiators used to say?"

"We who are about to die salute thee."

"That's it." Not a muscle of his face moved for a moment. "If I'm going to starve to death down here I salute you now. If I live—I may pay this peso back."

Their eyes met in a long steady gaze before Rennert turned and pushed through the curtains.

He made his way to the diner, where normal routine had again been restored.

At the first table on his right sat Miss Talcott, inscribing her order upon a slip of paper with firm steady hand. The ring looked heavy for her white fragile fingers. Beside her plate lay an unfolded newspaper and on the chair beside her the fiber bag.

Further forward sat Spahr and King, on opposite sides of the aisle. Spahr was leaning forward, his elbows propped upon the table, and gazing out the window with an expression of eagerness upon his fresh cleanly shaven face. King's face, in contrast, looked haggard and drained of vitality.

On the platform between the diner and the first-class coach Rennert came face to face with the army officer who had boarded the train at San Luis Potosí the night before.

The man seemed filled to overflowing with energy. He was freshly shaven and his dark olive face glowed. There were little particles of powder adhering to the lobes of his ears. His mustache and carefully brushed hair glistened with pomade.

He stood very straight and flashed pearl-white teeth at Rennert. "Ah, Señor Rennert!" he greeted. "I was wondering if you were awake. We arrive in Mexico City within an hour."

"Yes, I've been up some time."

"Good! We are about to move forward from this station. The delay here was unavoidable." His eyes rested on Rennert's with silent interrogation.

"The arrest was made, I see," Rennert answered him.

The officer shrugged delicately. "Yes, Señor, it was thought best to make the arrest before we reached Mexico City. Any unpleasantness is avoided, you understand."

Rennert nodded. "Jeanes made no difficulty about the arrest?" he asked.

"Jeanes?" The Mexican stared at him for a moment, then shrugged again. "Oh, yes, that was the name in which his passport was made out. It was not his real name." With a manicured forefinger he stroked gently the ends of his mustache. "I am not at liberty to tell you his real name. This is," he said carefully, "a very delicate matter for the authorities. It is the trouble with the Cristeros."

"I had guessed that this man's mission to Mexico was connected in some way with the Cristero movement rather than the strike."

"Yes, he has given us trouble before," the black eyes took on obsidian impenetrability. "He has been in the United States soliciting funds for aiding the Cristero revolt. We were notified by the authorities at the border that he was thought to be on this train. We feared that he would be warned by some of his friends along the way and make his escape. It was they, doubtless, who piled the ties upon the track, hoping to allow him to escape while the train was delayed."

There was a clanging of the bell of the engine.

The sound seemed to erase the veneer of reserve which had for a moment lain over the Mexican's manner and geniality flooded over him again.

"We are leaving!" he exclaimed. "In a few minutes more we shall be in Mexico City."

Rennert stared through the door and down the aisle of the diner. His thoughts were on Jeanes. He wondered if the man who had turned into the sunlight with a smile on his face would want pity. Probably not. He was going toward the martyrdom which his own ego had viewed as the only goal worthy of his striving. He would die with the same smile on his face, confident that he was now the peer of saints. Heroic, yes, and at the same time. . . .

He saw Miss Talcott rise hastily from her chair and walk with quick purposive step toward the rear. Her shoulders were held erect and her hands were straight down at her sides. In one of them she held the fiber bag clenched tightly.

"And now that this other affair has been disposed of," the Mexican's words broke into Rennert's thoughts, "there remains the matter of the deaths which have occurred in the Pullman. The police will be at the station in Mexico City to take charge of the investigation. The Embassy of the United States has been notified. There will be cooperation and," Rennert was afraid for an instant that the Mexican was going to embrace him, so eloquent was the gesture, "the best of feeling between our two great nations."

"I trust that the whole procedure can be carried through with as much quietness and with as little publicity as possible."

"Of course, señor, of course. These passengers will be taken directly to the Palacio for questioning. Unless," he put forward tentatively, "you know the person who is to be arrested. In that case—if you will indicate his identity the others need not be disturbed."

Rennert watched Searcey step into the diner and sit down at the first table to the right of the door, where Miss Talcott had been sitting.

"I am sure of the identity of the murderer," he answered.

"Good! In that case the arrest can be made as soon as the

train arrives at the station. This person is still on the train, I suppose?"

"Yes."

The other flicked an imaginary particle of dust from the cuff of his neatly pressed coat. "It is to be hoped!" he shrugged, "that he eats a good breakfast."

The bell clanged again and the train moved forward.

"Ah," the Mexican exclaimed again, "the next stop is Mexico City." He bowed to Rennert. "*Con permiso, señor.*"

He turned with a click of the heels and walked toward the first-class coach.

Rennert stood for a moment with his hand on the door of the diner. He watched Radcott come through the other door and walk up the aisle. Now that the end of the journey was at hand and the routine of existence was about to be resumed, he felt tired, as if he were finishing a race. *That,* he thought, *is exactly it. It has been a race, a race to safety, above all for one person for whom every mile of rails has been an approach to retribution.*

He opened the door and stepped into the diner.

Radcott had taken the table in front of King and was studying the menu. King and Spahr sat as before.

Rennert started down the aisle, paused for a moment, his eyes fixed on Searcey, then moved forward quickly.

Searcey had slumped in his chair so that his head rested awkwardly upon the back. His chin was thrust forward and the cords of his neck were tautened wires. His small delicate mouth was twisted and his blank glasses stared upward at the ceiling.

Rennert bent over him and felt for the pulse. Searcey was dead.

Chapter XXVI
MEMORIES OF TOMORROW
(9:40 A.M.)

IN THAT moment in which he stood there, his thoughts in chaos, Rennert was acutely conscious of the incongruous irrelevancies of the backs of heads.

The three men in the diner sat facing forward so that the backs of their heads seemed to stare at him like enigmatic masks. King's, with hair crisp and unruffled and iron-gray. Beyond him, Radcott's round skull, naked-looking beneath the sparse light hair that glistened and which ran down to the fold of pink flesh at the nape of his neck. Spahr's narrow head and slightly prominent ears and, like a furrow between them, a cowlick.

A muffled cry at the doorway behind him made Rennert wheel about.

Miss Talcott stood, one hand pressed against her mouth, staring at Searcey's body. The change which had come over her since Rennert had seen her seated at this table a few minutes before was incredible. She seemed to have shrunk within herself so that her flesh looked withered and lifeless. Her face was devoid of color and her eyes dull and glassy. (As dull and glassy, Rennert thought, as those of the corpse in the chair at her side.)

"Is he," she choked, "dead?"

Rennert nodded, his face grim. "Yes, Miss Talcott, he is dead."

She stared at him for a moment with eyes into which a slow look of horror crept, then groped toward a chair across the aisle. She sank into it and seemed to become absorbed in contemplation of the forward door.

Spahr had turned about in his chair and was regarding them curiously. He got up, put down his napkin and walked back with quick step.

"What's the matter?" his eyes went from Rennert to Miss Talcott. He glanced down at Searcey and his mouth fell open.

He raised suddenly fright-filled eyes to Rennert's face. "God!" he emitted a long drawn out whistle. "Another one!"

Silverware clattered against china and Radcott turned his head. King was on his feet in the aisle, a cigar held in trembling fingers.

Rennert looked from one of them to the other. "Will all of you," he ordered in a clear incisive voice, "go into the Pullman at once!"

He watched them go. Spahr's fingers were fumbling for a cigarette as he moved slowly forward, his eyes fixed sideways upon the face of the dead man. Except for one furtive glance downward King did not look to either side of him as he followed. Radcott got up, walked down the aisle and paused by Searcey's table. He stared down for an instant, then looked at Rennert. His blue eyes were queer and sharp.

"It was suicide, was it?" he asked in a strained voice. "He's the one who's been guilty all along?"

Rennert frowned impatiently. "In the Pullman, if you please, Radcott," he said sharply.

He looked at Miss Talcott, who sat very still and looked back at him with eyes that held no expression.

"I think," she said tonelessly, "that you want me to stay, don't you?"

He nodded, scarcely conscious of his action, and stood in the aisle with his eyes on Searcey.

It had come so unexpectedly, this man's death, that he was more than a little bewildered. He felt the need for a moment or two of quiet in order that he might get his thoughts marshaled into some semblance of order. Was this what had been needed to fit into place all those fragmentary little bits of evidence that he had been so carefully piecing together? Did this stamp irrevocably the mark of guilt upon the criminal? Or did it leave him at sea again, all his calculations strewn upon the waves of uncertainty?

He approached Searcey and scrutinized the table in front of him. There was an empty plate and silverware, unsullied by use. A napkin, unfolded. A Mexico City newspaper spread out flat upon the white cloth. An empty glass, its sides and bottom still moist with water. Rennert stared down thoughtfully.

He looked about the diner. The waiter was nowhere to be seen, busied undoubtedly in the kitchen.

He knelt and carefully surveyed the floor beneath the table and beneath Searcey's chair. There was nothing there.

He got up, a frown of concentration upon his face, and not without repugnance began to go through Searcey's clothing. He finished and stood back, still frowning.

He sat down at the table across the aisle and drew a cigarette from his pocket. He lit it and drew smoke into his lungs. He exhaled it very slowly, his eyes piercing the blue wraiths.

"You thought that he was guilty, didn't you?" the words, softly spoken, came to him from a distance, as if an echo of his own thoughts.

He looked across the virgin-white cloth at Miss Talcott. Her face was more composed now but held upon it the same lifeless expression. Her eyes were vague and clouded as they rested upon his face.

He was silent for a moment, surveying her. "Yes," he said.

She nodded. "I thought so." With a curious note of interest in her voice she asked: "Why did you think so?"

Rennert stared again into the cigarette smoke. He was conscious of a bit of relief at being able to voice his thoughts, to bolster his shaken suspicions by repetition.

"I don't see," he said slowly, "how it could have been anyone except Searcey."

"You mean because of the nature of these crimes? That they were the kind that a man of his type would have committed?"

"Partly, although twenty-four hours is too brief a period in which to judge a man's characteristics, particularly if he's watching every word and action of his own. Still, the whole business has had the marks of a man such as I think Searcey to have been—cool and level-headed yet with all of a gambler's daring, an aggressive personality that would never stop until his ends were reached. The man who carried through the Montes kidnapping without being detected, who struck with precise and deadly accuracy each time his security was threatened, could not have been nervous, hotheaded, or timid. Unless one of them is a better actor than I give him credit for, I cannot fit King, Spahr, or Radcott into that picture."

"No," Miss Talcott agreed slowly, "neither can I."

"In each of the three murders which were committed on this train as well as that on the platform at San Antonio," Rennert went on, "the evidence pointed directly to Searcey when one looked at it calmly and objectively. Take them in order. Graves, the federal man, was killed before the Pullman was opened, at nine o'clock. King and Miss Van Syle were the only ones of this group who admitted having been there at that time. According to Searcey's story he didn't step onto the platform until shortly before the train was due to leave, at nine-thirty. Yet he told me in the diner yesterday that he had seen Miss Van Syle on the platform at San Antonio the night before. If, as she said, she got on the Pullman as soon as it was opened he could only have seen her before nine o'clock, when he claimed to have been nowhere near the station."

"Miss Van Syle," Miss Talcott murmured. "It's better to leave her with that name, isn't it?"

"Yes," Rennert paused. "I'm wondering now about that incident in the diner, when Searcey thought he recognized her. Their paths may well have crossed at some time in the past, in Fort Worth or in the small town near by where she taught. Now the albino had become brown-haired and the drab Ollie Wright had become the fashionably dressed Coralie Van Syle. Small wonder that neither one knew the other."

A sharp exclamation in Spanish made him turn. The waiter stood in the aisle, staring at Searcey's body. A pencil and a pad fell from his fingers.

"Go into the kitchen," Rennert said to him quickly, "stay there until I call you. Do not say anything to anyone about this man."

"¿Está muerto, señor?"

"Yes," Rennert assured him, "he is dead."

The man turned and without waiting to retrieve the objects from the floor walked toward the door.

Rennert looked at Miss Talcott. She might have been in a trance, her eyes resting upon his face without seeing it.

"Go ahead," she said softly, "I'm listening."

"Very well," he resumed, "next comes Torner's death in the tunnel. As you know, all the evidence was against Searcey there. Jeanes' testimony about the corduroy trousers and his statement that the person who had stood over the seat before him went toward the rear of the car. Also the fact that the hatbox in which the needle was hidden stood in the aisle between Torner's and Searcey's seats."

"And if Jeanes hadn't felt my handbag against his hand you would have been more certain about Searcey at the time?"

"Yes," Rennert was scarcely conscious of the interruption. "My suspicions were strengthened, however, by Miss Van Syle's death. At first everyone except Spahr seemed to have an alibi for the period during which she was killed and her belongings searched. Spahr did go to her compartment but I'm satisfied—or," he amended thoughtfully, "I *was* satisfied that his story was correct, that he found her already dead."

Rennert paused and stared with slightly narrowed eyes into the smoke. Abstraction was in his voice when he went on.

"The alibis of two of the others were worthless, I ascertained later. King's seemed unshakable until Radcott revealed last night the fact that for a few minutes in the smoker King was out of his sight. Searcey, however, had an even longer time at his disposal. His story was that he remained in the diner the entire time that Spahr was there, that he left with Spahr and accompanied him to the door of the smoker. When I had them repeat their actions, however, I saw that Searcey had no alibi at all for most of the time between Radcott's and King's exit and that of Spahr. The latter's back was turned to him and he sat next to the door. The waiter was in the kitchen at the time and Searcey could easily have stepped out, gone to Miss Van Syle's compartment and returned, all unseen by Spahr, who would swear that he had not left the diner. Throughout, Searcey seemed a little too ready to direct suspicion against others. When he learned that Spahr was under suspicion, for instance, he emphasized the fact that the young man had been drinking heavily, suggesting that this might render him unaccountable for his actions."

Ashes fell unheeded upon the tablecloth as Rennert leaned forward. It was helping, this résumé, in clarifying his thoughts but it also was making him see straight ahead of him the *impasse* toward which he was headed: reaffirmed belief in Searcey's guilt.

"Then there was the murder of the porter, who was killed to prevent him telling me something about the conversation which the murderer of Torner held with the latter the previous night. While we were in Saltillo I questioned the porter about what passengers had been up and about in the Pullman late the night before, when King had overheard the talking at the rear of the car. We were standing then in the corridor outside the smoker. Searcey must have been in the smoker, since he was neither in the Pullman nor in the diner. A few minutes later, after he had joined me in the diner, he seemed much interested in the fact that it was the porter who had known that someone was engaged in conversation with Torner. He was evidently suspicious of the porter and what he might tell about the events of that night, when Torner threatened him with blackmail unless he were paid off at Monterrey. Regardless of the porter's evidence, however, the popcorn and the white horse stickpin which I found on the floor convinced me that it was Searcey who had sat there with the man who was murdered the next day."

"Oh, yes, the pin with the white horse," Miss Talcott murmured. "I'd been wondering about that. It was so grimly appropriate."

"Searcey, as I learned this morning, was practically without funds on this trip. I noticed that he ate very little in the diner and wondered at it at the time. He was strong and robust and looked as if he would have a hearty appetite. He must have seen the cases of samples which Radcott carried with him and filched several boxes of popcorn. Since he had the berth above Radcott one of the cases may have been put into his berth by mistake the first night. He was eating the popcorn while he talked with Torner and dropped the worthless premium and some of the corn on the floor. The ring and the tin whistle were likewise from boxes of popcorn which Searcey had eaten surreptitiously at various times."

"The whistle? I didn't know about that."

Rennert told her of his discovery of it upon the ground by the observation platform, where the porter had dropped it.

He smiled a bit shamefacedly. "I didn't realize at the time its real significance. I thought that the man was preparing to use it as a signal to the Cristeros, lurking in the darkness. When he told me that he had found it in the smoker while we were at Vanegas I remembered that I had gone into the smoker soon after the train stopped there and come upon Searcey with moving jaws, as if he had been eating something. He had tossed the whistle to the floor and the porter had found it while sweeping."

"I noticed that you showed the stickpin to several of the men. You were asking them if they could identify it?"

"Yes. Searcey said that he thought the Mexican had been wearing it in his tie after the train left San Antonio. No one else remembered having seen it. Spahr was positive that it had not been in the man's tie, which he had noticed particularly. It struck me then as likely that Searcey was anxious to account for the pin in the most logical manner, since he was aware that I knew Torner had been sitting in the seat where I found it."

Miss Talcott was frowning slightly. "But if Searcey were so hard up for money why did he take a Pullman instead of riding in the coach?"

"Probably because he knew that Pullman passengers are subjected to much less careful scrutiny at the border than ordinary travelers. After the hue and cry which had been raised over the Montes kidnapping he would want to pass the border as quickly and quietly as possible. He may not have trusted the effectiveness of his disguise too much."

"But what was it the porter had to tell you?" Despite the intelligence of the woman's questions Rennert had the feeling that her thoughts were far away.

"I'll never know exactly," he answered. "He may have seen Searcey in conversation with Torner, although I believe not. It was probably that he knew Searcey had been out of his berth after the other passengers had retired. According to his words to the conductor, the porter had been carrying a ladder for one of the passengers when he saw Torner seated at the rear of the car. Now, the only person to have an upper berth, and thus need the use of a ladder, was Searcey. At any rate, he was suspicious of what the porter might have seen and used Radcott's knife, which he had found upon the floor, to stab him last night when the lights were suddenly extinguished. My suspicion that this is what happened was confirmed last night when he informed me that Jeanes had had a knife in his possession. This was before the porter's body had been discovered, remember. When Searcey described a knife similar to the one found later in the porter's back he intended to throw the blame for the killing upon Jeanes, who he expected to make his escape and never be seen again. Actually, he betrayed his knowledge that such a knife had been used."

"And it was he, of course, who took my paper knife from my seat and hid it in the ladies' lounge?"

"Yes, he wished to keep a weapon handy in case he needed it." Rennert looked at her squarely. "Did it ever strike you as peculiar—the manner in which the murderer of Torner and of the porter was able to move about in the darkness?"

As if with an effort, her eyes centered on his face. "Yes," she said, "I had wondered at his being able to conceal the needle in the hatbox so quickly while we were in the tunnel."

"Exactly—and it is this matter of the darkness which still convinces me that Searcey was guilty."

"I don't understand."

Rennert crushed the end of his cigarette into an empty plate. "It was only this morning that I could understand why the murderer was able to strike with such deadly exactness, seemingly unhampered by the obscurity. Searcey was an albino."

"An albino?" faint surprise tinged her voice.

"Yes, his hair is dyed and the dark glasses hide his eyes. The lack of pigmentation of his skin isn't noticed except on close inspection on account of the sunburn."

"But I thought that albinos had weak eyesight?"

"In the daylight, yes, they are often shortsighted. But at night their sight is better than normal, owing to the greater amount of light reaching the retina. This explained why

Searcey was able to move about in the darkness with so little difficulty. I once had a friend who was an albino—a boy back in college—and I remember the uncanny way in which he could find his way about the dormitory after the lights had been turned off. Searcey told a story of having resorted to a disguise in order to obtain a job down here. This may be true or not, but there's no doubt that it also served to eliminate danger of detection at the border."

Rennert paused. The train was creeping between walls of pink and cream and white plaster, rendered flamboyant by painted signs. Voices and automobile horns and the clang of street cars poured through the windows.

"I was positive that Searcey was guilty, so positive that I was going to have him arrested when this train pulled into the station at Mexico City. And now my whole theory has fallen down unless it can be proven that Searcey committed suicide rather than face arrest. That would be the logical conclusion because I was standing at the door and am positive that no one approached his table after he entered the diner. On the other hand, there's nothing about his table, or his person or on the floor underneath to indicate how he did it. If it had been by means of a hypodermic needle the needle would have remained. If it had been poison there would be some trace of a container. His clothing and his luggage were searched yesterday and nothing of a lethal nature was found." Rennert got up. "So, you see, the affair, instead of being ended, is only beginning." He let some of the weariness which the prospect caused him creep into his voice.

Miss Talcott sat very still, her eyes fixed down the aisle and a vague half-smile upon her lips. Her hands rested upon the top of the table, as white as the cloth. Rennert noticed, with something of a start, that the ring which had adorned the third finger of her right hand was no longer there. (*She had left the diner,* his thoughts raced, *and had gone back into the Pullman. . . .*)

"All that you need, then, to make the guilt of this certain is evidence of how he died?" she asked in a low far-away voice.

"Yes, otherwise it will be another murder." *(She had returned from the Pullman a few minutes later.)*

"Here is the evidence."

She had opened the fiber bag. She took out of it a small pasteboard box and laid it upon the table. She opened it and pushed it toward him.

Rennert took it in his hands. It was empty. Upon the label pasted over the top had been written the word "Veronal." He had seen the box before, he recalled, when he had examined her bag.

He stared at it and then at her.

"The contents—all of them—were emptied into the glass of water which he drank," she glanced over at the empty tumbler on the table opposite.

"Before you left the diner?" he asked, with the curious feeling that the voice which was speaking was not his own.

"Yes."

Incredulity numbed him. "How did you know that he would sit at that table? That he would drink out of that glass?"

She stared at him oddly, then a convulsive movement seemed to spread over her face as if at the sudden snapping of a tautened wire. She leaned back in her chair and her laughter scaled for an instant into hysteria.

"You think that I meant the glass for him?" her voice was smothered. She leaned forward and covered her face with her hands.

She sat thus for a long time.

When she lowered her hands her face was composed again but retained its terrible lifeless look. She got unsteadily to her feet.

"I meant it for myself," she stood in the aisle, swaying slightly back and forth. "I never thought of anyone sitting there while I went to the observation platform. I wanted to take one last look——"

Rennert started forward but she raised a hand to stop him. He could see the way in which she steeled herself to force the same pleasant smile to her lips.

She reached over and picked up the newspaper from the table in front of Searcey. She folded it with careful fingers and handed it to him, pointing to a paragraph halfway down the first column.

She stood and waited until he ran his eyes down it.

Rennert did not look up for a moment. When he did his eyes were clear with understanding as they rested upon her right hand.

"The ring?" his voice was slightly husky.

She closed her eyes and smiled happily. "The baby has probably lost it in the dust by now," she said. "It doesn't matter—everything else has gone too. He may have gotten a moment of happiness out of it."

A long aching tremor passed through the train as it stopped.

Miss Talcott stood for an instant longer, as if in reverie, then opened her eyes. The smile died slowly from her face. She looked out the window and said in a matter-of-fact voice: "This is the Colonia Station. I must get my things together."

She turned, without meeting his eyes again, and walked with stiff erect carriage from the car.

Rennert stood and watched her go. Then his eyes fell to the newspaper which he still held in his hands.

The paragraph which he reread was a brief dispatch from Coyoacan.

"The residents of Coyoacan were thrown into a state of panic yesterday noon by an explosion which occurred when a truck loaded with nitroglycerine ran into the wall of a private home in the suburbs. The driver of the truck was blown to bits and two passers-by were severely injured. The residence which was destroyed is believed to have been empty at the time since the owner, an American lady by the name of Talcott, is at present in the United States. It was known locally as La Casa de los Alamos, from the poplar trees which surrounded it, and its gardens of flowers were the most beautiful in the city."

THE END

DISCUSSION QUESTIONS

- Were you able to predict any part of the solution to the case?
- After learning the solution, were there any clues you realized you had missed?
- Did any aspects of the plot date the story? If so, which ones?
- Would the story be different if it were set in the present day? If so, how?
- Did the social context of the time play a role in the narrative? If so, how?
- Trains were a popular plot device in Golden Age mystery fiction. Why do you think that is?
- This book has frequently been compared to Agatha Christie's *Murder on the Orient Express.* If you've read that other book, what do you make of this comparison?
- If you were one of the main characters, would you have acted differently at any point in the story?
- Did you identify with any of the characters? If so, which?
- What characteristics make Hugh Rennert an effective investigator?

OTTO PENZLER PRESENTS

AMERICAN MYSTERY CLASSICS

Dorothy B. Hughes

Dread Journey

Introduction by
Sarah Weinman

A movie star fears for her life on a train journey from Los Angeles to New York...

Hollywood big-shot Vivien Spender has waited ages to produce the work that will be his masterpiece: a film adaptation of Thomas Mann's The Magic Mountain. He's spent years grooming young starlets for the lead role, only to discard each one when a newer, fresher face enters his view. Afterwards, these rejected women all immediately fall from grace; excised from the world of pictures, they end up in rehab, or jail, or worse. But Kitten Agnew, the most recent to encounter this impending doom, won't be gotten rid of so easily—her contract simply doesn't allow for it. Accompanied by Mr. Spender on a train journey from Los Angeles to Chicago, she begins to fear that the producer might be considering a deadly alternative. Either way, it's clear that something is going to happen before they reach their destination, and as the train barrels through America's heartland, the tension accelerates towards an inescapable finale.

DOROTHY B. HUGHES (1904–1993) was a mystery author and literary critic famous for her taut thrillers, many of which were made into films. While best known for the noir classic *In a Lonely Place*, Hughes' writing successfully spanned a range of styles including espionage and domestic suspense.

"The perfect in-flight read. The only thing that's dated is the long-distance train."—*Kirkus*

Paperback, $15.95 / ISBN 978-1-61316-146-3
Hardcover, $25.95 / ISBN 978-1-61316-145-6

OTTO PENZLER PRESENTS

AMERICAN MYSTERY CLASSICS

Ellery Queen
The Siamese Twin Mystery

Introduction by Otto Penzler

Ellery Queen takes refuge from a wildfire at a remote mountain house — and arrives just before the owner is murdered...

When Ellery Queen and his father encounter a raging forest fire during a mountain drive, the only direction to go is up a winding dirt road that leads to an isolated hillside manor, inhabited by a secretive surgeon and his diverse cast of guests. Trapped by the fire, the Queens settle into the uneasy atmosphere of their surroundings. Then, the following morning, the doctor is discovered dead, apparently shot down while playing solitaire the night before.

The only clue is a torn six of spades. The suspects include a society beauty, a suspicious valet, and a pair of conjoined twins. When another murder follows, the killer inside the house becomes as threatening as the mortal flames outside its walls. Can Queen solve this whodunnit before the fire devours its subjects?

ELLERY QUEEN was a pen name created and shared by two cousins, Frederic Dannay (1905-1982) and Manfred B. Lee (1905-1971), as well as the name of their most famous detective.

"Queen at his best . . . a classic of brilliant deduction under extreme circumstances."
—*Publishers Weekly* (Starred Review)

Paperback, $15.95 / ISBN 978-1-61316-155-5
Hardcover, $25.95 / ISBN 978-1-61316-154-8

OTTO PENZLER PRESENTS
AMERICAN MYSTERY CLASSICS

Clayton Rawson
Death from a Top Hat
Introduction by Otto Penzler

A detective steeped in the art of magic solves the mystifying murder of two occultists.

Now retired from the tour circuit on which he made his name, master magician The Great Merlini spends his days running a magic shop in New York's Times Square and his nights moonlighting as a consultant for the NYPD. The cops call him when faced with crimes so impossible that they can only be comprehended by a magician's mind.

In the most recent case, two occultists are discovered dead in locked rooms, one spread out on a pentagram, both appearing to have been murdered under similar circumstances. The list of suspects includes an escape artist, a professional medium, and a ventriloquist, so it's clear that the crimes took place in a realm that Merlini knows well. But in the end it will take his logical skills, and not his magical ones, to apprehend the killer.

CLAYTON RAWSON (1906–1971) was a novelist, editor, and magician. He is best known for creating the Great Merlini, an illusionist and amateur sleuth introduced in *Death from a Top Hat* (1938).

"One of the all-time greatest impossible murder mysteries."
—*Publishers Weekly* (Starred Review)

Paperback, $15.95 / ISBN 978-1-61316-101-2
Hardcover, $25.95 / ISBN 978-1-61316-109-8